He set his hat on the table, shook his head. His hair was a bit longer than gentlemen wore, but it shimmered in such a rich, lovely shade of chestnut brown she would not think of advising him to have it trimmed.

"She might come over later. Just now she is writing a letter to Ma and Pa."

"Mother and Father." She felt something of a harpy pointing it out. But she had committed to his transformation. Since she had decided not to comment on his hair, she could not let his language go uncorrected. "A gentleman would say, 'Mother and Father.'"

"Seems awfully formal. They'd have a good laugh if they could hear it."

"Rather say, 'It does seem awfully formal. They would laugh if they could hear me.'"

"That's what I said."

"Yes, well, nearly." She was a shrew. The truth was that she was beginning to find she quite enjoyed the way he spoke. However, needs were what they were. "Gentlemen do not use contractions."

"I fear, Lady Shaw, that my instruction will be a challenge to you. Please do not lose patience with me."

If only patience was all she had to lose. Her fear was that she might lose something more costly. Such as her self-possession, her levelheadedness... her very heart.

Author Note

Thank you for picking up *The Making of Baron Haversmere*. If you have read the stories leading up to this one, I appreciate it! In *The Earl's American Heiress* you will have met Olivia Cavill Shaw. Perhaps in the beginning you were not all that fond of the bitter widow, but I do hope you can see into her heart of hearts. She has been horribly wounded by her late husband. I'm certain Olivia is not alone in putting her trust in an unworthy man. In *The Making of Baron Haversmere*, we see her face who she is now, strive to rise above her brokenness and become again the girl who knew how to love.

You might recall that at one point in *The Earl's American Heiress*, Olivia jokingly—and yes, sarcastically—stated to everyone at the dinner table, "Perhaps I should wed a cowboy..." Those were her exact words. Well...perhaps she ought to! Conveniently, such a man has moved into the apartment across from where she lives at Fencroft House. Not only that, but her small son, Victor, is convinced the cowboy is a gift from his late uncle. What do you think, dear reader? Could he be the gift Olivia needs to rise above her distrustful nature and open her heart to love and joy again? If Victor has his say, she will. But what does Cowboy Joe have to say about the matter?

We shall see...

CAROL ARENS

The Making of Baron Haversmere

ISBN-13: 978-1-335-50554-5

The Making of Baron Haversmere

Copyright © 2020 by Carol Arens

Harlequin Enterprises ULC
22 Adelaide St. West, 40th Floor
Toronto, Ontario M5H 4E3, Canada
www.Harlequin.com

Printed in U.S.A.

Carol Arens delights in tossing fictional characters into hot water, watching them steam and then giving them a happily-ever-after. When she is not writing, she enjoys spending time with her family, beach camping or lounging about a mountain cabin. At home, she enjoys playing with her grandchildren and gardening. During rare spare moments, you will find her snuggled up with a good book. Carol enjoys hearing from readers at carolarens@yahoo.com or on Facebook.

Books by Carol Arens

Harlequin Historical

Dreaming of a Western Christmas
"Snowbound with the Cowboy"
Western Christmas Proposals
"The Sheriff's Christmas Proposal"
The Cowboy's Cinderella
Western Christmas Brides
"A Kiss from the Cowboy"
The Rancher's Inconvenient Bride
A Ranch to Call Home
A Texas Christmas Reunion
The Earl's American Heiress
Rescued by the Viscount's Ring
The Making of Baron Haversmere

Visit the Author Profile page
at Harlequin.com for more titles.

Dedicated to Wade Matthew.

Your quick-witted humor keeps us laughing;
we are blessed by your loving spirit.

Chapter One

London—third day of spring, 1890

Lady Olivia Shaw kept a tight hold of her five-year-old son's hand even though he was capable of keeping pace beside her. This early in the morning fog swirled along the path, twining eerily among the tombs of Kensal Green Cemetery.

Naturally she did not expect a vaporous spirit to slither into view. That was nonsense.

What was not nonsense was the possibility of there being a thief—or worse, a kidnapper—lurking in the mist. Yes, any mother with an ounce of caution would be aware that a man of evil intent might be listening to their footsteps and waiting to pounce.

Perhaps she ought to have waited until the fog lifted and there were other mourners to keep company with.

Of course she could not have. Her appointments for the day were a few too many as it was. In order to visit her late brother's grave, it must be done at this early hour.

With all her family aboard ship to America, the running of Fencroft fell to her and she intended to do a first-rate job of it.

If only birds would awake and sing, the mood of the place would improve dramatically. Birdsong had a way of brightening any situation, of cheering the bluest heart.

'Mother...' Victor wriggled his fingers from her grasp '...you are holding too tight.'

She gazed down at her only child, pinned him with a stern look, then reclaimed his hand, gripping it even more firmly.

'Perhaps so, but you do have a habit of disappearing, my boy. If you pull such a stunt here, I'll have the devil of a time finding you.'

If she could have, she would have left him back at Fencroft House in the care of his governess, but he no longer had one. The lady had up and married without warning and left Olivia at a loss.

'I miss everyone,' Victor said, dragging his feet, which indicated he was about to express a complaint. 'Why did we not go to visit America with them?'

'Because it is a very long way across the Atlantic Ocean.' She could scarcely credit that her sister-in-law, Clementine, had taken her fourteen adopted children on such a journey. 'They will be gone for a long time. Someone must stay behind and see to the affairs of Fencroft.'

Poor Victor was naturally bored and lonely.

'But there are cowboys in America!' Add envious to bored and lonely.

He yanked his hand from hers yet again. Where was her adorable toddler? The one who wanted nothing more than to gain his mother's approval? Left behind somewhere between his fourth and his fifth birthday, she supposed.

Oh, but he was a handsome child. She cupped his upturned face in her palm. His wavy blond hair and his sky-blue eyes were quite her undoing. She would be for ever grateful that he looked nothing like her faithless late husband.

It was his uncle, Oliver—Olivia's twin—she saw blinking up at her.

'You would only be disappointed if you met one, Victor. Cowboys are not the bold heroes you read about in your storybooks.'

'Yes, they are, Mother. I know it!'

Around a bend in the path a stone angel kneeling in prayer at the foot the Fifth Earl of Fencroft's tomb came into view. How odd that it appeared to move when fog whorled about cold damp marble.

It was only good common sense that made her certain it was a trick of shadow and mist that made the wings appear to tremble. If she did not know better, she would think they were about to unfurl and take to the heavens.

To fly away suddenly, just as Oliver had. But it had not been so sudden, really. Her brother had been sick for most of his life. It only seemed sudden because he had been laughing and smiling over a game of whist—and then he was just gone.

'Here we are.' She knelt, placing the bouquet of roses she carried at the foot of the tomb. 'Would you like to say something to your uncle?'

'Where is he?' Victor frowned at the sculpture. If she knew her son at all, and she did, he was wondering if his uncle had somehow turned into a marble figure.

'That is not him. Uncle Oliver is in Heaven.'

'Then why are we here? Ought we not go talk to him in Heaven?'

'That is not how it is done. We talk to him here and he hears us there.'

'Oh,' he said with a nod. 'Good morning, Uncle. I miss you. I suppose you know all your dead neighbours by now. Might there be any cowboys here I can talk to?'

'Victor Shaw!' Even as she opened her mouth to scold her son, she heard, not with her ears, of course, but rather a faraway echo in her heart of her brother's laughter.

Oliver saw humour in everything.

'I'm sure there are no cowboys in Kensal Green.'

'Might be.'

There was more likely to be a criminal lurking about than a cowboy. She glanced about, wishing her nerves were not so on edge.

Perhaps she ought to have accepted her carriage driver's offer to accompany her, but Mr Creed had spent a late night in the stable with a newly purchased horse who was nervous about unfamiliar surrounds. It was only right for him to remain in the carriage and get some rest while she paid her call on Oliver.

Now though, with the cemetery grounds so damp and still, with shadows that might be hiding—things— she rather wished for his large presence.

Even knowing, as she now did, that the Abductor who was rumoured to have plagued London recently was not in fact an actual villain, she had been scared by the incident. London was a large and dangerous city. There might still be evil men who would kidnap innocent children—her innocent child, not to put a fine point on it.

The mother of an adventurous boy could not be too careful.

'I'm going to have a few words with your uncle. You can play nearby, but only where I can see you.'

'May I have a puppy, Mother?'

'What? No, you may not!'

'If I had one, he could follow me and when you wanted to find me he could bark.'

'How would he know—? The point is, you will stay close by while I speak with your uncle.'

'Heaven is quite far off. I do not think he will hear you.'

'Oh, but he will, my dear, with his heart. Hearts hear things that ears cannot.'

'Dogs can hear everything with their ears and mostly cowboys have dogs.'

What was there to do but shake her head, sit on the bench beside the tomb and laugh inside at his persistence?

Perhaps she would get him a small pup, after all. Getting him a cowboy was quite beyond her, but a puppy, yes, she could manage that.

'Hello, Oliver,' she murmured softly, staring at the cross which the angel knelt in front of.

The marble bench felt chilly, hard and cold even through layers of clothing. She would speak with her brother for a short time and then take her son back to the coach, to warmth and security.

Really, she ought not to be so fearful. She was sturdier than that. Or had been at one time.

Life—the behaviour of men, to be more precise— had changed her. The brother she was here to visit being one of them.

There was Heath, of course. She did trust her

younger brother, but he was off to America. Which left her feeling more vulnerable than ever. Until he returned, any problem that arose for the estate would be hers to deal with.

'You left quite a mess behind when you died. I was angry at you for a time. But you needn't worry. I have forgiven you and it has all been sorted out thanks to the Macooishes from America. Our brother went through with the marriage which you had intended to be our financial salvation—not to Madeline, but to her cousin Clementine. It is because of her that the destitution you left us with is settled in our favour. I cannot imagine why you thought that college chum of yours was qualified to handle the estate funds. Did you know that creditors came knocking upon our doors? Yes, but I did say I forgive you and I will speak no more of it. Everything down here is going rather splendidly for now. Although all the family has sailed off for a holiday in America. And when I say all—well, let me tell you how the family has grown...'

Fog in this cemetery was a different breed of mist than what Joe had grown up with in the wilds of Wyoming. A body would expect London fog to be a more docile sort, citified and tame, but it wasn't so. Back home the stuff was fresh, cool and moist to breathe.

This creeping vapour was neither. There was a yellow taint to it that made a man cough if he breathed too deeply.

He figured it hid a lot of secrets.

'It would, I reckon,' he said to Sir Bristle. The wolfish dog trotting beside him glanced up, swishing his broom-like tail. 'It is a graveyard.'

One which he would rather not be visiting. Wouldn't

be if it were not for the fact that the woman who gave birth to him was laid to rest here.

Joe's boots, the leather well worn and feeling more familiar to his feet than bare ground did, crunched the gravel and broke the early morning stillness.

Reading the names on the tombstones while he walked, he tried to summon an image of his mother. It was a sad thing that he could not.

It hurt that he did not recall what she looked like, or smelled like even. What had her voice sounded like singing him a lullaby? He knew none of the things a boy should know.

All he did know was what his father had told him. Mother was as pretty as a porcelain doll, more angel than woman. Father's heart had shattered when she died a month before giving birth to their second child. Not of the complications of childbirth as sometimes happened, but of a lung ailment.

Grandmother Hampton blamed her daughter's death on Pa. Had he not brought her delicate child to such a damp place, she would not have sickened. It was because of Lady Hampton that Mother was buried here in London and not at the estate near Grasmere.

Pa always said her grief had been bitter and so he had allowed his wife to buried in London, hoping to give the woman a bit of relief.

"'Evan Green, Viscount Clament",' he read, then passed by searching the shadows for the one he sought. "'Lady Emily Thornton"—not you either.'

Pa had told him to look for a standing angel, her marble arms wrapped about a woman cradling her infant.

'Sure are a lot of stone angels.' The dog huffed a soft woof in apparent agreement.

Joe passed by no less than a dozen marble guardians keeping eternal watch.

A small path turned off the wide, central one he strode down. It looked pretty, lined with trees whose newly leafed branches formed a wisp-like canopy in the fog.

He turned down it. The gravestones here were less ornate than the ones on the central path. Barons did not rate as high as dukes, he'd been told. Growing up, Joe had never paid a lot of mind to life across the ocean. As an adult, cattle ranching took up the greater portion of his attention.

As interesting as he found London to be, he longed to return to the great open spaces of Wyoming, where the land was as big as the sky, where he could gallop across open ground on his horse, to shout out loud and feel one with the wind.

'What do you think, Sir Bristle? Will we go home by summer's end?'

Drizzle caused by the heavy mist tapped the brim of his Stetson.

The dog shook himself, but did not answer one way or another.

'I suppose it depends upon how long it takes to—'

Ah, just there. The tomb he'd been searching for loomed suddenly in front of him. He took off his hat, held it in his fist and read the name on the marker just to be sure.

'"Violet Hampton Steton, Baroness Haversmere".'

He hadn't expected his heart to weep, but it did. Somehow seeing his mother's name upon the stone brought tears to the corners of his eyes.

Being not quite three years old when she died,

he could not recall anything about her, but he must remember…her.

There was not a bench to sit on so he settled on the wet grass beside the tomb. He touched the marble, Sir Bristle pressed close beside him, whining and trying to lick his face. 'I reckon you were expecting Pa.'

He didn't know for a fact that his mother could hear him, but he went on as if she could. It was a thing folks did in a cemetery, speak out loud to the dead. For some reason it seemed right.

'Pa wasn't feeling up to making his usual trip so he sent me to tend to business at Haversmere.' Maybe Joe ought to have made the trip to England with his father once or twice, but Pa had needed him to remain on the ranch and keep it going in his absence. 'He said to tell you not to worry about him. He's only feeling tired and will pay you a call when he comes next year.'

A sudden breeze came up, ruffled his hair, then faded as quickly as it had risen. It was the oddest sensation, almost as if his hair had been tenderly stroked.

'Was that you?' he asked over the lump swelling in his throat.

It had to have been a trick of imagination, but he did wonder why Sir Bristle suddenly looked up and thumped his tail.

He'd caught the scent of a squirrel foraging his breakfast, more than likely.

'I wish I remembered you…you and me…together.'

He sat silently, trying to.

It wasn't as if there had not been a woman he called 'Ma' for most of his life.

His father had left Haversmere behind, having been being broken with grief and guilt over his wife's death. What if the climate had been the cause of it just as her mother claimed? He'd purchased a ranch in Wyoming hoping for a new start.

He'd got one. When Joe was seven years old, Esmeralda Viella came into their lives. She healed what was broken in both of their hearts. When she and Pa added Roselina to the family, life became complete again.

'I could use some help, if you are able to influence anything here below.'

He listened for a moment, but nothing happened to make him think she was able.

'I need to find a husband for Roselina. You might know that she is my sister.' Again, no breeze, no odd turning of a leaf, gave hint of what she did or did not know of this conversation. 'My stepmother has given me the task of finding her a suitable fellow. She's set on her daughter making a society marriage.'

Ma had worked towards this goal for the better part of two years. She had even hired an instructor to teach Roselina proper deportment and current fashion.

His sister took to the training well, but Joe wasn't sure if she went along with the tutelage because she wanted to be a 'lady' or if she longed for a bit of adventure.

In her eighteen years on the ranch she had seen little of gentle society. Parties were few and far between. If Joe made a guess, his sister was looking for fun more than marriage.

For all that Ma had told him not to bring her home without a title, he was not sure this was anything he had control over.

He could not help but wonder why Ma would want this. If his sister did marry a British fellow, she probably would not come home.

The thought made him hope he did not succeed in finding her a husband.

He might not, especially once they made the trip north to the Lake District. He wasn't sure how many eligible nobles would come calling at Haversmere. Wasn't London the place they looked for brides?

For all that he had never been to Haversmere, he understood the area to be sparsely inhabited, with more sheep than folks.

Sir Bristle had never seen a sheep. Joe couldn't help but wonder how he would react to seeing a critter as woolly as he was.

All of sudden the dog stood up, cocked his big head, ears twitching.

'What is it, boy?' Joe came to his feet, glancing about.

The dog took this stance when there was something he felt Joe needed to attend to. More often than not it was a straying calf. Once it had been a lost kitten, but once it had been Roselina, so Joe always paid attention to the dog's message.

'Take me to it.'

With a woof the dog set off at a trot. Joe dashed after him, back to the main path, then down a narrower one that twisted half-a-dozen times. The further down it he went the darker it got. This part of the cemetery appeared to be neglected and densely overgrown with vegetation.

'Good boy,' he said to the dog.

It was always amazing to Joe that Sir Bristle was able to hear a sound from so far away and find his way to it.

After five minutes of twists and turns, the dog stopped, sniffed the ground, then disappeared behind a chipped and mossy tomb.

'Wolf!' a young, high-pitched voice screeched.

On a dash, Joe rounded the grave. A young boy crouched on the ground, his face buried in his arms while he wept in apparent terror of the beast sniffing his shoulder.

'Howdy, son,' he said. 'Get yourself lost?'

The boy looked up. His tear-streaked face broke into a wide grin.

'And so, last autumn was an adventure since our brother did turn out to be the Abductor. But, of course, he was not the fiend people believed him to be.' Olivia glanced up from her story to make sure Victor was still hunting for bugs under damp stones. 'Victor? Come out where I can see you. As you can expect, Heath was arrested when his wife accidentally—Victor?'

He ought to have answered by now. What on earth was she to do with him? It was one thing for him to wander off at the town house, but quite another out here where— 'Victor!'

She sprang up from the bench, spun about looking left, then right. Was it her imagination that the fog had grown even thicker while she spoke to Oliver?

It was not! How could she have failed to notice the change? Worse, how could she have failed to hear her son sneak away?

What a thoughtless, inattentive mother she was! She knew her son's proclivity to hide and she had let down her guard.

He had sneaked off to find a cowboy. She would bet her life on it. But who might he have come across instead?

'Victor!'

She dashed along the path, trying to stave off the

panic constricting her chest. So many smaller paths led off from this central one. Which could he have taken?

Was he still in the cemetery or had someone carried him off? How was she to go on if he had been...?

No! She could not think it.

Her sweet, precious boy—she would give anything to see him run from the tombs, laughing at the grand trick he had played.

Winded, she stopped, braced her hands on her thighs and tried to catch her breath.

Fog was supposed to lift as the morning wore on, but today it only grew worse. She could see no more than fifteen feet in any direction.

Anxiety made her sick to her stomach—lightheaded and half-faint. She would not crumple! She could not. She was a mother, not an inexperienced girl. Her child depended upon her.

The sound of shoes crunching the path brought her upright.

These were not Victor's light, quick steps. The footfalls coming towards her hit the ground boldly and with long, purposeful strides.

There were other steps as well. They sounded like something having four feet—or possibly paws—large ones, and whatever they belonged to panted heavily.

She ought to run away, hide until the possible danger passed. Of course she could not. There was but one thing to be done. For Victor's sake she must stand her ground.

A dark-looking figure began to emerge, the fog swirling and receding about it. Second by second the silhouette of a man became more defined, beside him trotted some sort of large beast—a canine of some sort.

She readied her legs to leap, her arms to fly in defence of her child in the event the man had captured him.

The closer the man strode, the clearer his image became. And there was Victor, perched in the crook of his arm.

'Look, Mother! I found a cowboy and he isn't even dead.'

Chapter Two

'Howdy, ma'am. I reckon this young'un belongs to you?'

Had to. The lady looked like she might faint on the spot…or attack him.

Either way, he figured he ought to set the child down.

She lowered her arms to her side, uncurling her fingers one by one.

No doubt she was surprised to discover she was not alone in the cemetery at this early hour. He sure had been surprised to come upon the boy.

Did she realise her mouth sagged slightly open?

Blamed if he would mention it, though. Not only because pointing it out would be rude, but because the expression looked extremely fetching on her pretty, heart-shaped face.

The brim of her hat dipped low on her forehead, but did not hide what her round blue eyes had to say. Glancing between him and Sir Bristle, they revealed her fear—and her courage.

She wanted to flee, but held her ground. Not that he could blame her for feeling frightened. A little thing like her coming across a stranger and what would appear to be his wolf, and the stranger in possession of her boy?

Motherhood was a miraculous thing in his mind. Common sense would urge her to run. Mothers, he'd noticed, were fierce in defending their young, be they animal or human.

To put her at ease he offered a friendly smile and set the boy down.

Her brow lowered, her lips pressed together. It was hard not to stare at them because they looked like a satin bow with dimples at each corner.

No doubt to the boy she looked stern, but to Joe she looked as pretty as a morning rose with dew drops on her petals. Clearly this woman was a rose with a thorny stem, but it was the delicacy of her features that appealed to him.

Part of her thorniness might have to do with the fact that her child was clutching tight to the fringe of his coat sleeve when he ought to be rushing to her.

'I'm Joe Steton, ma'am.' He dipped his hat in formal greeting. 'I found young Victor crouched behind a tomb and lost as can be.'

'I'm very grateful, Mr Steton.'

He was glad to see her expression soften slightly with her thanks. She had the most arresting eyes he had ever seen. A man could get lost in how blue they were, in how round and wide. Even more in how they seemed to slant ever so slightly at the corners, giving them a pretty cat-like appearance.

Joe had always been fascinated by cats.

Too bad for the boy, though, being on the wrong end of that look. He had some sort of punishment coming. One could hardly blame his mother for needing to teach him a lesson about wandering off.

'Victor Shaw, come to me at once. And step well wide of the wolf.'

'But, Mother! Uncle Oliver sent me a cowboy. He's mine to keep.'

It was fair to say the statement left the lady as stunned as he was.

'I beg your pardon, Mr Steton.' A wisp of fair hair slipped out from under her bonnet when she shook her head. 'My son is only five years old and has quite a fascination for cowboys.'

He could only hope that she secretly shared it. The fact was, he could not recall when he'd had such an instant fascination upon meeting a woman. There had been a few who'd intrigued him, but none of them as suddenly or as intensely as this woman did.

'Victor, no person belongs to another.' Since the child seemed loath to release Joe's sleeve, his mother walked forward and snatched his hand. 'Mr Steton has a life of his own. You cannot simply lay claim to him.'

'But Uncle Oliver—'

With the woman's attention settled upon the boy, it was clear there was no other thought in her mind but what to do with him. It had been wishful on his part to hope she might return his interest.

He'd wager she had not even noticed it.

Perhaps if they had met under other circumstances? London was a very large town, so he doubted the odds of them crossing paths again were great.

'Son, I haven't met your uncle. I was only here to pay my respects to my mother.'

'There, you see? It was only coincidence that he was here.' She flashed him a smile of appreciation which gave his heart a turn. 'Now, thank Mr Steton for rescuing you and we will be on our way.'

'But, Mother, didn't you hear? He called me son—that means Uncle Oliver did bring him here for me.'

'Come along, Victor, we will discuss this later and not take up any more of Mr Steton's time.'

'Please allow me to walk you to your carriage.' He wasn't ready to be quit of her company yet.

'It is not necessary, truly. But thank you again for finding him. I am for ever grateful.'

With that she walked away. The boy pulled, resisting her lead.

'Uncle did give him to me! You said he hears us from Heaven and when I was lost I asked him to make a cowboy find me. And there he is!'

Joe stood watching, while she half-dragged the boy along the path.

What the child said gave him the oddest feeling in his belly because what he stated was not exactly wrong.

Here he was.

He had been there—a cowboy.

Leaning against the doorway between the governess's bedchamber and the nursery, Olivia watched her son sleep. The softly glowing lamp, placed a safe distance from his bed, cast a golden aura about his face, giving him the appearance of an angel.

Which he was, a five-year-old cherub who was blessed with a vivid imagination.

How was she ever to convince him that Oliver had not given him his very own cowboy?

She had to, of course. The fact was, the man had just happened to be in the cemetery and had just happened to find her lost child. Olivia's late brother had not a thing to do with it.

There was that echo of his laughter again. She felt

it go through her as vividly as she would have heard it with her ears.

'If it was you, what do you expect me to do now?'

Rain tapping on the window was all the answer she heard. No mysterious voice in her heart took credit for her predicament.

Had it really been Oliver, he would have.

In the morning, she would explain it all to Victor, somehow find the words to do it gently and not break his heart.

It would not be easy since, against all reason, the cowboy had been there. It was not as if she could tell him that it was a common thing to be rescued by a man like Mr Steton. In thirty-two years of life the only cowboys Olivia had seen were in storybooks.

Even they had not been as dashing and—

Her mind conjured the boldness of the cowboy's smile before she could swat the image away.

Spinning from the doorway, she crossed the room and sat down at the dressing table. She drew her hair over her shoulder and began to plait it.

At least Victor had not asked his uncle for a pirate. The boy had been quite enamoured of them until he discovered the existence of cowboys.

Had she crossed paths with a pirate in the graveyard, well, she might have collapsed on the spot.

As it was, she nearly had collapsed, but in an intense blend of relief and astonishment.

Once she had seen that Victor was not only safe, but deliriously happy, and that the wolf was not going to attack, she had truly noticed the man.

Noticed things about him that she had no business noticing.

Her hands fell from her hair to her lap while she

stared at the water drops gently tapping the window behind the mirror.

But even she, a mature and wary woman, could see how uncommonly handsome he was. No gentleman of her acquaintance looked quite so rugged or had fine lines at the corners of his eyes that squinted in suppressed humour. Oh, and his voice—it had been so deep and rich sounding when he'd called her 'ma'am'.

She would be a liar if she said that her nerves had not tapped a flamenco dance under her skin.

She was nearly certain that he had been biting down a bark of laughter during the encounter in the cemetery.

The words he spoke were supportive of her motherly authority, but under it all she would bet he found the situation amusing. And, honestly, it was.

Once she understood her child was safe, she could hardly fail to see the humour. Not that she could let on that she did. As far as her son knew she was quite angry over his disappearance.

Oh, but the cowboy—Joe—she had been quite mistaken when she told Victor that meeting one would only cause him to be disappointed. That they were not the heroes romantic tales told of.

Mr Steton was every bit a hero. And a dashingly handsome one to go with it.

Too handsome, in fact. If he were hers, she would never have a peaceful moment. Not a single unworried thought. Dozens of women would be fawning over him, hoping to become his mistress.

Certainly a dashing fellow like Cowboy Joe would have one—perhaps even two—whether he was married or not.

One thing was certain: no matter how bold or handsome he was, Olivia Shaw's heart was one that would never be broken again.

If her late husband had left her with anything of value, it was the lesson of keeping her heart to herself.

Giving it away would only cause it to be crushed, as ruined as an egg fallen from a bird's nest.

She stared at the mirror, watching her head nod in forceful agreement.

What she noticed, though, was how very plain her hair was. It was straight and not in the least bit interesting.

She lifted a hank and twirled it about her ear. What if she took to styling a loop here or a whirl there? It would be quite dramatic in comparison to the severe bun she typically wore.

Hmm, it did look rather pretty. It had been a very long time since she felt pretty.

The problem was, feeling pretty led to feeling flirtatious.

What was the point of feeling flirtatious unless one wanted to attract the attentions of a man?

She let the loop slide out of her fingers.

By no means would she stray from her good staid bun.

Roselina arched a brow at Joe, shrugging one shoulder while they walked along Bond Street.

Had he been carrying one more package he would not have been able to see her shoot him the glance that said, *This is your own fault.*

'Were you dressed like a gentleman, no one would be staring at you.'

'These clothes have always been good enough.' He tried to glance down to reassure himself it was true, but the boxes got in the way and the lacy pink bow on the hatbox tickled his nose. 'I don't see any reason to change.'

'Good enough for Cheyenne, Big Brother.' Roselina's attention snagged eagerly on the perfumery they were passing by. She crossed in front of him so suddenly he nearly dropped the stack of treasures his sister had purchased this morning. 'If you hope to find me a husband, you will need to act more of a gentleman.'

'I am a gentleman.'

'Yes, you are.' She glanced back at him over her shoulder, her teasing frown raking him, Stetson to boot toe. 'But you will need to look like one.'

Blame it! His good sturdy clothes were just fine as far as he was concerned. Anybody else's concern didn't matter all that much.

'If you buy one more thing, we are taking a carriage back to the rooms.'

She winked at him. 'But we will not call for one. Walking gets us seen.'

If he did need new clothes, as Pa had warned him he would, he'd have Roselina do the shopping. She revelled in what to him was a tedious ordeal.

He was pretty certain they had spent more than an hour in the perfumery even though his sister insisted it had been only a quarter of one.

Finally outside in open air, she carried her prize close to her heart, smiling happily over it.

A bee buzzed about Joe's nose and no wonder. With all the scents sticking to him he must seem like a huge blossom drifting down the street.

'Tonight at the Duchess's ball I will smell like my name—Rose. People will remember me because of it.'

It was not as if she needed the scent to be remembered. Roselina Anne Steton was unforgettable.

She was a bright spirit, a joy to everyone. She had been since the day she was born. If folks at the ball did not remember her for that, they would for her appearance. She'd got Pa's mossy green eyes and Ma's nearly black curls. Her lithe, pixie-like form he thought was all her own.

His sister could not help but be noticed tonight. That was not his worry.

What concerned him was that he was not acquainted with any of the gentleman who would be doing the noticing. It was going to be a tricky thing to determine which of them was worthy of courting her.

With the pavement crowded, Joe scanned the faces of the younger gentlemen passing by. He watched their behaviour. There might be a few strolling along Bond Street who would attend the Duchess of Guthrie's gathering.

He'd heard it was to be a lavish event.

It wasn't likely he would learn anything of value by staring at passing faces, but it only felt natural to be on the lookout.

All of a sudden he was aware that it was no longer the young men's faces he was studying. Without being aware of his attention drifting, he realised it was the ladies' faces he sought.

One face in particular. The mother of the boy he had found in the cemetery.

A thought struck him, nearly making him trip over his boots.

'Mrs,' he mumbled under his breath. For some reason when he met her, the idea that she might be married had not entered his mind.

It ought to have, first thing.

While the lady never said so one way or another, the fact that she had a child ought to have alerted him that there was very likely a husband.

Good God forgive him if he had been indulging in inappropriate thoughts about a married woman.

Blame it! How did he expect to make a judgement on his sister's suitors when his own clear-headedness was in question?

Most of the time what his gut told him was spot on. What it said, even now, was the lady seemed too vulnerable to have a man who stood with her. Perhaps she was a widow.

He might not know the truth of her marital status, but what he did know was that it was not for him to wonder about.

In the instant a young fellow swaggered past, his manner arrogant, a hint of last night's bourbon on his clothing, and his half-cocked smile resting squarely on Roselina.

His sister responded with the bright smile she gave everyone, but—

Curse it! Just there, he spotted a twinkle in her eye—a flash of returned interest.

And like a wisp of smoke blown in the wind, thoughts of Victor's mother scattered.

While he'd understood part of his reason for being here was to see Roselina well wed, in his heart she was still his baby sister. Baby sisters did not return the flirtations of grown men.

Olivia tapped her fingers on the arm of the chair while she waited for Miss Hopp, the next candidate to be interviewed for the position of Victor's governess, to be escorted to the terrace.

Idleness, she observed for the third time in less than a quarter-hour, was hardly a virtue.

Even with the sun shining down to warm her shoulders, no matter that a hundred birds sang pleasantly to each other and the fountain tapped soothingly in the garden pond, she found it impossible to relax and enjoy a tranquil moment.

All she could think of was the next thing to be done. Her sister-in-law seemed to have no trouble indulging in peaceful interludes. Clementine seemed content to sit in the garden and write poetic words, even with so many children needing her attention.

Perhaps if Olivia liked poetry she could do the same. But she did not. Fancy words expressing silly sentiments was all it was.

It was better to focus her mind on attending to Fencroft business.

With the family on holiday to America, it fell to her to keep the estate in order. She would not fail in the task as Oliver had.

'Look at me, Mother!' Victor called.

She would if she could see him. A sudden rustle of leaves told her he was peering at her through one of the terrace trees.

'Come down at once, Victor Shaw. It is not safe for you to be up so high.'

'I bet my cousins visiting America are climbing great tall trees.' Branches lower down began to shimmy.

'They are still aboard ship. They will not see a tree for at least a week.'

'May I have a steer?' A pair of short, swinging legs came into view, dangling from the lowest branch.

'You only just asked for a dog.'

'My cowboy already has a dog, so I think a steer with great long horns would be splendid.'

No doubt her child was thinking it would be great fun to swing from those long horns.

Where in the dickens was Miss Hopp? If she did not arrive momentarily, Olivia would be late for her appointment with the accountant, which in turn would make her late in preparing for the Duchess of Guthrie's ball.

Which then, in turn, might cause her to be short with her maid. She did want to avoid that at all costs.

There had been a time in her life when kindness came to her as naturally as breathing did. She had been a sweet and trusting girl full of hope and romantic dreams of the future.

Marriage had changed all that.

It had taken an American—Clementine—to show her what a shrew she had become, especially when it came to dealing with the servants. She was doing her best to make up for it, but even still she noticed the servants looking at her apprehensively on occasion.

'My steer could stay in the stable at night.' Dropping from the tree, Victor ran for her, then climbed on to her lap.

'What would you do with it during the day?' She hugged her boy tight. How long would it be before he considered himself too old for cuddling?

'Me and my cowboy would play with him. Rope him and ride him and have quite a merry time, Mother.'

'Victor, you must know that Mr Steton is not your cowboy. He is simply someone we crossed paths with at Kensal Green.'

'But that isn't so. I was lost and Uncle Oliver sent him to find me. I know it!'

It hurt her deeply to have to crush his dream, but what help was there for it? She could not allow him to believe this fantasy.

Especially since her sweet son was no doubt seeking the father he had never known. The one who chose a harlot's bed over hers—a stranger's affection rather than—

Well, that no longer mattered. What did matter was keeping that man's wicked choices from hurting her innocent boy. No matter what, she would not allow Henry Shaw to shatter Victor's heart the way he had shattered hers.

Just because the man was stone cold in his grave did not mean it could not happen.

'Do you know what a coincidence is?' she asked while fluffing his short blond curls.

He shook his head. The silklike strands pulled away from her fingers.

'A coincidence is when something occurs by happenstance. It might appear meant to be, but it is not at all. Mr Steton just happened to be there when you needed him. Your uncle hadn't anything to do with it.'

'Did too.'

'I know you want it to be so and I wish for you that it was. The thing to keep in mind is that you did indeed get to meet a cowboy—to be rescued by him. That is a lovely memory to hold on to. But you must prepare yourself for the fact that you will not see him again.'

'But I will.'

This conversation was more difficult than she imagined it would be.

'Of course you will in your heart—'

'I see him with my eyes.' Victor leapt from her lap, hopped up and down, wagging his finger. 'Right there by the fountain! He's giving that lady a kiss on top of her head. She could be his Indian princess.'

'You do have a vivid imagination,' she said with a half-laugh while pivoting about on the chair. 'You—'

By the saints! There he was!

Tall and bold-looking with his hat dipped low on his forehead. He was indeed kissing the crown of a small woman whose dark hair fell in waves down her back.

The girl, for she was little more than that, swatted his arm, then laughed, exposing a playful-looking dimple on one side of her mouth.

She looked far too happy to be married. She must be his mistress, then—or one of them.

He must be keeping her in one of the sets of rooms across the way.

This was highly inappropriate. Olivia would have a word with the landlord as soon as possible. As long as Fencroft House and his property shared the garden, she did have some say in the matter.

The very last thing that was going to happen was for innocent Victor to associate with such a man—to think he was some sort of hero when in fact he kept a woman.

In any event she had learned an important lesson. She could scarcely imagine what had come over her, if only briefly. To allow her mind to wonder about a man, to fantasise and imagine that he might be better than most, was folly.

There were faithful men, of course. Her brother Heath was one. And, she thought Clementine's cousin, Madeline, had a devoted husband, as well.

But to sort out which men were honourable and which men were not? No, Olivia would not do it. She had no intention of taking such a risk again.

Chapter Three

Joe stared out of his chamber window, watching rain tap on the garden two storeys below.

Through the drizzle he could see the wavering image of the large home on the other side. He'd been told it was the residence of an earl. Fencroft, he thought the butler had said. He wondered if the Earl would be attending the ball tonight.

If he was, would he be wearing the same sort of stiff-looking clothing that had been delivered to Joe this afternoon?

The formal garments lay across his bed in a precisely arranged line. He'd bet the price of a steer gone to market that his toes were too wide for the gentlemanly boots.

Were it not for the fact that his sister set a great store in appearances, he'd wad it all up in a heap and toss it out of the window.

After all the stares he'd got during the outing to Bond Street she had become convinced he could not be presented to society garbed as an uncivilised rancher.

Being certain of it, Roselina had sent the butler to

buy the fancy duds he could not look at without feeling itchy.

He hadn't wanted a butler but it seemed as if the fellow came with the place. Joe did not think this could be a common practice, having a servant as part of a rental arrangement, but it was one the landlord had insisted upon. His sets of rooms were for ladies and gentlemen of distinction and standards must be upheld.

Since the landlord did not forbid Sir Bristle's presence Joe accepted the butler in turn.

From what Roselina had to say, the fellow had experience in serving Americans. The last tenant had been a wealthy industrialist who married his granddaughter off to the Earl who lived on the far side of the garden.

Evidently, Mr Bowmeyer would take pride in dressing Joe in the fancy garments that seemed more foreign to him than the moon.

He didn't have to turn to see the shiny black top hat, its absurd image was reflected in the window glass.

How tall would he be if he wore it? He'd probably collide with a chandelier and set the ballroom ablaze.

Maybe he ought to pretend to be ill. If he were forced to wear the thing, it would not be a lie.

But no. He would not find a noble husband for Roselina by hiding away at his room.

The sooner she was betrothed, the sooner he could travel to Grasmere, see to business at Haversmere and then go home—home to Wyoming, a vast open space where what he put on his head was no one's business but his own.

The ranch in Wyoming was where he grew to be a man. It suited him. The busy streets of London with everyone strolling along to be seen, greeting each other so properly, so mannerly, it all felt very foreign to him.

Perhaps if Pa had ever brought him along on the yearly trips to England, he would not feel so much like a fish gasping on a riverbank. But Pa had felt it best for Joe to remain at home to watch over Ma and Roselina and tend to the business of cattle ranching.

One distant day from now Joe would become Baron, although he tried not to think about it much because it would mean—

Once again he put the thought away. Every time Pa taught him about Haversmere, about raising sheep instead of cattle, Joe shied from the lesson. It wasn't that he had anything against sheep, or Haversmere, but the ranch was home—the place in the world his roots grew deep.

While he had shied from those lessons in his heart, he had paid attention to them. On the far-off day he became Baron he would need to know.

He wondered if by then he would have a son of his own who would care for things at the ranch while Joe made the journey to Haversmere.

Just like Pa did, he would remain at the estate for a few months, meet with folks, make plans with the estate manager, then go home where his heart lived.

A soft knock rapped on his door. It slid open without a squeak and his sister's head poked into view.

'Mr Bowmeyer is ready to serve tea. You must come at once.'

'Tea?'

'Yes, and little sandwiches. You'll like them.'

'I'll hate them. Is there at least coffee?'

She shook her head.

'You go ahead without me.'

She came inside and snatched his sleeve. 'You are my

guardian. You must learn to take tea in a proper way. Mr Bowmeyer has offered to instruct you. It is quite a kind gesture and we will not offend him.'

'Quite?' He could not recall ever hearing his sister use the word that way. 'When did you start speaking so properly?'

'I've had lessons. It just never seemed right to speak so formally at the ranch.'

'You sure you really want to marry a society fellow?'

'Yes.' She nodded confidently, hauling him towards the door. 'Quite.'

'All right. For your sake I will learn, but I'm not wearing that top hat tonight. There are some things a man just can't do.'

'Every other gentleman will be sporting one and feeling fashionable.'

'The difference between them and me is that I'm not a gentleman.'

'As the son of Baron Haversmere, you most certainly are.'

'Heaven help me.' He shook his head going down the stairs. 'If I didn't love you and Ma so dang much, I'd hightail it to Haversmere tonight. Pa does say it is a bit of paradise.'

'I love you, too, Joe. I recall that, as much as Pa loves the ranch, he always says he left a piece of his heart here. I suppose it had to do with your mother as much as anything.'

Mr Bowmeyer stood beside the parlour door, stiff and proper looking. He nodded when Joe passed by him.

'Mr Steton,' he greeted him with a nod. Joe caught sight of the small sandwiches. He'd eat one in a single bite. Didn't figure he'd even need to chew.

It was the teacup that worried him, though, being as dainty a piece of porcelain as he'd ever seen. If he didn't snap the fragile-looking handle off, he'd consider it a wonder.

Had Olivia been invited to any other ball this evening she might have remained at home. She had hired Miss Hopp as governess and the lady had already begun her service.

It would have been good to stay close at hand to be sure that Victor and Miss Hopp got along. Luckily Mrs Hughes had agreed to keep an eye out and Olivia had faith in her housekeeper's judgement.

Since an invitation from Her Grace was a summons more than a request, she instead found herself on the short carriage ride to the Duke and Duchess's Mayfair estate.

The rain had cleared, giving way to a lovely starry sky. Olivia might have easily walked the distance, but to go out at night without a man to accompany her would be folly even for a widow.

Within moments she found herself mounting the steps, wondering who would, and who would not, be in attendance.

Now that she was entering the house, the vestibule sweet with the scent of spring flowers and gaslight from the chandeliers casting the room in an elegant glow, she was glad she had come.

Having become used to the company of Clementine and her brood, Fencroft House seemed too quiet.

The company of others would be just the thing. Of course, even after all this time there would be those who looked at her with pitying glances because of what her late husband had done. She had become accustomed to it and for the most part managed to smile past the shame.

In fact, she was not at all uncomfortable walking into the grand ballroom without having a man's arm to cling to.

That was one advantage of being a widow. She had quite a bit more freedom than a debutante did in her Season.

It felt rather nice to be off the marriage market. Wedded bliss was a myth and she was glad to be done with it. While there were gentlemen seeking widows as brides, Olivia had no fortune of her own, nothing really to offer, and so felt quite safe from their attentions.

There was not a gentleman present tonight who intrigued her in the least. Oh, to be honest, if Victor's cowboy sauntered in he would capture her attention. Luckily that was not going to happen. The very last thing she wanted was for him to notice and remember her.

Indeed, it was fortunate that earlier today she had managed to whisk Victor into the house before her son had a chance to call out to him. It would have been embarrassing if he, again, claimed the man as his own.

Only steps into the ballroom, Olivia spotted a face she did not wish to see. A former mistress of her husband's. Not the one whose bed he had died in, but another.

Fortunately, in that moment Her Grace spotted her. The Duchess hurried forward, her hands stretched in greeting and a welcoming smile upon her round face.

'My dear Olivia! I feared you might not come without someone of your family in attendance, but I'm so pleased that you did.'

'You seem like family to me, Your Grace.'

The Duchess slipped her arm through Olivia's, leading her deeper into the ballroom.

'And you to me, my dear. We have a fine gathering tonight. So many people coming in from the country.'

'Everything looks enchanting, as it always does.'

'I do adore a bit of enchantment, as I know you do as well.'

Yes, in a decorative sense. But in matters of the heart, well, she'd learned better.

'It is quite delightful.'

'Now that you are not in mourning for anyone, I do believe it is time for you to find a husband.'

'I've no interest in that, I assure you.'

'Hmm…' Lady Guthrie glanced about the room. 'There is Lord Nelby. Rather nice looking and a decent sort. Or perhaps his brother. You would not mind a younger son?'

'I would mind any son.'

'Nonsense. You are young and beautiful. And your dear little boy needs a father. It is time you put the past away. What Mr Shaw did to you was unconscionable, but you cannot let that cripple you. You must go on with your life.'

'My life is adequate as it is.'

'Living on the good graces of your brother and his wife? Again, nonsense.'

'To marry again or not is my choice, Your Grace.'

'Why, yes, of course it is. And you will choose more wisely this time.'

While she spoke, the Duchess's canny gaze swept over the guests. The woman was a matchmaker to the bone. Even her garden seemed designed to encourage romance, having lovely winding paths and secret alcoves.

More than one marriage had been instigated by a visit to the Duchess's garden.

'Look! The Earl of Grayson has come. He is just out of mourning and is no doubt here to seek a wife. Come along, we will have a word with him.'

'I'm rather thirsty all of a sudden. I believe I will find my way to the punchbowl.'

'Wait over there by the palm near the garden door. I'll have Grayson bring you a cup.' Olivia nodded, but had no intention of waiting anywhere for the Earl.

'Oh!' The Duchess spun back on her tracks, lowered her voice. 'Flirt with any eligible gentleman who takes your fancy, but be aware that the Marquess of Waverly has returned to town and is present tonight. You must not encourage him.'

Any woman with a pinch of wariness would not. Waverly was a predator. Too many foolish widows had fallen victim to his handsome face and the compliments he used to lure them.

Once that hunter had a lady in his sights, there was no getting away. His focus upon her became all but— demented, yes, that word suited superbly.

Nothing would deter him from prowling after her skirt, not even the fact that he already had a perfectly lovely wife. Olivia wondered if Lady Waverly had heard the rumour that her husband had portraits painted of his mistresses. After spurning them he hung their likeness on the wall of his secret room, along with the mounted heads of game he had hunted.

Further rumour had it that he boasted of having a tiger's head and a zebra's tail on said wall. That was one rumour she never intended to discover the truth of.

She would be sure and keep the full width of the room between them given that she was a widow and his favourite prey. He might consider her a great challenge since she was known to scorn any type of dalliance.

All of a sudden people began to whisper. The drone of shushed words became a hum from one end of the room to the other.

'Obviously American,' she heard, then words such as, 'Cowboy, uncouth interloper—not a gentleman.'

Oh, dear. It could only be the one man in all of London—or creation—she did not wish to encounter. Joe Steton.

From the corner of her eye she saw Lord Grayson approaching, a cup of punch in each of his hands. It would be the height of rudeness to leave him standing alone beside the palm but, really, she did not want to encounter the cowboy.

The reason she did not want to disturbed and confused her.

What she wanted little mattered since there he was, as bold as a man could be, his confident-looking strides carrying him into the ballroom. His companion, the pretty young mistress he had consorted with in the garden, clutched his arm, her face going from pink to cherry-red the further into company they came.

Not everyone expressed dismay at Mr Steton's rustic dress. Clearly many of the younger ladies found his cowboy attire to be dashing.

Indeed, the way he tipped his black hat to them in greeting?

Despite herself, it made her heart beat faster and her palms grow damp.

Spinning about, she strode outside into the tranquillity of the sweetly scented garden.

* * *

Joe felt the full weight of the mistake he had made as soon as he walked into the ballroom. The eyes of a hundred people settled upon him, judged and weighed him.

Roselina had warned him to don gentleman's clothing, but in the end he could not bring himself to do it. No, curse it, he'd stubbornly refused to give up the familiar comfort of his Stetson, boots and buckskin coat.

Even Bowmeyer's frown of censure had not been enough to get him to stuff his feet into those polished shoes and yank the fashionable hat on his head.

'Fashion be damned' had been his exact words to the man.

Now Roselina was paying the price for it.

This ought to have been his sister's shining moment, her grand presentation into polite society.

He greatly regretted that the attention was focused so intently upon him that she went all but unnoticed beside him.

There was nothing for it now but to push on and locate their hostess. Perhaps being a woman—a duchess and a friend of his father's—the lady might know how to set things right for Roselina.

First he would need to locate her. She might be any one of the gaily bedecked matrons in the room.

Father had written informing Lady Guthrie that ill health prevented him from making his yearly trip and that he was sorry to miss visiting with her. Joe had read the letter his father had written, knew it explained that it would be Joe coming in his stead. Most of the letter, though, had to do with Roselina finding a husband.

He could only hope the Duchess would know more how to go about it than he did.

Blamed helpless was how he felt. Like a trout trying

to make his way downstream in the midst of spawning salmon going up.

'There she is,' Roselina murmured, her voice sounding relieved.

His sister nodded at a group of woman who openly gawked at him. Some seemed merely confused while others judged him harshly.

'How do you know?'

'She has a regal bearing about her. I can just tell.'

The woman his sister indicated appeared at ease in the company and yet elegant in bearing.

The Duchess cast a frown at the ladies, who had no doubt been discussing his crass appearance. They fell silent, looking owl-eyed at each other rather than at him.

Everything about the lady told of her position as Duchess.

Leaving the group she had been with, she glided towards him and Roselina, her hands extended in greeting. Her smile had to be the most reassuring thing Joe had seen in some time.

'You can only be Josiah!' She squeezed his hands, then turned her attention to his sister.

'Your Grace.' His sister gave a small, pretty curtsy. When had she learned to do that? Ought he to have bowed or some such thing? 'It is a great pleasure to meet you.'

'You, my dear, are as lovely as your father boasted you were.' The Duchess leaned forward, kissed Roselina's still-flaming cheek. In a lowered voice she said, 'I've got you under my wing, sweet bird. Do not worry about a thing.'

Roselina tipped her chin in his direction, her brows arched in worry.

'He'll clean up rather well, I think.'

Clean up? He'd bathed only hours ago. His leather was well worn, but he was certain it did not reek.

'You must feel rather out of your element, Josiah. Life here in London is far from what you will be used to.'

'Yes, ma'am, it is.'

For no good reason, Roselina stepped discreetly on his toe. Her skirt covered the movement so the Duchess was not aware of the assault to his boot. When his sister shot him a glare he realised his faux pas.

'Your Grace,' he amended and noticed Roselina's sigh of relief.

'As I said, Josiah, our ways must be quite foreign to you. At times they are a puzzle, even to me. But come along, your sister must be introduced to the young men.'

'I wonder if I'd best stay back.' The last thing he wanted to do was disgrace his sister more than he already had.

'That will not do—no—Roselina will be making a formal introduction to her prospective suitors. They will need to understand that she is not to be dallied with, but has a fierce guardian.'

He wished the guardian was Pa and not him. Pa would know how to thwart a disrespectful fellow without laying him out flat. What would be acceptable in Wyoming would no doubt get him banned from polite society here in London.

'I wonder, Your Grace—how did my father handle it? I know he is Baron Haversmere, but I have only ever known him as a rancher.'

'He is a gentleman to the core. He was raised for the position, although I rather think it would have been interesting to know him as a rancher. I will say, the Duke and I missed him terribly when he went away. We both tried to convince him to purchase an estate closer to London. But his grief was intense, you understand, and along with that his mother-in-law never ceased berating and blaming him. In the end he must have felt putting an ocean between himself and everything here was the only answer.'

'Did you know Josiah's mother, Your Grace?'

Joe nearly tripped on his boot toe. In eighteen years Roselina had never called him anything but Joe, nor had anyone else.

'Indeed.' Her Grace stood still, looked back and forth between him and his sister. Compassion suffused her face. 'Since she was a little girl. Everyone adored Violet. She was a bright spirit, but a delicate one. Something like you, Roselina, although you do not share a blood connection with her.'

'The truth is, I am not a bit delicate. My size is quite deceptive and does not reflect who I am.'

The Duchess cupped Roselina's face with her palm. 'You will do amazingly well here, my dear,' she whispered. 'Every gentleman could benefit having a lady with spirit.'

Releasing his sister, the Duchess smiled at him, the twinkle in her eye pronounced. 'Perhaps we shall find such a lady for you.'

'As much as I appreciate the thought, Your Grace, I'll be going home when my business here is finished. I suspect the fine women here would not be comfortable in Wyoming.'

'I wonder if you will change your mind once you see Haversmere. It is one of the loveliest places on the planet for all that your grandmother detested it.'

'Pa says she blamed my mother's death on the wet climate.'

'I suppose she needed to blame it on something. Her resentment towards your father for taking her daughter to Haversmere was not sufficient for her grief. It was a shame she was so consumed by it. In rejecting him she forfeited knowing you.'

'I wish we had met her,' Roselina said, gently squeezing his arm. 'Perhaps if she had known Joe, it might have helped.'

'Of course it would have. I grieved when your grandmother passed away. Not only for her death, but for the life she never truly lived. Ah…and it was such a shame about your grandfather. Did your father ever speak of him?'

'He seldom spoke of either of them.'

'One can hardly blame him for that. Tragedy is not to be dwelt upon. But your grandfather perished in a shipwreck while travelling to France. There was a great storm, everyone aboard was lost. It happened only two years after your mother died and it quite did Lady Hampton in.'

The Duchess was quiet for a moment, giving him time to let the news settle, he figured.

'But here we are,' she said brightly. 'Grateful to be together on this lovely night and looking forward to your happy future, my sweet girl. Shall we continue on?'

'Oh, yes!' Roselina did indeed smell like her name, just as she'd hoped to. The pink blush of excitement in her cheeks made her resemble a freshly bloomed rose, too.

Joe followed along, meeting gentleman after gentleman, looking stern and feeling—lacking.

As soon as the opportunity arose, he would sneak out the open doors and into the peaceful-looking garden.

* * *

For all that Olivia had believed she wanted company, she found the solitude of the garden to be a balm. The spring air was crisp, but not frigid as it had been only weeks ago.

Without clouds to block them, the stars made a brilliant show. She stood still at a bend in the path, looking up and feeling overwhelmed.

How far did they go on, blinking and shooting across the heavens? Just to look at them, she guessed it was for ever.

All of a sudden she felt the air stir ever so slightly, heard the crunch of a boot step around the bend of the path.

'Lady Olivia, how delightful to come upon you like this.'

It was not delightful. It was beyond unfortunate.

'I see you enjoy stargazing just as I do,' he said while stepping too close.

'Indeed. I also find it is better a solitary activity, Lord Waverly. I'll bid you good evening.'

'Surely not!'

He took another step closer. She shook her head, narrowed her eyes so he backed up, but half a step only, which made it appear that he was retreating when, in fact, he moved closer.

'I find stargazing with a beautiful woman to be more entertaining.'

'Is your wife in attendance, Lord Waverly? I've no doubt she would enjoy the sight.'

'She would tire too quickly. She is in her confinement and I find I am rather lonely tonight. Please say you will walk with me.'

'I've finished with the stars. I'm going back inside.'

He stepped around, blocked her way.

'I imagine you are lonely as well. How long has it been since your devoted husband died?' He smiled, but there was nothing remotely friendly in the gesture. 'Oh, but as I recall he was not devoted. Yes, there was some nasty business of him dying in another woman's bed.'

'Step out of my way.' Heat flared through her, made her feel like a match newly struck.

A gentleman would move aside, heed the warning in her indignant expression. She was accomplished at this particular sneer, but he seemed indifferent to it.

Instead, he took an indulgent posture, leaning against the trunk of a tree, arms crossed over his chest and head tipped as if he were judging how best to entrap fresh prey.

Somehow even lounging on the tree he managed to block her retreat. Clearly he was skilled in this game.

'I imagine you were a lonely woman well before your husband's sad demise.' Now he was staring at her chest while slowly straightening away from the tree. 'I'm lonely, too. Surely we can find a bit of pleasantness this evening.'

There had to be something to hurl at him other than a sharp tongue.

'Are you such a coward then that you cannot look me in the eye when you suggest such a vile thing?'

'Come now, Lady Olivia. Step with me into this alcove and I will give you the most pleasant few moments you have ever spent.'

'Clearly you think highly of your prowess, Lord Waverly. For all that my late husband was a disloyal lout, he did manage better than a few moments.'

Perhaps she ought not have poked his pride, but it

was what was at the heart of this confrontation. Not romance or pleasure—but egotism.

The more feminine conquests he made, the more powerful he felt.

Olivia Cavill Shaw was not going to be a conquest. Although, having insulted him, she might now have to take the brunt of his indignation.

He smiled in response, but the gesture appeared feral with his white teeth grinding behind shapely but wooden-looking lips.

It seemed that words were not going to convince him to step to the side.

A weapon was what she needed. Glancing about, she spotted a twig, a grey feather and a tuft of newly sprouted grass.

Her shoe it must be, although the toe was rounded more than pointed. The heel might do, being a small block of wood.

Reaching down, she plucked it off, waved it in front of his nose. The shoe would not disable him, but perhaps it would dissuade him. No gentleman would want to return to the ballroom with his face scratched. Questions would be asked.

'My dear, dear lady.' He caught her wrist, squeezed hard until she dropped the shoe. 'You need not disrobe for what I have in mind.'

She struggled against his mean grip. She ought to scream. She truly ought to, but she had faced so much shame already she could not bear any more.

If people believed she was assaulted in the garden, there would be no end to the pitying looks.

She kicked his shin. He snared her waist, trying to drag her while she dug her feet into the gravel path.

Something pierced her heel. She yelped because it stung like the dickens.

To her everlasting astonishment, a fist ploughed over her shoulder from behind, then slammed into Waverly's nose.

She spun about, gazing straight into the enraged face of her—Victor's, rather—cowboy. She was only vaguely aware of Lord Waverly swaying on his knees and clutching his bleeding nose.

Chapter Four

'My dear, dear lady, you need not disrobe for what I have in mind,' Joe heard a voice say the instant before he rounded a corner of the garden path.

He stopped, wondering how to best retreat without intruding upon the couple.

Then he heard the scrape and scramble of feet, a man's low, predatory laugh.

He dashed around the bend, saw a woman being dragged towards an alcove.

Red haze flashed in his brain. He did not consider consequence, only the need to act. He curled his fist, reached over the woman's shoulder and gave the villain a solid punch in the face.

With his free arm, he tucked the lady behind him, even while the blow crunched bone.

The fellow went down on his knees, grasping his nose. Blood spurted through his fingers and dripped on his fancy shirt. It sounded as though he might be choking back a sob. He made no move to rise and defend himself.

Coward. He'd seen men like this. All huff and blow

to women, but they ran tail-tucked from a fair fight with a man.

Since the scoundrel no longer seemed a threat, Joe shifted his attention to the lady.

'Have you been harmed, ma'am?' For the first time his mind registered more than seeing a threatened female. He sucked in a sharp breath. 'Mrs Shaw?'

She shook her head while tucking strands of hair back into the strict-looking bun they had fallen loose from.

'I'm cursing myself for a fool. I knew Lord Waverly was in attendance, but I walked out alone in spite of it.' Her wide blue eyes blinked—she seemed to be looking for something on the ground. 'Things would have become quite ugly had you not happened by. I thank you, Mr Steton. It seems I am in your debt once again.'

While the fellow on the ground did seem deflated, Joe thought it best to put several steps between him and Mrs Shaw.

'I reckon a lady ought to be able to take a walk without being set upon.'

'Are all cowboys so noble-minded?' she asked while still looking for something on the ground.

He shrugged one shoulder. 'We are men like any other.'

She looked up from whatever she was searching for, gazing intently at him.

'I wonder,' was all she said.

'What are you looking for?'

Far in the distance he heard a dog barking. Could be it sensed what had happened and was distressed over it. If the animal was anything like Sir Bristle, it could smell trouble from half a mile out.

'My shoe. I meant to hit him with it.'

Mrs Shaw's words sounded as brave as any he'd ever heard a lady in peril speak. The nearly imperceptible shiver of her fingers said she was putting on a courageous face.

He greatly admired her for it.

A flash of blue caught the moonlight. He strode halfway back to the man, snatched up the satin slipper, then came back and handed it to her.

The dog's barking sounded louder and more urgent— a mite closer, too. Joe figured it must have got out of its yard and was being chased by its owners.

Mrs Shaw slid the delicate-looking shoe over her foot, but uttered a muffled 'ouch'.

The cad behind them was slowly coming to his feet.

'Are you injured?' The furrow between her brows said so. The way she pressed her lips together confirmed it.

'A splinter in my heel, that's all.'

'I hope your husband won't mind, but I'm going to carry you back to the house.'

He swept her up before she had time to say no. She circled her arms about his neck for balance, but it was obvious she was reluctant to do so.

That was something to admire as well. Who did not adore a virtuous woman who recognised necessity without putting on maidenly airs of protest?

'My husband will not care a whit. I'm a widow.'

'Oh, well, I'm sorry to hear it.'

He wasn't though, not completely.

'Don't fret over it, Mr Steton. I'm far better off without him.'

Blame it, he should not be toe-tapping in his boots to hear it. He was going home as soon as he was able.

The last thing he was going to do was tangle with a pretty widow.

'I'm sorry to hear that, too.'

It was the truth in spite of his immediate reaction. A fine woman like her ought to have been appreciated.

'Wolf!' a voice from inside the house screamed.

Screeches and the crash of breaking glass spilled out into the garden.

He started to curse, but sucked the word back because of the lady in his arms.

'You have a wolf, do you not, Mr Steton?'

'Sir Bristle is only a quarter-wolf. The rest is just dog.'

Men shouted. It sounded as if items were being hurled, clattering off walls.

'But he does appear to be a wolf. There is a very good chance he belongs to you.'

'Is it too much to hope there is an actual wolf prowling Mayfair?'

'A bit much, yes.'

In an explosion of fur and barking, Sir Bristle burst upon the terrace. Roselina ran behind him, waving her arms and shouting at him to sit.

The dog rushed past him and Mrs Shaw, who clung suddenly tighter to his neck. Although congenial at heart, the dog could look fierce when the need arose.

This was clearly one of those times.

Lord Waverly had not quite made his feet when Sir Bristle knocked him flat again.

The dog growled, baring his long teeth. Waverly covered his face with his arms...and whined?

'Come,' Joe stated. The wolf-dog gave a soft huff in the villain's face, then trotted over to sit at Joe's side and sniff Mrs Shaw's skirt. 'Good boy.'

'You wouldn't say so...' Roselina stood in front of him, grasping her middle, breathless from the chase '... if you saw the ballroom. Who is that?'

'Fellow called Waverly.' Joe cast a scowl at him. 'As far as anyone is to know, Sir Bristle knocked him over and he hit his nose on a stone.'

Roselina glanced about at the shrubbery. She walked to a camellia, then reached under and came up with a good-sized rock.

'This one?' She tossed it at Waverly's feet.

Joe nodded, grinned. 'That very one.'

'Would it not be best if you set the lady down before everyone comes outside?'

'She has a splinter in her foot.'

'Lend her your arm, then.' Roselina petted Sir Bristle's head without having to lean down to do it. 'It's more seemly.'

Blame it if she wasn't right. He did set Mrs Shaw down, but felt some reluctance in doing so. The woman had intrigued him from the start.

For some reason she was staring slant eyed at Roselina.

Perhaps because they had not been properly introduced?

Mrs Shaw's feet touched the path only an instant before the Duchess and a crowd burst on to the terrace. One fellow carried a rifle at the ready.

Joe supported Mrs Shaw with a hand under her elbow.

Roselina stood in front of Sir Bristle, spreading her skirt. The dog was at least partially hidden from view.

With a sidelong glance, Roselina smiled at Mrs Shaw. 'Hello, I'm Roselina.'

'Mrs Shaw,' he said while watching the agitated,

chattering group on the terrace surge forward, 'may I present my sister, Miss Steton?'

Sister?

Not a fledgling mistress?

With everything that had transpired within the past moments, this was the one that riveted her attention?

Not the Marquess on the ground. Not a supposed wolf invasion. But the discovery that Mr Steton was not keeping the girl.

It was nearly impossible to determine whether she was relieved or distressed. It was very likely that she was both.

Add to that feeling miserably guilty. For someone who was striving to be a more amiable person she had failed completely—once again she'd been a judgemental shrew. What she had witnessed between Joe and his sister in the garden had been sweet and tender. She was the one to have made it lurid.

She would simply have to strive to be better.

'I can scarce believe my debut has come to this,' said Mr Steton's sister Roselina, with a great, resigned sigh. 'No man will want to court me now.'

The child was so fresh, so blooming with hope. Olivia had to fight the urge to warn her to be cautious.

She might as well advise herself of the same thing, standing beside Mr Steton, leaning against his strong arm, her emotions off kilter. On the one hand her stomach had the pleasant sensation of small butterflies flapping about. On the other hand she was quite irritated that it did.

Well, she would sort out the confusion later tonight in the quiet of her bed.

In the moment she must decide how best to navigate away from scandal.

Nelson Waverly might go along with the story of hitting his nose on a stone. He would hardly want it known what he had really been about and that he had been thwarted by a common cowboy.

But no—hardly common—she knew this even if she did not want to admit that she did. Not only was the man Victor's hero, but he had acted her champion—twice.

If only he had indeed kept a mistress, she would not be so flustered. He would be just one more unreliable male. As it was, well—she had best focus on the Duke and Duchess who were presently charging forward at the head of their guests.

Somehow this must all play out for the good of Mr Steton's sister. Way back in a corner of Olivia's mind, she remembered how it felt to be a debutante, the magic and the thrill.

Of course it was all a very long time ago.

The crowd halted a prudent distance away from Sir Bristle, who decided to stand to greet them. The fact that his tail was wagging failed to keep most of the lords and ladies from looking agitated.

'Is this your beast?' demanded the Duke with a severe glare at Mr Steton.

It was as much a surprise to see the Duke at the ball as it was the wolf. Ordinarily he shunned social gatherings.

'I beg your pardon for the disturbance,' Mr Steton said.

'Sir Bristle is not accustomed to being away from the ranch,' Roselina explained while she knelt beside the beast, her arm draped over his shoulders. 'He really is the sweetest creature.'

'This is very irregular.' The Duke looked at his wife, his brows lifted as if asking for direction in the matter.

'It is not unheard of for an animal to create havoc at a ball.' Olivia was grateful to see the Duchess smiling, but she was the only one to be doing so. 'Do you not recall when we attended a ball in Derbyshire? Oh, how many years ago was that?'

'I do not recall the event.'

'As well you might not, my dear. It was rather a long time ago. Lord Dalton was quite into his cups and took it into his head to charge into the ballroom on his great beast of a horse while singing "God Save the Queen". Everyone was scattering and screaming. It was very much like tonight.'

'I ought to recall that.' The Duke blinked as if trying to summon the memory.

'Do not fret over it, my dear. It really was so long ago.' She patted the Duke's arm. 'No one has been harmed except perhaps Lord Waverly. Would you kindly explain to us how you find yourself thus?'

Olivia turned to look at the lecher. He seemed about to speak, so she did it first.

'I was walking in the garden, Your Grace. I saw what happened.'

'Please enlighten us.'

'The dog bounded to Lord Waverly, to lick his face in greeting, but the Marquess was terrified. He tried to run, but he tripped over his feet. When he fell he hit his nose on a stone.'

'I see…' Olivia was quite certain that the canny woman knew very well the story was a fabrication. She would not reveal her suspicion since she would not want the scandal to taint her gathering, or Olivia. Much better to have the party enlivened by a supposed wolf.

'I imagine encountering a predator in the garden would be distressing. Shall I have your carriage summoned, my lord? No doubt you will recover from the ordeal more easily at home, with your wife to console you.'

'Thank you, Your Grace,' Lord Waverly muttered while dabbing his nose on his sleeve. 'You are most thoughtful.'

'May I touch your beast, Mr Steton?' the Duchess said, skilfully turning everyone's attention away from the villainy of the evening. 'I adore dogs and I have never seen one so large.'

'Certainly, and he's only a quarter-wolf. The other three-quarters is pure lovable dog. Same as every other one, he wants attention however he can get it.'

'Well, Sir Bristle, you quite resemble your name. I've no doubt your appearance here tonight will be spoken of for years.'

'I'll take him home. And again, I apologise.'

'Do let him stay.' Then in a quieter tone she added, 'It's always a boon to have a noble beast flush predators out of the garden.'

Joe's admiration for Her Grace was immense. He'd never met anyone who could twist a situation and make it come out to her liking the way the Duchess could.

The way things had unfolded in her garden made him think of a herd of stampeding cattle running for a precipice. Then there was Her Grace, neatly swirling a rope and lassoing the beasts, bringing them to order.

He was certain she suspected the truth concerning Waverly. She'd said as much and dismissed him without openly revealing anything.

Unless Waverly was a dimwit, he had to feel chastised.

By sugar, the lady could match wits with any lawyer and best him. If that had not been enough to earn Joe's eternal respect, she had shown the courage to touch the beast who had wreaked havoc through her home.

And havoc he had wreaked.

Trailing the other guests back inside the ballroom, Joe winced seeing half-a-dozen broken vases, flowers splayed across the floor and puddles of water pooling everywhere. There was an overturned sofa and probably more ruin than that, but the servants had already set to work righting things.

Still, had the dog not come charging in, there would have been no easy way to explain away what had happened to Waverly's nose and Mrs Shaw had made it plain that she did not care to have it made known.

'Come, all three of you.' The Duchess swept her hand in a gesture which left no doubt that this was an order and not a request. 'There are matters to be resolved.'

'I'll pay for every bit of damage,' Joe promised, following the Duchess down a long elegant hallway with gas sconces casting golden light on the rug.

'Indeed you will, my boy.'

About halfway towards a set of backstairs the Duchess opened a door and indicated they should follow her.

Joe was nearly taken aback at the elegance of the library. It was huge, having hundreds of volumes displayed on shelves. Rich wood and a snapping fire made it a place one would want to linger in, to take down every volume of poetry and take all night reading it.

'Pay no mind to the Duke. He sleeps like a stone.'

Sure seemed so. The fellow lay sprawled on a big stuffed chair with his feet on a footstool. His hands were crossed over his comfortably sized belly. If Joe was not mistaken, his face reflected a pleasant dream.

Being able to fall asleep so deeply and quickly was something to be envied, in Joe's opinion. It had been only moments since they had come in from the garden.

The Duchess indicated that Joe, Roselina and Mrs Shaw should sit on a divan. She sat across from them in a chair that was a match to her husband's.

As promised, the fellow was no more aware of their presence than a rock was of the lizard lounging upon it.

Her Grace's attention settled first on Mrs Shaw. 'I regret what happened to you, my dear. I can promise it will not happen again. I hope you were not hurt.'

'Just a splinter, my lady.' She still hadn't put her shoe on. The injury must still be causing her pain. 'It might have been worse had Mr Steton not come to my aid.'

'Indeed.' The Duchess's glance back and forth between them was interesting—speculative—he thought.

Joe wondered when she would come to the point of telling him how much he owed for the damage done by Sir Bristle.

'And you, my poor girl!' The Duchess fixed her attention on Roselina. 'To have your evening end in such a way! However, it started rather ominously, did it not?'

Had it? Joe could not recall what ominous thing the Duchess might be referring to.

'However, the mess can be salvaged. When all is said and done you will be sought after by every eligible young man.'

'Am I correct in assuming you have a plan, Your Grace?' There was the faintest crease to Mrs Shaw's lips, an ever-so-slight narrowing of her eyes that warned him she suspected something might be amiss.

'Naturally. I always have a plan. This one is particularly good.'

Did everyone fall into step with the Duchess's 'plans'?

Joe cringed, wondering how much was he going to end up paying for the night's events.

'First we will correct the impression that Roselina is less than refined. You, Josiah, will see to it.'

He nodded cautiously, not at all sure how he was to go about it. The fine hairs on the back of his neck went to attention because it was apparent that the Duchess did know how. He had a suspicion he might not like it.

'Beginning tomorrow, you will learn to present yourself as a gentleman. You will dress the part, speak it and act it.'

Not if it meant putting on the tall shiny hat.

'Olivia, you will be his instructor.'

Pushing open the nursery door, the phrase pounced upon her again—for perhaps the hundredth time since it had been uttered.

'Olivia, you will be his instructor.'

Everything since the moment of decree had been a something of a blur. Had it been in her best interests to do so, she would have come home from the ball at once.

As it was, she remained for another three hours, chatting and making it appear as if nothing untoward had happened.

Or if it had, it was nothing to do with her.

Had she fled for home, people would remember there had been three of them in the garden when Lord Waverly injured his nose. They would wonder, they would speculate, they would gossip.

Her dearest hope was to have a quiet life, a modest existence where she would not be the object of idle tongues.

Being lashed by idle tongues clearly didn't bother

Mr Steton. He had not felt it expedient to remain behind and keep up appearances.

Oh, no! Upon exiting the library, he had caught his
sister's arm, whistled for his one-quarter wolf and, quite
without a thought for what anyone might think, gone
home.

Was that what America was like? A country of people doing what they pleased without a thought for social
consequence? Would her family adopt that attitude and
return home to toss propriety to the wind?

It was true that society was changing, one saw it
every day. In some ways for the better, but in other
ways—well, things were not as they had always been.

Ah, but here she was, home at last and gazing at the
face of her sleeping angel. Miss Hopp looked rather
like an angel as well.

A weary young angel, asleep in a chair beside the
bed, her feet propped upon a stool and a storybook
open on her lap.

Olivia did not need to look to know the book would
be the one about Cowboy Earl—'the surest-shootin',
fastest-ridin', damsel-rescuin' hero of the West'.

It spoke well of the new governess that she had not
simply put Oliver in the nursery and left him to his own
devices at bedtime. Seeing her exhausted devotion, Olivia found it easier to overlook the girl's tendency to be
tardy on occasion.

'Miss Hopp,' she whispered.

The girl jolted upright in the chair. The book hit the
floor and what was left of her coiffure plopped in a
brown wave across her face.

'Oh, dearie me. I did not intend to fall asleep, my
lady.'

'It is quite all right, Miss Hopp. I will take over from here. You may retire to your quarters.'

Miss Hopp stood, curtsied and, while in a bent-kneed position, snatched up the book. She placed it on the bedside table, then hurried towards the door.

'Thank you, Miss Hopp. I appreciate coming home and finding Victor well tended.'

Until Clementine came into her life, Olivia could not recall having thanked a servant for doing what they were paid for.

Now, it only felt right and proper. Treating servants with deference was one change she felt had been too long in coming—if not to society at large—to Olivia Victoria Cavill Shaw.

'Oh, but truly, he is a delightful little boy. Good night, Lady Olivia.'

After kissing Victor's slightly damp curls, Olivia proceeded to her chambers.

Since Miss Hopp would by needs use the bedroom next to the nursery, Olivia had moved into the chambers Clementine had briefly occupied before she moved into the master's chamber with Heath.

Before Clementine, the quarters had belonged to Olivia's mother, although that had been many years ago. Even though Olivia had redecorated the room for her new sister-in-law, she kept her mother's chair where it had always been beside the large bay window.

It was late so, rather than waking her maid, she undressed herself, donned her sleeping gown, then fell into the chair.

Looking out the window at the garden cast her back in time to when she and Oliver sat on Mama's lap while listening to her tell stories. Tonight, just as it had then, moonlight sparkled on the water fountain. Trees and shrubs seemed streaked with fairy dust. She could all but hear Mama's voice speaking of beautiful princesses and their handsome princes.

When she was five years old fairy tales had been lovely. In fairy tales a prince would permit himself to be trampled by a herd of rats before he stole a princess's joy.

She drew her knees up to her chest, pulled a soft blanket over her shoulders.

'Olivia, you will be his instructor,' she mimicked the Duchess's autocratic voice.

Would she be, when it came down to it?

She did owe him a favour. Two favours, in fact. All things considered she was in rather large debt to the cowboy.

If only he were not a cowboy it would make the decision easier—because she did believe she had one—in spite of the edict.

Had Mr Steton been a sea captain or a chimney sweep, Victor would not be so enamoured of him. The very last thing she was going to allow to happen was for his young heart to be broken—by anyone.

As far as broken things went, there was Roselina to be considered. Through no fault of her own, the girl's hopes of a successful marriage were endangered. The happenings of the night were no doubt being discussed even now by husbands and wives in their beds, by other young ladies riding home in their carriages—by just about everyone who was still awake.

And by tomorrow the story of the cowboy, his sister and their marauding wolf would become even more embellished.

With any luck Lord Waverly and his bleeding nose would be mostly overlooked.

What could not be overlooked was the fact that when she had been desperate with fear because Victor was missing in the cemetery, Mr Steton had walked out of the mist and delivered him safely to her. Nor could she overlook the fact that she had been quite defenceless against the advances of the Marquess until Mr Steton had punched him in the nose.

Oh, indeed, she did owe him a debt. Unless she wished to remain beholden to him, she would need to repay it.

A lamp flickered on, illuminating a window on a second-floor room across the garden.

Someone stood at the window, looking down. Olivia was not able to see features from where she sat, only the dark silhouette of a petite woman.

The lady appeared to be plaiting her hair while gazing at the garden in serene contemplation—of course it might just as well be silent worry.

Certainly worry if she happened to be Roselina Steton.

All of a sudden a hairy creature bounded into the room, reared up and placed his great paws on her shoulders. He licked her face.

It appeared that she laughed, then ruffled his ears.

Another figure strode into view. Tall, muscular, his strides long and with purpose even in the small space of what must be the parlour.

Mr Steton. It could be no one else.

Gazing at him now, laughing with his sister and plucking the dog's paws from her shoulders, she felt ashamed.

She had judged them both quite wrongly. She was no better than the people who were, even this minute, judging Roselina for the appearance and manners of her brother.

Really, Olivia had no choice but to help her.

Yet it was the appearance and the manners of the man which made the decision difficult. He was far too handsome for her peace of mind. Why, his smile alone would bring any female to her knees, that was, if she was not already there by having looked too deeply into his rugged, greenish-brownish eyes.

Olivia Steton was one woman who had no wish to brought to her knees by a man. No—never again.

Roselina said something to him. She reached for an item on the table beside her. Olivia could not tell what it was until she plunked it down on her brother's head.

A top hat, clearly that was what it was. He shook his head. Roselina nodded, her hands fisted on her hips.

He plucked the hat from his head and tossed it over his shoulder. Roselina made a frustrated gesture with her hands and then walked out of the room, the dog trotting loyally behind her.

Mr Steton was left alone to stare down at the garden.

If watching Mr Steton's silhouette in a window made her heart beat faster, if seeing him lift his hand and yank it through his hair made her insides quiver, how would she manage spending time with him in the flesh?

What a poor choice of words! Flesh? Even if she did not utter it aloud, those five letters made her blush.

Spending time with him instructor to student, yes, that was far more fitting.

Flesh! Why ever had she thought it?

All of a sudden she had the distinct feeling that he could see her, was looking directly at her.

He could not possibly be. Her lamp was out, she was under a blanket.

And yet she felt him—his gaze settled upon her. No matter that she was hidden by a blanket and completely concealed from his gaze, she shivered in a disquieting way.

She had spent years sequestering her heart from such temptation. The only sensible thing to do was refuse the Duchess's dictate. The risk was too great. Not only for herself but for Victor.

What a shame that the sensible thing was not also the honourable thing, the compassionate thing.

But perhaps the appointed hour for his first lesson would come and go without him. What was to say he was willing to become a gentleman? He might not want it. There was every chance that he was content as he was.

If noon came and he did not come knocking, she would be greatly relieved. Indeed she would. But what if she was disappointed?

The thought did not bear thinking about, so she would not. Instead she would—

She tossed the blanket over her, huffed.

Under the dark privacy of the wool, she sensed that whatever happened tomorrow would change her. And perhaps not for the better.

Chapter Five

Joe's gut felt as sour as a tub of lemons until he heard Roselina laughing from the parlour. The sound had a way of setting things right inside him. It had ever since the first time she'd smiled at him while he held her and tickled her fat baby feet.

'That's a mighty fine fur coat you have on, Little Sister,' he said, coming into the parlour and seeing Sir Bristle express his adoration by reaching for her face with his great pink tongue.

'Help me take it off!'

He lifted the dog's paws off her shoulders, then ordered him to sit.

'What made him come charging into the party like he did, do you think?' Roselina petted the wide head, gazing into the dog's amber-brown eyes as if she might find an answer.

'He's got a sense for trouble and Mrs Shaw was in it.' He shrugged.

'It's possible, I suppose. And she is not Mrs Shaw. She is Lady Olivia. Her father was the Earl of Fencroft— it's her brother, Heath Cavill, who is now, though. They live in the big house on the other side of the garden.'

'How do you know all that?'

'It is important to know and so I do.' She reached for the table beside her, plucked up the blamed fancy hat. She set it on his head, then gave it a tug. 'Honestly, Joe, did you not wonder why our appointment for noon tomorrow is at Fencroft House?'

'I've been trying to figure a way out of it more than where to go.'

He snatched the hat off his head and tossed it over his shoulder. Let Sir Bristle chew it to threads was how he felt about the thing.

Roselina glowered at him. She curled her hands into fists, slammed them on her hips when he knew full well where she would rather slam them.

She'd been brought up a lady and so contented herself with a glower.

'Don't act a beast, Joe.' With that she spun about and flounced from the parlour, her half-plaited braid swinging.

A beast? Just because he didn't wear fancy shoes and walk with a dapper cane did not mean he was a beast.

There was the bit about punching a man in the face. If that made him a beast, he'd do it again.

He only hoped that Lady Olivia—not Mrs Shaw, but Lady Olivia—was recovered from the ordeal. No woman ought to go through what she had.

Yet he sensed she had been through worse. It seemed to him the looks folks gave her after the Sir Bristle episode went deeper than the situation called for.

As if perhaps she had been at the heart of something unfortunate in the past.

He could ask Roselina, she claimed to know so much.

Perhaps not, though. Lady Olivia's secrets were hers to share or not.

If they met again, which was likely since she had been ordered to be his instructor in all things restrictive, she might confide in him.

Once he agreed to be tutored in the art of looking like a gentleman, camaraderie might strike between them.

The problem was, he didn't think there was a blamed thing wrong with who he was. Putting on satin breeches would not change him.

By sugar, if it wouldn't change him, why was he fighting the idea?

He had promised Ma and Pa that he would find Roselina a husband. Not just any fellow either. One who deserved her and would make her happy.

It was not as if Pa hadn't warned him to purchase clothing more appropriate for a London drawing room. He just hadn't figured it would be so all-fired necessary.

In spite of his sister's warnings, he'd marched into that ball all pride and bluster, feeling that who he was inside was who folks would see.

He sure hadn't expected to feel every eye judge him before he had even said howdy.

Even now he felt looked at. Which was odd since the sensation of feeling watched was immediate, not a memory.

He glanced at the garden. A pair of cats frolicked in and out of the bushes, but that wasn't the cause of it.

No lamps glowed in the windows over at Fencroft House, which did not mean he was not being watched from a dark one.

He looked from one to the next, studying shadows.

Ah, just there!

Something shimmered in a shaft of moonlight. He squinted, saw a skein of fair hair catching the light.

Someone was sitting in a chair beside the window, but it was too dark to make out who it might be.

A chill skittered over his skin. Since it was a pleasant chill, not one warning of danger, he suspected it might be Lady Olivia.

When he thought about it, though, just because a sensation was pleasant did not make it less dangerous. Could be it was more so.

He liked the woman. Liked her child, too.

It would be prudent to keep in mind that he was only here until his business was completed. After that he was going home. The last thing he wanted was to tow a broken heart across the ocean. Most especially Lady Olivia's broken heart.

There was something about her that drew him. And it was not only the fact that she seemed vulnerable—a pretty widow in need of someone to watch out for her. No, it was more the 'pretty' part that tugged at him. And yet, it was more than that even. He had met many pretty women in his life, had been in love with one of them even. Whatever drew him to the widow was more than her lovely frown, the slant of her sky-blue eyes.

He did not know her well enough to know precisely what quality about her tickled his attention but, by sugar, he felt it.

The fact that he could not quite get her out of his mind did not change his feelings about leaving heartache in his wake. There was a time and a place for romance and this was neither of those.

If he decided to keep tomorrow's appointment, and he was beginning to think it was the right thing to do, he would have to keep close rein on his heart.

It wasn't so hard to imagine the pretty widow lassoing it and holding it captive.

* * *

The fellow who admitted them into Fencroft House looked more of a gentleman than Joe did.

When a servant appeared more dapper than the son of a baron, challenging times lay ahead.

Hopefully Lady Olivia was up to the chore of transforming this tumbleweed into a pruned hedge. A hedge that would just as soon present thorns as a willing stem.

'What are you thinking, Josiah? I don't like the look of it,' Roselina whispered while they followed the butler past an open set of doors that looked as though it ought to be a drawing room.

The house was huge, every inch of it elegant.

'That I do not want to be addressed as Josiah.'

'Perhaps not, but remember, Lady Olivia is not likely to be any happier about having to train you than you are to be trained.' A twittering of birds ushered out of an open door up ahead. 'But trained you will be. Once you go home you can be as thorny as a bramble, but just for a while, please Joe, learn to act a gentleman.'

'I'll do my best,' he said because promising was more than he could manage.

They followed Mr Ramsfield into the most amazingly green and leafy indoor place Joe had ever seen. It was as if the outside had grown inside. The only thing to distinguish one from the other was a glass wall. What separated the ceiling from the sky was more glass.

The birds were caged, but he wasn't sure they were aware of it since the aviary was nearly large enough to take a stroll in.

The air was heavily scented with some sort of blossom.

'Look,' she whispered. 'I think that's an orange tree.'

'Could be.' He'd never seen one, but knew they were plentiful in parts of the United States. He'd never thought to see one for the first time in London. Who would have expected that?

In the next second, he didn't think of another blamed thing.

The widow stood near a door that must lead to the garden separating her house from their apartment. Lady Olivia was bent over from the waist, industriously cleaning a smudge off of Victor's cheek.

The show of maternal devotion shot straight to his heart.

But why?

He'd seen mothers with their young countless times and he'd never felt struck dumb over it.

It must be because he had a connection of sorts to them due to the fact that he had reunited the two of them in the cemetery, had felt a part of the deeply moving event.

'Lady Olivia, your guests have arrived,' the butler announced, each syllable crispy enunciated.

'Good afternoon. What a pleasure it is to see you again.' Her greeting was even more properly delivered than the servant's had been, so much so that he could not tell whether it was sincere or not.

Probably not, which just might illustrate the first lesson of the day. Recite what was expected. Speak with courtesy even if the words you want to express are less than hospitable.

Truly, he hoped this was not the case. That her welcoming smile was actually an indication that she was pleased to see him.

Because he was more than pleased to see her. It was the single bright spot in this situation.

'Yee-ha!' Young Victor began to dash towards him, but his mother caught his collar, drawing him back firmly. 'But, Mother, it's my cowboy!'

'You may not claim people as yours. You know this. Apologise to Mr Steton at once.'

'But I claim you as my mother.'

Clearly Lady Olivia was at a loss as how to respond. She looked into her son's eyes for the longest time while she seemed to be searching for a logical response.

'How about this, Victor?' Joe felt compelled to speak up. 'You claim me and Roselina as your friends. If your mother approves, there is no harm in it. Folks claim friends every day and are proud to do so.'

'Yes, that will do.' He could not help but notice she said so rather reluctantly.

Roselina stepped forward and extended her hand to the boy. 'May I claim you as my friend?'

'Yes, miss.' Victor did not shake her hand, but executed a gentlemanly bow over it.

Joe figured that was lesson number two. Do not shake a lady's hand in greeting.

'Good day, my lady.' He tipped his Stetson in the same show of respect he always paid a woman.

She tilted her head to the side, her brow lifted ever so subtly in question.

Ah… He removed the hat, tucked it under his arm, then executed the bow, although not as skilfully as Victor had.

'Are you willing to take instruction from me, Mr Steton?'

'Oh, he is, my lady!' Roselina answered for him, no doubt fearful that he would refuse.

'Yes, Lady Olivia. Willing and grateful.'

* * *

Very well then, where to begin?

Watching her son pull on Mr Steton's sleeve while tugging him towards the orange tree, it was obvious.

Teaching the cowboy to execute a proper greeting would be a difficult thing while Victor insisted everyone watch him climb the tree.

The smile on his round, fair face all but broke her heart. It was not a cowboy her son yearned for. It was a father.

She could hardly blame him for wanting one of his own—but what was she to do about it?

With Miss Hopp having the day off to tend to family matters, it was evident that Olivia would simply need to carry on as best she could with Victor consuming her pupil's attention.

'May I take Victor out to play in the garden, Lady Olivia?' Roselina asked.

'That would be an excellent idea,' she said. Apparently Victor thought so. He leapt from the second limb of the tree, landed on the ground with a thump and a grin. 'Thank you, Miss Steton.'

'Oh, but please call me Roselina! It would give me the greatest pleasure if you did.'

Many people made such a statement without meaning it. Proper words to be uttered was all it came to.

Not so with this fresh young lady. It would be impossible not to be touched by her sincerity.

'You have a lovely name, Roselina. I will be happy to call you by it, but only if you call me Olivia.'

By allowing the familiarity there was a bit of a risk. It would only follow that she be on the same terms with her brother.

What was it about him that she feared? Nothing that

had to do with him, certainly. He seemed to be a decent young man.

Looking at her feelings truthfully, she knew it was her own weakness she feared. Josiah Steton made her feel things she had not felt in a very long time—if she had ever genuinely felt them.

There was a picture in one of Victor's books that depicted a cowboy throwing a lasso. The noose end of it twirled through the sky with whatever it meant to capture not drawn on the page.

It was rather too easy to see her heart as the target. If she were not vigilant in her feelings, she feared that rope might catch her.

If only Josiah Steton was not so handsome. More than that, if only he were not so decent.

Oh, but he was both decent and handsome.

Dangerous. She could nearly hear the hiss of that rope coming towards her.

As soon as he became a 'gentleman' young women would be tripping over their skirts for his attention.

It would be wise to keep her heart safely sequestered, the same as it had been since her husband's death.

'Might we play with Sir Bristle?'

Roselina looked at Olivia, dark brows lifted, waiting for consent.

Instinct warned against it. He was a large beast and part-wolf. But Roselina and Mr Steton seemed to trust him, so perhaps…

'All right, yes. Just stay close by where I can hear you.'

Roselina clapped her hands with as much pleasure as Victor did. They dashed outside, then raced each other across the courtyard towards the house next door.

Hearing their laughter warmed her, brought back memories of when she had been light of heart.

And then she had wed.

What would happen when Roselina married? It was too sad to think about. Better to direct her attention to the task at hand.

'Well,' she said, gazing up into a pair of eyes, not quite green, but not quite brown either. Straightforward, honest-looking eyes that might be her undoing if she allowed it.

'Well?'

Well! She had completely lost her train of thought—jumped aboard the one that led to getting lost in a masculine smile. She knew too well where that locomotive would derail.

'Shall we sit?' She indicated the small table set for luncheon.

He pulled out her chair for her. She sat, wondering how to proceed.

'It is my thought that, in spite of—' She indicated his clothing with a sweep of her hand. 'In any case, you are at heart a gentleman already. All that is needed is a spot of polish in your dress and your speech.'

'Yes, ma'am. It's what Roselina tells me.'

'Your sister is a lovely young woman. I believe Victor is a bit smitten with her.'

Josiah Steton actually winked at her! 'Everyone is.'

Her heart beat triple time responding to the genuine warmth in that expression. The lasso came for her, she ducked.

Of course, this would not do. If he executed that gesture in a social situation debutantes would swoon. The floor would be littered with skirts and petticoats of all colours.

She would need to correct this behaviour first thing, just as soon as her light-headedness passed.

'Do you not worry that she will—' it really was none of her business, yet it was not right to remain silent when sweet Roselina might fall victim to the same fate Olivia had '—be taken advantage of?'

'My sister is a canny judge of character. She's had to be with so many seeking her attention.'

'I hope that is true.' Prayed it was.

'Lady Olivia, I have to ask—is it truly necessary for me to turn into someone I am not in order for her to marry well?'

'The Duchess believes it is and so here we are.'

'I would like to know what your opinion of it is.'

'I agree. If gentlemen of quality are to court your sister, you must. The more suitors you have to choose from, the better off she will be. But may I speak bluntly?'

'I imagine you always do.'

'I do, of course. I've learned that I must and—'

'Didn't mean to say I don't approve. I do. So speak as bluntly as you like.'

'Oh, all right then—I only think, if she is set upon marriage that you must be diligent in whom you choose for her. Be wary of philanderers.'

His chest rumbled in a deep, subtle chuckle. She nearly had to catch her heart in cupped hands to keep it from—no matter, she did catch it.

'The fact is, I've little choice in which fellow she sets her sights on.'

'Oh! But you must. She leads with her heart, I think, she cannot give it away without due consideration—by you, Mr Steton. No matter how she believes there is no other man—'

Olivia clapped her hand over her mouth. How had

she let those words escape her? She had all but admitted her greatest mistake.

But that was not right. Had she not gone through what she had, she would not be Victor's mother. Nothing could make her sorry for that.

Which did not mean she ought to bleat it all out to a stranger.

'Will you call me Joe? Given our situation, it would be fitting.'

No doubt it would. Refusing would be a simpler thing had she not already set a precedent with his sister.

Calling him Joe would make him less of a stranger. This undertaking would be best accomplished by keeping him one.

He tilted his head in askance. The gesture made his eyes twinkle and his mouth quirk. The man was a tease.

What was wrong with her? She ought not to even be looking at his mouth.

She could not possibly call him Joe—not aloud at any rate. And yet, given how much time they would be spending together, Mr Steton did feel rather formal.

'But your name is Josiah, is it not?' It was what she had heard the Duchess call him.

'It is what I was born with, but no one calls me by it.'

'I will call you Josiah.' Yes, it was perfect—not intimate in the least. 'You must get used to it. Since it is how the Duchess refers to you, other people will as well. And it does sound rather distinguished.'

'It's my pa who is distinguished, not me.'

'Is he? May I ask why he is?'

'For being Baron Haversmere.'

Haversmere! Josiah's father was known in society, for all that his visits to London were for only part of the year. The Baron was congenial and well liked.

It all made sense now. Roselina was not simply an American wanting a title. She was a lady by birth. It was only fitting that she wed for social position.

'I'm acquainted with your father. But he is not here with you?'

Josiah pursed his mouth, his brows furrowed. A shadow deepened his expression.

'His health prevented it this year. So here I am.'

'To find a suitable match for your sister…'

'That first. But once I've done it, I'll go north to the estate and see to matters there. After that I plan to sail for home.'

Lord Haversmere had always seemed vigorous, so healthy and strong. She dearly hoped his illness was not serious.

She would never forget his compassion when Oliver died. He had attended the funeral. His sadness over her brother's passing had been quite sincere.

Now understanding Josiah's connection to Haversmere, she did not feel he was such a stranger.

Which did not mean she would call him Joe. Josiah was a fine name and she would use it.

'When you do return home, please give Lord Haversmere my best regards.'

He nodded, smiled, but under it she sensed that he would give anything to be there now. London must be vastly different than where he had come from.

'You and I will succeed in this business of spinning you into a gentleman, Josiah. Your father will rally at once when you tell him of the fine match Roselina has made.'

Knowing who he was—who he was connected to—put her more at ease.

However, she did not necessarily want to be at ease—not with a cowboy.

At least knowing he intended to go home made her job easier. Or, if not that, safer. It would be a simpler task to resist becoming overly familiar with a man who would only be in London for a short time.

Yes, indeed. He would be here and gone quicker than that wink of his could capture her. Because certainly it had not already done so. She was far too prudent a person to allow that to happen.

The sooner she transformed him into a dapper gentleman, the sooner he would succeed in his business and depart—which was what both of them wanted.

Was it not?

'I suggest that the first thing we need to do is get you used to finer clothing.' She smiled brightly at the idea. 'As they say, clothes make the man.'

'I was born bare as a jay. Wasn't any less of a male child for it.'

Funny how a frown did nothing to detract from his handsome appearance.

'After that we will begin lessons in genteel speech.'

'Yes, ma'am.'

Hmm. With work, she would educate him in proper speech.

But the grin, the wink? She doubted it could be tamed.

Worse. She suspected she would rather it not be.

Joe watched the garden from his bedroom window. Sure was a lot of rain in England. He didn't mind it so much since it kept things clean and refreshed.

But the reason he was standing here staring out the

window didn't have to do with the weather. It had to do with getting a glimpse of Olivia Shaw.

He should not be thinking about her, how blue her eyes were, how they slanted up at the corners and yet only looked sharp when she was out of sorts. He hadn't known her long, but already he knew this about her.

He'd also noticed how her lips were shaped like a bow, sitting merrily atop a gift. When she tried to press them in severity, they still looked agreeably plump.

He ought to turn away from the window, do something else. It was not likely that she would venture into the garden in a downpour.

But wait! A movement caught his eye in the window directly across the garden from this one.

Victor had spotted him and was waving his arm while bounding up and down.

Sir Bristle must have sensed it because he trotted up, shoved his nose under Joe's hand, then thumped his tail against the desk. Joe caught a vase of flowers just as it began to topple.

A young woman came to the window, glanced at the rain, then picked Victor up and carried him away.

Since it was unlikely that he would see Olivia before their appointment this afternoon, he gave up the effort.

Maybe he shouldn't call her Olivia, even in his mind, since she had yet to give him leave do so. Blame it if he wouldn't, though. Who was in his mind to hear it but him?

Now that he had agreed to being gentrified, he did want to succeed at it.

It might please his instructor if he came knowing something, even if it was only how to greet her in a proper way.

Sir Bristle followed him out of the bedroom.

'Mr Bowmeyer has brought the mail,' Roselina greeted him with a frown while shuffling though the envelopes one more time. 'There is nothing from Ma or Pa.'

'You can't expect there to be. We haven't been here long enough. Besides, the spring calves will keep them busy sun up to sundown.'

'But I miss them, Joe.'

'Are you sure this is what you want? You can go home and marry an American fellow.'

'I am sure and I'm thrilled as can be to be here—do not think I regret coming. I just miss them.'

So did he. He missed them and every acre of land on the ranch. The sooner he accomplished what he'd come for the sooner he could get back to the place he called home. The place where he intended to raise a fine family, to help their roots grow deep in rich Wyoming soil.

He'd always known in a vague way he would enjoy having children of his own, but now, knowing Victor, seeing the bond between him and his mother—by sugar, the idea of having a family tugged at him in a very real way.

He only hoped he could find a woman as fine as Olivia Shaw to be their mother.

'Will you teach me something?'

'Depends upon what it is, I suppose.'

'It's something gentlemanly. I would like to surprise Lady Olivia this afternoon. Show me how to greet her properly.'

'What will you be wearing when you greet her?'

'What I have on.'

For all that he had agreed to become 'refined', he found it hard to commit to stuffing himself into the clothing it required.

'You will not succeed, then.'

'Just tell me what to say. I know it's not "Howdy, ma'am".'

'It is all very complicated, Joe. While you were learning to rope cows, other gentlemen of rank were learning manners.'

'Not the fellow in the Duchess's garden—Waverly—wasn't that his name? Seems he was learning something else.'

If Joe caught him even glancing at Roselina or Olivia, he would do worse than bloody his nose.

'You know quite a lot considering the short time we've been here. Have you heard anything about him?'

'He is a marquess. That's one down from a duke, so folks act deferential to him. But they do talk.'

'What do they say?'

'Nothing pleasant. He's married, his wife is expecting a child—their second. He is a wanton rake who preys on defenceless widows. He charms the bloomers off them and leaves them to their shame.'

'I doubt if saying "charms the bloomers off them" is proper etiquette.'

'Quite so, but I am speaking to you in the privacy of our rooms. What polite people do say is that he dallies with affections. You can tell by the whispers and frowns it's worse than that.'

'You must keep away from him.'

'Oh, I've nothing to fear. I'm a virgin debutante. He would have no interest in me.'

'Virgin debutante? Is that a respectable phrase? I doubt it.'

'Again, it's only us. In society I would be referred to as an innocent young lady.'

'You are an innocent young lady.'

'Who had the advantage of growing up on a ranch. I know what goes where and why. I'm quite safe. It's our friend Lady Olivia he has his sights set on.'

Not if Joe had a say in the matter.

Blame it, he did not! Except that he was a gentleman, regardless of his clothing or speech. A gentleman protected a lady, belonging to him had nothing to do with the obligation.

Roselina might consider herself safe. Joe did not. It was going to be a tough thing for him to agree to let her marry any man.

'What do I say instead of "Howdy, ma'am"?'

'Try this. "It's a pleasure to see you again on this fine day, Lady Olivia." And be sure and remove your hat when you say it.'

He would if he could bring himself to put the blamed thing on.

'It's not a fine day. It's raining.'

'The weather has nothing to do with it. It is a fine day simply because you are in her company.'

It would be fine for him. He was not certain Lady Olivia would feel the same way.

The widow was grateful to him. He figured it was the only reason she agreed to help him—except, maybe gratitude was not all there was to it.

There was something between them, shimmering under the surface of caution.

They were wary of each other. And yet it was as if whatever that thing was, it was drawing them together. It wasn't logical. They barely knew each other. Perhaps that was why the feeling was so downright bewildering and yet—compelling.

He feared to discover what it was, but not as much as, maybe, he wanted to.

Chapter Six

Olivia walked into the garden room, plucking the curl bouncing at her temple. It felt unnatural, irritating.

What had possessed her to ask her maid to create it? Fleeting madness was all she could think. A dash of insanity which she now regretted.

No matter how she tried to tuck it away, it sprang back into place. No doubt Helmswaddle had been beyond pleased for the opportunity to try something creative with Olivia's hair.

Pleased and wondering why her mistress would ask for something so out of character.

Indeed, why would she?

'Mr Steton has arrived, my lady,' Mr Ramsfield announced, standing in the doorway looking proud and refined as his position in the household indicated he should be. She was extremely grateful the butler had chosen not to visit America along with the family as some of the staff had done.

'Thank you, Mr Ramsfield. Please do show him in.'

Moments later, she heard her visitor's boots striding down the hallway. Mr Ramsfield's steps tapped quickly, trying to lead the way.

The door frame looked dwarfed with Mr Steton standing in it. Somehow he managed to appear a gentleman without losing that rugged presence he had about him.

Oh, yes—she knew exactly why she had asked for the curl.

She might not welcome the strange shiver under her skin at the sight of him, but it was there none the less. She was clearly in rebellion with good sense.

What she needed to do was put up a more determined fight! Be strong, just as she had trained herself to be.

Oh, but truly, watching him walk towards her in a well-turned-out suit, his Stetson dipped low on his forehead—well, the wonder was that she had not asked for two curls.

Or perhaps three! Who would have imagined cowboy boots worn with tailored trousers would be so—well—it was more than appealing.

The ensemble might seem foolish on another gentleman, but on Mr Steton, it looked outstanding.

He stood in front of her, neither too close nor too far. He removed his hat, then, with a congenial smile, tucked it under his arm. He dipped his head in a greeting as refined as any born-and-bred gentleman's.

'It is a pleasure to see you on this lovely day, Lady Olivia.'

'It is a pleasure to see you again, Mr Steton.' She nodded her head in approval. 'But did you not notice it was raining?'

'Oh, I noticed. I said so to Roselina, but she pointed out that it was the lady who made the day lovely, not the weather.'

'Indeed.' She glanced away because it was a charming thing to say. It would not do for him to see that she wished it was sincere.

'My sister was correct.'

Oh, dear, oh, dear, oh, dear—why must he smile at her that way? He was clearly flirting with her. She was, to her distress—or her pleasure, she was not sure which—enjoying it.

Oh, please let her outward expression not reveal it— whatever 'it' happened to be.

'She did not accompany you?'

He set his hat on the table, shook his head. His hair was a bit longer than gentlemen wore, but it shimmered in such a rich, lovely shade of chestnut brown she would not think of advising him to have it trimmed.

'She might come over later. Just now she is writing a letter to Ma and Pa.'

'Mother and Father.' She felt something of a harpy, pointing it out. But she had committed to his transformation. Since she had decided not to comment on his hair, she could not let his language go uncorrected. 'A gentleman would say Mother or Father.'

'Seems awfully formal. They'd have a good laugh if they could hear it.'

'Rather say, "It does seem awfully formal. They would laugh if they could hear me."'

'That's what I said.'

'Yes, well, nearly.' She was a shrew. The truth was that she was beginning to find she quite enjoyed the way he spoke. However, needs were what they were. 'Gentlemen do not use contractions.'

'I fear, Lady Olivia, that my instruction will be rather a challenge to you. Please, do not lose patience with this humble cowpoke.'

If only patience was all she had to lose. Her fear was

that she might lose something more costly. Such as her self-possession, her level-headedness—her very heart. Which she had no intention of giving away. There was her son's heart to consider even more than her own. Victor would not suffer the loss of another man in his life.

'Speaking of cowpokes, where is Victor this afternoon?'

Had he read her mind? Surely not. Mental—or spiritual—connections were found in fairy tales. No woman with a grain of sense would entertain such a frivolous notion.

Olivia Victoria Cavill Shaw was not frivolous. In spite of the ridiculous ringlet bobbing beside her eye she was as sensible as—as—she just was.

'You look lovely today, Lady Olivia.' He was gazing at the curl when he spoke. 'I hope it is proper to say so.'

'Oh.' Well, what was she to say to that? His comment did not feel in the least offensive, yet had the Marquess stated it offended would not begin to describe how she felt.

'That is difficult to determine. Some ladies will be highly complimented. Others will not. It would be safer to make a comment about, oh, perhaps the feather on her hat, or the colour of her gown. Once you are better acquainted with the lady you might say so, but feel your way in the situation.'

'I'll—I mean—I will—take that advice to heart.'

She would have commended him on correcting the contraction, but he winked after he spoke.

She sighed—but on the inside where no one was privy to it but her—and really, that was one person too many.

Certainly she ought to say something. Rain pelting the glass only served to accentuate her silence.

'Do you enjoy watching birds, Josiah?' What an inane comment to make. Surely he would know that he'd left her disconcerted by the flirtatious gesture.

With any luck he took her silence to mean she was thinking of a way to tell him that it was not quite polite to wink.

He might have thought it had she not sidestepped and asked him about birds.

'I enjoy birds.'

'Come, then, we'll have a look at the aviary.'

'Is it permissible for ladies to use contractions, then?'

The confounded cowboy had her tripping all over proper speech.

'I think in private conversation it would be acceptable for either gentlemen or ladies. However, we are here this afternoon to teach you how to act in public.' She led the way to the aviary.

They watched dozens of small, colourful birds flit about, listened to them chirp.

'I would greatly enjoy a private conversation with you.' He turned his attention away from a yellow finch, settled those greenish-brownish eyes on her.

Oh, my. The birds were not the only ones fluttering. Something was very wrong here. She did not feel at all herself.

She felt better.

The thought insinuated itself into her brain before she could think more wisely of it. But there it was and it was not untrue.

What was she to do with that? Embrace the lovely sensation and risk her heart being broken, or snuff it out and go on as she had, bitter and lonely?

Humph! Until this moment she had not considered

herself to be lonely. The lovely sensation twinkling within her neatly pointed out that she was.

It would still be some time before tea was served and she did not intend to spend it staring into his eyes.

'Would you enjoy a walk in the rain?' She indicated the umbrellas that were kept at the ready beside the garden door.

Snatching his hat from the table, he put it on his head, then, walking over, plucked a pair out of the stand.

He nodded, held the door open for her. Even though he did not wink, his smile alone left her muddle-brained.

Once outside, rain hit the umbrellas with a steady thrum. Water sluiced off edges but not so loudly that they could not hear each other.

'On the subject of propriety, tell me, when is it appropriate for a gentleman and a lady to address each other by their given names?'

'Whenever it suits the gentleman and the lady involved.' She suspected he was asking for more a reason than vague enquiry. Presently the only man who called her anything other than Lady Olivia was Heath. Oh, and Clementine's grandfather. James Macooish called her 'my dear' or 'my girl'.

'Would it suit for me to call you Olivia?'

She would be a complete fool to allow it. She could not possibly.

'Yes, Josiah. I would enjoy that.'

There were many ways to be a fool. One of them was to lie to one's self.

'Thank you, Olivia, for letting me and for—' he glanced down at his clothing '—all of it.'

'We both know it is what the Duchess assigned me to do. But I would have tutored you, regardless. Victor and I do owe you a great deal.'

'It was simple luck that I happened to be in the cemetery. As for the Duchess's garden? Again, I was lucky enough to be there. Any man would have come to your aid.'

'Not according to my son. No matter how I try, I cannot convince him that you are not a gift from his late uncle.'

'A kid can imagine all sorts of things. I did. When my stepmother used to hold me on her lap and read to me, I always thought I heard two voices. I have impressions of my mother, but no memories. When I was little I felt the loss keenly. But the first time Esmeralda smiled at me, called me son, I forgot I'd ever felt it.'

Cold wind came up, pitching raindrops under the umbrellas. Dots of water speckled Josiah's face. The moisture did nothing to discourage her curl. It held as steadfastly as when it came out of the iron. No doubt Helmswaddle would crow about it for weeks.

'I'm sorry for all the adoration my baby heaps upon you, but he feels the loss of a father, just as you did a mother. It is why he has taken it in his mind that you belong to him.'

'How would you like for me to deal with his affections? I wouldn't—would not—want to wound him.'

How indeed? One way would be to marry her and become her son's father.

Sometimes, lately, her mind conjured the most ludicrous thoughts. It was unsettling to know they mostly had to do with this American.

'I wish I knew. The last thing I want is for him to have a broken heart. I fear it cannot be avoided, though.'

Josiah nodded, gazing through the rain at the fountain. Its spray mingled with raindrops, making one indistinguishable from the other.

'If I encourage his friendship, well, I'll be going home. If I do not encourage it, he might feel that I do not care. But I do care. I can't think which course of action would be worse and I am sorry for it.'

'Do not be. This is not your fault in any way. If his own father had been—'

It occurred to her that she was in danger of facing the same heartache as Victor did.

She could encourage friendship with this man. But if she did it would not be confined to simple camaraderie. There was an indefinable energy that quivered between them. Should she allow the spark to ignite, she would get burned.

Even if the man did not leave her for another woman's bed, he would, understandably, leave her to return home to his home in America.

Misery—either way she turned she was bound to end up feeling wretched. Having suffered a bleeding heart once before, she was loath to do so again. She had been a very long time healing from it.

Oh, but had she healed? Standing here in the rain, so close to Victor's cowboy, she wondered. Had she merely coped with heartache by mounding a heap of bitterness on it?

Perhaps such a wound could not be healed that way, but rather by having the courage to boldly step out and give one's heart away again.

Which, she feared, she did not have the courage to do.

They had stopped walking without her noticing. Josiah was looking at her questioningly.

What was it they had been discussing? She had completely wandered from the conversation. Oh, yes—Victor's father.

He might as well know. Everyone else did. And not a one of them had the power to bring her child joy—or sorrow.

It felt as though a precipice lay before her, admitting her marital failure to him. She took a deep breath, then stepped to the edge.

'How much do you know of my late husband?'

'I know that he is dead. Roselina probably knows more, but she hasn't said what.'

'He died in his mistress's bed.'

Josiah shook his head, his expression hard to read. When he took a step closer to her the rims of the umbrellas overlapped. The noise of the rain became fainter.

'The man was a fool, Olivia.'

'Perhaps he was. But I was more of one.'

'Don't believe it. He was your husband. When a man takes vows he ought to honour them.'

'Josiah Steton, you are as naive as I was when I wed.' It was not prudent to confide anything but the black and white of what had occurred, and yet— 'I was so in love with that man. I could not see past the stars in my eyes. I began to have suspicions, how could I not? I heard rumours of his infidelity, plenty of them. But I refused to see, or hear, anything I did not wish to. Would you believe it, I even found a bit of poetry he wrote to his mistress—his second or perhaps his third. I did ask him about it and he claimed it was written for me. It did not matter that the object of his adoration had "eyes the colour of rich brown velvet" and "hair the shade of deepest obsidian", I blindly chose to believe him. Did you realise it's possible? To know something and yet refuse to acknowledge that you know it?'

'I know that you did not deserve to be treated so

callously. And Victor? The child deserved the love of his father.'

'Henry Shaw's love would have been warped. It is better that Victor was only a baby and never knew the loss.'

What was there to say to that? His silence indicated that he did not know any more than she did.

'If your boots are anything like my slippers, they are soaking wet.'

'Are your toes getting numb, too?'

'I can't feel them.'

'I reckon you ought to hold on to my arm and keep me steady,' he suggested.

With a grin he extended his elbow. She must be mad, but she slipped her hand into the crook of his sleeve. She very nearly sighed because it felt so solid and warm under her fingers. More than that, it set her heart pounding and her blood singing.

There was one more thing she wanted to say while they had this quiet moment of friendship between them, while she was not his instructor and he was not her student.

'There is something I need to tell you. It has to do with your sister.'

'Roselina?' he asked, looking surprised.

'Do you have another?'

'No.' His brows arched, small lines creased his forehead. 'But what about her?'

'Not her so much as men. She is so innocent and sweet—I fear they will— But perhaps she is not as naive as I was and all will be well.'

'I'll tell you, she is all that. But she also knows her own mind.'

'Have a care for her, though, won't you? There are all sorts of pitfalls for a young woman.'

Coming in the garden door, Olivia found Mr Ramsfield striding past the orange tree, a severe frown cutting his professional demeanour.

'Lady Olivia, you have a caller.'

She had not expected anyone. 'I do not recall receiving any cards this morning.'

'Lord Waverly claims he did leave one, but I assure you he did not.'

Waverly. Joe's blood went cold even though it pumped hotly through his veins.

It's how it went when he was riled, hot and cold all at once.

'I shall inform him that you are indisposed.'

'I would rather not receive him, so, yes, please do.'

'May I receive him, Lady Olivia?'

Joe was not sure which part of his temper would greet the fellow, the hot or the cold, but the butler was smiling so maybe it didn't matter which.

'That would be wildly inappropriate.' Olivia's complexion was pale when she said so, which made him more determined to meet with the Marquess.

Joe was not bound by society's folly. He did not care who in society was valued more than whom and all that rot. Any American worth his salt knew that a cowboy was equal to a marquess, a duke, or an earl.

As far as Joe was concerned it was character that made a man. And that being the case, Waverly was on the waste heap of humanity, sharing the muck with Henry Shaw.

'I will not let the incident be known, nor do I believe Mr Ramsfield will. Am I correct?'

'Anything that might occur in the parlour will go unseen by this employee. Or any others, I dare say.'

'But you cannot mean to—'

'I do mean to.'

'Yes,' she murmured, her eyes narrowed upon him, the upward slant sharp with censure. 'It is abundantly clear that you intend to throw aside everything proper and shame me in my own home.'

'Shame you in front of whom?' He took her shoulders gently in his hands, made sure she was looking at him, which was no doubt an act more scandalous than receiving her caller was. 'The man knows no shame. My sister told me about him. Roselina believes she is safe from him, but that you are not. I saw for myself that is true. I intend to make it clear that both of you are under my protection.'

'No one gave you the right to protect me.'

'What about Victor? Will you give me the right to protect him? What happens to you happens to him.'

After a long, scathing glance, she twirled out from under his hold.

She walked past her butler, who was grinning broadly. 'I will walk ahead of you.'

Joe winked at the butler in passing. The man nodded, then brought up the rear.

'I saw what you did, Josiah Steton. Kindly do not subvert the staff.'

Odd, he was heading for a showdown with a grin on his face. He would need to school his features before bursting into the parlour.

Going before them, her strides long, her back straight as a pole and her chin lifted, she was the image of authority.

The problem was, from his point of view, she was

more than that. Olivia believed she was expressing outrage while she paced ahead of him. She had no way of knowing that her affronted strides caused her skirt to sway in a provocative swish.

By sugar, he would not be the one to inform her of it.

Olivia marched into the parlour. Joe could not recall a woman he admired more than this one.

He and the butler remained in the hallway, but out of the man's line of vision.

Joe needed to know what Waverly's attitude towards Olivia would be before he confronted him.

There was no danger to Olivia, given that he and the butler had a clear sight into the parlour and were ready to act when the need arose.

If Waverly had come to beg her forgiveness, his posture did not indicate it. Rather than standing, hat in hand and head bent in shame, he lounged indolently on the sofa, ankle crossed over knee. He gripped his walking stick in one fist, tapping it on the floor as if the wait had made him impatient.

At least his arrogance was offset by a bruised nose and black eye.

Olivia did not greet him, warmly or otherwise. She stood silently, her hands folded in front of her.

Waverly did not change his posture, but allowed his gaze to slide over her, his opinion of his superior social rank evident.

In Joe's opinion, Mr Ramsfield, a man of no social rank, was the superior man.

'Is this how you welcome a caller, Lady Olivia? No pleasure at having a gentleman paying his respects?'

'I do not welcome you, my lord. If you suppose I find pleasure in your visit, you are greatly mistaken.'

He laughed, came to his feet, but did not take a step towards her. 'But of course, you are playing coy.'

'Not at all. You are deceiving yourself if you think I welcome your lurid advances.'

'In spite of your sharp tongue, I find you enticing. You challenge me.'

'What you may find is your way out of my home.'

The tap, tap, tap of his cane sounded on the floor.

'Is it true that your family has gone to America and left you alone?'

'Perhaps the blow to your face has left you forgetful of the way you entered. The front door is behind you, down a short hall, then to the left.'

'My dear lady, I am willing to forget the unpleasant episode in the Duchess of Guthrie's garden.'

The fool advanced a step. Joe would have liked to see Olivia retreat one, but she did not. She stood with that proud heart-shaped chin lifted, all but challenging the Marquess.

'There is no reason for you to be alone.'

The wretch lifted his hand.

Joe had no idea what he meant to do with it, only what he would not. He stepped into the room.

'Lady Olivia is not alone.'

In spite of his dandy walking aid, the Marquis half-stumbled while retreating a few steps.

'You,' he hissed, but the sound was not nearly as impressive as a snake's buzz.

'Indeed...it is me. Mr Ramsfield and I are both present.' At that the butler entered the parlour, presented a bow, but Joe figured it was not enough of one to show respect.

'Lady Olivia, if you require the presence of a gentleman, I will be happy to attend,' Waverly uttered with a smirk.

'Mr Ramsfield,' Olivia said. 'It is apparent that not only has this visitor forgotten his way out, but he cannot discern a gentleman from a rogue. I fear you must show him the way.'

'Yes, Lady Olivia, indeed.'

'Oh, but, Lord Waverly, it occurs to me that perhaps you do not recall your way home, either. I'm certain your wife will be beyond distressed if you lose your way. Shall I call for my coach to deliver you safely to her?'

'I believe, Lady Olivia, that my own coachman recalls the way.'

'Does he? It is said that he becomes lost at times, delivering you to doorsteps that are not your own.'

The Marquess's neck and face flamed, the hue a near match to his cravat.

With nothing to do but admit defeat at the tongue of the valiant Lady Olivia, Waverly pushed past Mr Ramsfield, his retreat punctuated by the slam of his cane on the floor.

'I imagine that is the last we will see of that philanderer,' she observed.

Olivia's smile over her victory looked triumphant, as well it should.

Joe would feel a great deal better about it if he believed the man had given up his pursuit.

More than likely, Waverly's interest in her had only been escalated.

Chapter Seven

A balmy breeze blew in the office window from the garden. It lifted the lace curtain and carried the scents of rose and lavender.

Sitting at the desk, Olivia felt the essence of spring caress her face, tickle the hair at her temple.

She held a pen in her fingers, all but forgetting she meant to dip it in the ink bottle.

Victor's laughter carried into the office along with Miss Hopp's.

It had been a very long time since she paid attention to the beauty of the Season or to beauty in any form, except Victor's smile, of course—and his laughter.

She closed her eyes, listened while inhaling a long, slow breath of sweet air.

She could not recall the last time she had indulged in such a common pleasure.

'Lady Olivia?' Olivia glanced across the desk. Mr Small, her accountant, pointed to the tip of the pen hanging limp in her fingers. 'You are dribbling ink on the invoice.'

'Oh, of course. I was just…' How could her attention have wandered so far afield?

'Spring is in the air.' He smiled, his gaze slid to the garden. 'One must allow for it.'

Spring being in the air had not caused her undue distraction since before her marriage. She could not imagine why it would now.

There was nothing different about this spring day than any other—and yet it seemed more vibrant.

It was unlikely that this day was any different than the next. More likely, she was different. For so long it seemed that she had been asleep and was now beginning to stretch and open her eyes to the beauty all around.

Much like the yellow rosebud beyond the windowsill, she was opening. She could not prevent it from happening any more than she could stop the imperceptible spread of the petals.

Just because it was happening did not mean she wished it to. Opening up made her vulnerable, and she disliked being vulnerable. Surely one could imagine dancing among the newly budded leaves and not lose oneself. One could, if she was able to purge the image of an American cowboy from her mind.

Oh, my word! She no longer had an image of him on her mind, she had it on her eyes. He came out of the house next door, sat on a bench beside the fountain and opened a book.

She felt one of her petals tremble, reach for the sunshine.

Mr Small indicated that she should sign something. She gave him her attention for the moment it took to neatly write her name. The instant her pen lifted from the paper, her gaze returned to the garden.

Victor spotted his hero and scampered away from his governess. Without apparent invitation, he clambered on to Josiah's lap.

She heard a slip of paper slide across the blotter, set the pen to it.

'An inch higher, Lady Olivia, if you please.'

'Yes, of course.'

She dragged her attention away from the window, but what she had seen would not go away. No, rather the image burned itself on her heart.

Victor leaned his curly head against his cowboy's chest, snuggled in. Josiah's calloused hand settled on her child's back while he read to him.

What an easy thing it was to imagine Victor having the father he wanted so badly. Easy to imagine, yes, but reality told a far sadder story. Her child was giving his heart to a man who did not call London home.

She dashed at her eye, hoping Mr Small had not noticed the moisture welling.

'Are you well, my lady?'

'Oh, yes quite well. A bug has flown in, that is all. It caught in my eye.'

'We are nearly finished, but I can return later if you would like.'

Spring was in the air—she feared it was creeping further into her heart. Returning to Fencroft's finances at a more convenient time would not help in the least.

'Let us carry on, Mr Small. How much did you say we owe the grocer?'

'"The ice was here, the ice was there,"' Joe read over Victor's shoulder while the child snuggled on his lap. He felt a tremor shiver through the boy. '"The ice was all around: It cracked and growled, it roared and howled, like noises in a swound!"'

'What is a swound, sir?'

'Something akin to a swoon.'

'Seems like an odd swoon, cracking and growling. What happens next?'

'"At length did cross an albatross, Through the fog it came; As if it had been a Christian soul, we hailed it in God's name."'

'But could they not tell a Christian soul from a bird?'

'Indeed.' A shadow fell across the pages of the book. 'What nonsense are you reading to him?'

'It's not nonsense, Mother.' The child shifted so that he sat on only one of Joe's knees. He patted the other, indicating that she should sit there and join them. 'It's poetry and there's an Ancient Mariner with a long grey beard and a glittering eye!'

Joe jiggled his knee in teasing invitation. He should not have but, by sugar, some playful devilment urged him to and he did.

'Poetry is a waste of good time. Look, here comes Miss Hopp to take you to the nursery for your nap.'

'But, Mother, I'm too old for a nap and I need to find out what will become of the wedding guest sitting on a stone and forced to listen to the tale.'

'I'm certain he will be fine. Now here is Miss Hopp, go along with her.'

Victor let himself be led away, but turned to frown at his mother. 'He's probably going to swound.'

'We can only hope the poor wedding guest fares better than that,' she said, glancing at Joe's knee and then quickly away.

'We can read it together and find out.' He patted the bench beside him. He actually did know what happened to the wedding guest. *The Rime of the Ancient Mariner* had been his favourite since he was Victor's age.

'Poetry is romantic nonsense,' she huffed.

'It is when it is written by fools.' She had to know

he was speaking of her late husband and his adulterous missives. 'To my knowledge Samuel Taylor Coleridge was gifted.'

'I've no time for frivolity.'

As improper as it was to do so, he caught her hand, drew her down beside him on the bench.

Her bare hand was smooth and warm. He would have let go of it at once had he not felt a shiver skitter through her fingers.

She was such a fine lady. What her husband had done to her was a crime.

'Do not let your past blind you, Olivia.'

'One's past teaches wisdom for the future.'

'Wisdom, my friend? Or fear?'

'Caution more than that, I think.'

'Will you cautiously sit beside me on this lovely afternoon and listen to the poem?'

She glanced down at her lap, nodded, but so quickly that he nearly missed the twinkle in her eye. 'I do not promise that by listening I will become a fan of nonsensical phrases.'

'Now, where were we?'

'Hailing an albatross in God's name.'

He gave her a nod and a wink to put her at ease. '"It ate the food it ne'er had eat, And round and round it flew…"'

Joe knew the poem well, could recite it without opening the book, but there was something about seeing words on the paper, reciting them aloud that made a story come alive.

Sliding a glance at Olivia, he saw that she had closed her eyes. A smile flitted across her lips. He slowed the pace of his words because he did not want this moment with her to end when the poem did.

Spending time together, friend to friend rather than pupil to instructor, was a fine thing. Funny how simply sitting beside her made him feel good. Better than good—better than he had ever felt sitting beside a woman. Even the one he had considered proposing to, once upon a time.

Watching Olivia's face, turned up to catch the sunshine, he was glad he had not.

He'd write a poem about the moment, about spring and her pretty face, if he had any talent with words.

As lengthy as *The Rime of the Ancient Mariner* was, it was coming to a conclusion far too quickly.

"'He prayeth best, who loveth best,'" he recited slowly. "'All things both great and small; For the dear God who loveth us, He made and loveth all.'"

She opened her eyes and smiled at him. 'Is that all of it?'

'There's a bit more about the mariner's bright eye and hoary beard and the wedding guest being a sadder but wiser man.'

'Not swound, then. Victor will be glad to hear it.'

'You must be proud of him.' If Joe had been blessed with a son he would hope him to be like Victor. 'Of yourself, too, for raising him to be so fine.'

'Oh, he is sweet enough, but full of the dickens.'

'As a boy ought to be.'

'Were you full of the dickens?'

'It's what Ma and Pa—Mother and Father, I mean—tell me. I only remember having fun.'

'Oh, to be a child again.' Her sigh seemed soft with remembrance.

'Tell me, what did you do for fun?' The more she spoke of good times, the happier she would be. It only stood to reason.

'Tormenting my brother Oliver, I suppose.' Her lips tugged up. He was certain she nearly laughed. 'He was my twin and I forced him to be a prince to my princess. Even though I know he would rather have been running about the estate with Heath, he played court to me. Of course, had his health been better, he would have run off and left me to invent a prince.'

Joe knew about Oliver Shaw, at least as much as Roselina had told him. He had been the Fifth Earl of Fencroft and had died young. He had trusted a college chum to keep the accounts for the estate. The man was inept and Fencroft had faced financial peril. Heath Cavill, the younger brother, had inherited a broken estate, a title and a wealthy American bride.

From what Joe could tell it had all worked out fine. The estate seemed to be thriving and the Cavills had adopted fourteen children and opened a school for orphans.

'Victor says you were visiting his grave when we first met.'

'Yes, it had been too long since I had.' She shrugged, no longer smiling. 'I resented him for a while even though I loved him and missed him desperately.'

'I can imagine why. Roselina told me what happened with the estate and your other brother.'

'I'm afraid my family is often the talk of the town.'

'None of it deserved.'

'It hardly matters.'

'Olivia.' He touched her chin, turned her face towards him because she had looked away. 'It matters greatly when it steals your joy. Look around us. There is so much to be happy about. Sunshine, birds singing—you and I reading poetry and you not hitting me in the head with the book.'

'I might do it yet.' He knew she would not because her lips twitched, right at the corners. Anyone with such pretty dimples was not likely to assault him with a poetic masterpiece.

If he was fancy with a pen, he would write about those dimples first. They were quite his undoing, made him feel like a weak-kneed boy wondering if he might kiss them.

'I'll make you a bargain,' he said. 'You let loose of that smile you are choking on and at our next lesson I will wear the blamed ugly hat.'

'Oh…well…' She covered her mouth, shook her head. In spite of the effort not to, she did laugh.

But the agreement was that he should see her smile. With one hand he caught both of hers and drew them away from her face.

If only she would do it more often. 'You have the loveliest smile I have ever seen. And that is not flirta- tion—just a statement of fact.'

'You can't mean that.'

'Since I've never said it to anyone before, I reckon I do mean it.'

'I nearly believe you, Josiah.'

That was something, he figured, since she hadn't much cause to trust men in the past.

'I don't say what I don't mean.'

'Do not,' she corrected him, then stood up, smooth- ing the folds from her skirt. 'Next time I see you it will be in that hat.'

By sugar, she was still smiling when she walked away.

'Olivia? How long has it been since you had fun with a man?'

'Since Oliver was my prince.'

Somehow it broke his heart that she did not even give it a bit of thought. Her brother had been her prince a very long time ago.

'That is going to change.'

She nodded, but so circumspectly that if he had not been looking for it he would have missed it.

'Do not forget the hat.' She winked, and his knees felt like slush.

What had she done?

Standing in the garden room watching Josiah walk across the garden, she knew, of course. She had winked.

The question was, why had she done it?

Because he had made her laugh with his silly bargain? Or perhaps because it felt so wonderful to feel silly again?

Honestly, she had all but forgotten how to. Even with her own child. When was the last time she had laughed freely at his youthful antics?

Most of the time she reprimanded Victor for hiding under tables and climbing trees. She wondered if she truly knew his mother.

How could he when she had all but forgotten who she was, or used to be? She was beginning to see the person she had turned into and did not like herself overmuch.

Olivia Cavill Shaw had become dry as dust—drab and gloomy.

Yet, watching Josiah saunter across the garden, not wearing the hat but scowling at it while he carried it under his arm, she found herself grinning.

No one unbalanced her as this man did. The problem was, Dreary Olivia feared what he was doing to her. Gloomy Olivia warned her to be wary because the cowboy had every intention of returning to America.

If she was not on her guard, he would take her heart back with him.

As soon as he opened the terrace gate he spotted her, gave an exaggerated bow, then slapped the tall hat back on his head.

He grinned and Light-Hearted Olivia gave Gloomy Olivia a shove. Lady Gloomy did not topple over, but she did step aside.

'You look very dapper, Josiah,' she commented, while opening the door.

Indeed he did look like a gentleman, but he smelled robust, as if he carried the scents of prairie grass, cattle and campfires with him. Not that she knew what those things smelled like, but she was certain it was so.

'I feel like an undertaker.'

'You could never be that dour.'

'I knew a jovial undertaker once.'

'I don't know, Josiah. It seems to me that would make the chap rather ghoulish.' She indicated the table beside the lemon tree, which was set for tea.

'When I was little I'd hide under my bed because I'd dreamed that he was nailing my coffin closed while he grinned and chuckled.'

He pulled out her chair, then sat across from her.

'I hope you are making that up.'

'I'm not. Charming Wendell was what folks called him. For all his smiles, he didn't have many friends.'

She poured tea, then added the three cubes of sugar he liked in his. She added a dollop of milk to hers.

Coffee was what he preferred to drink, black coffee, which she found interesting since he needed so much sugar in his tea. What she found even more interesting was that knowing this small thing about him gave her such satisfaction.

Having pleasant feelings for a man was something she had not experienced in a very long time. For all that it was pleasant it was also unsettling.

'You look worried, Olivia. I will not tell Victor about him.'

Oh, she hadn't thought—but no doubt Victor would be fascinated, not repelled. Luckily Josiah would not know that her expression had to do with him, with her ever-slipping battle to keep her heart from taking a risk.

'I appreciate that. Now, shall we get down to the business of the afternoon?'

He still wore the hat. He dipped it at her as if it had been his Stetson.

'You are doing splendidly. Except that you ought to have removed the hat when you first came in.'

'Wish I'd known sooner.'

'Sooner than the one moment we have been inside?'

'It's like wearing a pipe on my head.' He snatched it off, giving it a scowl as he did.

How could she not laugh at his offended expression even if doing so put her on treacherous ground? Too hard a giggle might shake her resolve to keep him at arm's length. One slip and she would fall—

On her feet was where. Squarely and solidly on her feet.

'It will soon be time for you and Roselina to be seen in public again.'

He lifted his teacup and, taking a sip, wagged his little finger at her. Then he winked. Was this a tic of some sort? He did it fairly often.

'You must not do that in public. People will think you are a terrible flirt.'

'But I am flirting, and blatantly expressing my appreciation of your effort on my behalf—and even more on Roselina's.'

'Perhaps appreciation would be better accomplished with a simple "thank you".'

'Thank you, Olivia. When will you begin to call me Joe?'

He well knew she would not and there was no point in belabouring the issue. 'The best place to get you and Roselina seen is at the opera.'

'Went to an opera once. I fell asleep in spite of all the noise.'

'Many people do not appreciate the music, but it is where one must go to see and be seen.'

'Sure hope they do not see me snoring.'

'We have two weeks in which to finish polishing you.'

'How much more socialising will I need to do once I'm polished?'

'There is always something to attend. But the most important will be another ball of the Duchess's a bit later in the Season. A proper presentation on that evening is extremely important for your sister's future in the marriage market. All the entertainments before this one are of a getting-to-know-you nature. It is known in society that this ball marks the point where suitors become serious. It is what we are working for here.'

And after that?

After that he would no longer need her. There would be no reason for him to visit daily.

She rather thought her life would be a great deal more dull.

Dull had always suited her splendidly. There was no risk in leading a dull life.

* * *

Stepping down from the carriage in front of the Theatre Royal, Covent Garden, Joe felt spit-shined and, with the blamed hat perched on his head, no less than seven feet tall. There was no doubt about him being seen.

No doubt about Roselina being seen either. Taking her hand as she stepped out of the conveyance, he figured she was the prettiest flower in the bouquet of young beauties attending tonight's performance.

Of course, Olivia had yet to step out of the carriage.

They were attending tonight's show in the company of the Duchess of Guthrie and a few others. Apparently it was the custom to attend the opera as a group. They would share the Duchess's balcony—from this vantage point they would be quite visible to anyone who cared to look.

Olivia had informed him—warned, rather—that everyone would be looking.

The last thing he was going to do was disappoint her after all her hard work in getting him to this point. No matter what, he would not doze off—or wink.

Even though the carriage driver stood by to help, Joe ignored him and assisted Olivia down the steps. He wanted to touch her hand again even if it would be encased in a glove.

'Is it normally this windy?' he leaned close to ask.

The front of the opera house looked like a scattering of spring blossoms with colourful skirts being tossed this way and that.

'I imagine a storm is coming.' Olivia had to go up on her toes and lean close to his ear to be heard over the gust buffeting them. Her breath was warm. It smelled slightly of cloves and spice from the meal they had taken at the Duchess's before departing.

He was trying to think of something else to ask so she would have to keep whispering in his ear, but the coachman was assisting the rest of the party down the cab steps.

Ladies laughed, trying to press down their skirts against the wind howling along the ground while the gentlemen of the group ushered everyone towards the entrance.

'I've never seen anything like this!' Roselina hung on to his arm while pointing to the opera house they hurried towards. 'Those great tall columns all lit up from behind—and really, Joe, have you ever seen a building made of glass?'

She was referring to the huge horseshoe-shaped structure beside the opera house.

'It is called Covent Garden and, yes, it is made of glass.' Olivia stepped up beside them, then slipped her hand into the crook of his other arm to steady herself against the wind.

All of a sudden Joe felt like a king, all gussied up and escorting a pair of special ladies into what looked like a palace.

Once inside they were ushered upstairs to a box with seating for ten.

Her Grace took the seat in centre front as was her due as owner of the box and her rank as Duchess. She motioned for Roselina to sit on her right, then waved Joe to the seat on her left.

Luckily Olivia swept into the seat beside him.

'What do I do with the hat?'

Noise from below rose up like a hum of bees so that Olivia had to lean close in order for him to hear the answer.

'Is it an opera hat, do you know? If it is, it will collapse.'

'It's a blamed nuisance that no one can see over it, is all I know.'

'Hmm, it is rather tall. You had best remove it.'

'Who is that who just sat down beside Roselina? He was not with us at dinner.'

'The Earl of Grantly's son, Viscount Mansfield. I imagine he saw her when we were coming in and is hoping for an introduction.'

'Should I allow it?'

'Our hostess will decide. But don't worry. No one can set up a match like Her Grace can.'

Until this moment the whole business of seeing his sister wed had been theory. Now there was a young man gazing at her frog-eyed and Joe was not certain he cared for it.

Once she married, she would set up a home here—in London.

The thought of not having her nearby hit him like a punch in the gut. It was very likely he would go years without seeing her.

Pa was the one to make the yearly trips to London while Joe stayed home to tend the ranch. It had always been that way and he saw no reason for it to change. From all he knew, Pa enjoyed the few months he spent here.

'She will meet many young men. He might not be the one she chooses so you can stop glaring at him.'

'It's not to do with him, more it has only just truly hit me that, when she marries, we will be separated by an ocean. We've only ever been separated by walls before.'

The hum of voices from below buzzed in his ears. He closed his eyes, trying to shut it all out.

But then warmth covered his hand. Hesitantly, Olivia twined her fingers in his. She drew their joined hands close to her side, then yanked her skirt over them.

'I'm sorry for it. It's such a hard thing to be separated from a sibling. At least when Heath comes home it will be to stay.'

Even he knew publicly holding hands was not proper behaviour, even with gloves on. But by sugar, if no one knew it but the two of them, what did it matter?

If he liked it—and he did if the quick flip in his stomach was anything to go by—and she was the one to begin it, he was going to hold on as long as she would allow it.

All of a sudden he felt the longer this performance lasted, the better, which was a far different opinion than the one he had coming in.

With his hand feeling right at home holding Olivia's, he glanced down at the merriment going on below.

Apparently it was true that folks came to the opera to see and be seen. Ladies and gents craned their necks this way and that, taking note of who was where and who they were with.

He could not help but smile because looking down on it all gave a better vantage then looking up. No one down there would know he and Lady Olivia were touching fingers.

Apparently the hat was good for something after all. If he shifted it just so, it more fully covered their discreet hand-holding. Even those sitting in the chairs behind them would be unaware of the indiscretion.

The quite delicious indiscretion.

The Duchess cast him a pointed, sidelong glance. Surely it could not mean she was knew what was happening under the hat.

More likely, it had to do with the fellow sitting beside his sister.

Did she know the young man to be a wastrel?

He arched a brow at her in question. She arched one back at him before turning her gaze towards the stage. In doing so she smiled! Surely he had not imagined it, but he blamed sure could not figure it out.

What was going on? At times women were a puzzle with a piece missing. He did not understand them.

Who he did understand were young men. He would need to have a word with Roselina's admirer and determine for himself if he was worthy.

The theatre lights dimmed. Seconds later lights illuminated blue brocade curtains which swept open to reveal a woman standing in what appeared to be a pasture. Live sheep grazed happily about her. While she sang a sweet, lyrical melody to her flock a man dressed as a wolf could be seen creeping through the grass.

Joe could not help but glance at the fresh-faced fellow sitting beside Roselina. He might look harmless, but he could be a predator in the opera brush.

Even if he was the most noble of peers, Joe would still not warm to him. He might be the one to sweep Roselina away. He never had been able to understand why Ma encouraged her to marry a titled fellow in another country.

He returned his attention to the stage and the shepherdess serenading her flock. As much as he could since the greater part of his attention was on how warm Olivia's hand was.

When his gaze swept the audience, he noticed one face was not looking at the stage.

While the stage's wolf was actually harmless, the one watching Olivia was not. The Marquess had not forsaken his pursuit of her. In all likelihood, his interest in her had increased since her rejection of him.

Joe let his gaze slide discreetly over the man. He did not want Olivia to notice anything untoward.

Perhaps he should not take the protection of this woman so personally. He ought to care for her well-being in the same way he would for any woman.

But 'any woman's' hand was not resting in his, so small and trusting.

And trust did not come easily to her, he knew well it did not.

So, yes, this need to watch out for her was deeply personal.

It thrummed through him like a drumbeat, a primeval need to protect his woman. Although she was not his woman. He was simply holding her hand.

Since as far as he knew there was no man in London to defend her, he took the job upon himself.

While he might not be looking directly at Waverly, Joe knew the instant that the man turned his attention to the stage.

Let him believe himself to be slinking through the grass, creeping and thinking to pounce upon Olivia Shaw. He could not know that he was the one being pursued.

Chapter Eight

With the opera over and everyone filing out of the box, Olivia was proud of Josiah for not falling asleep. Perhaps he had found it to be entertaining.

Even had Olivia thought the performance dull she would not have nodded off. How could she have with her hand taking odd turns at shivering and steaming, gloves notwithstanding?

There had been a point when she had half a mind to slip the glove off, feel Josiah's warm flesh curled around hers.

She would not—no, never. It had been a very bold move to do what she had. Even so, she could not say she regretted it.

She had never simply held a man's hand for the sheer tenderness of it.

Her husband had not been one for tenderness, at least not once the vows had been recited, but, no, even before that he had only play-acted at it. As naive and open-hearted as she had been, she had not known the difference between genuine and false.

She knew it now.

There was no doubt that Josiah Steton's attentions towards her were an expression of open-hearted—*some-thing*—and whatever it was, it was quite genuine.

Indeed, every bit as genuine as the reason she had taken his hand in the first place. The man needed comfort for the loss he feared coming. She wanted to give that comfort. She was adept at giving comfort—did she not give it to Victor daily?

Somewhere between the first and second act of the opera, something had changed inside her. The something was not at all maternal.

What had begun as a compassionate gesture had quite turned on her.

Indeed, compassion did not lead one to wonder what his large rough hands would feel on other parts of her person. It certainly did not make one's pulse race and her heart feel like a melted lump, all sweet and gooey.

She watched him going down the stairs ahead of her, filling the role of the Duchess's escort.

Light from the sconces along the walls made his hair gleam a rich and engaging brown. She thought to tap his shoulder and remind him to put on the hat, but if he did she would not be able to appreciate his hair, wonder what it would be like to touch it, smell it.

'What do you know about him?' Roselina nudged her with an elbow.

What? Oh, Lord Grantly's son, of course.

'I have not heard any scandal involving him. He is Lord Grantly's heir. The family is respectable. But take care, Roselina. Many men will seek an introduction. You will be sought after, but, please, do be more cautious than I was.'

'Yes, I will be. And may I say something, as a friend? For we are, are we not?'

'Indeed we are and you may.'

'Good, then, because I tell you this in all affection. I have heard about your first husband. But you can trust Joe. My brother is as loyal a man as you will meet.'

Having been acquainted with him for some time now, she did believe it. But who would he be loyal to?

Just because they had touched hands all through the opera did not mean it would be her. She had lost count of how many ladies had glanced appreciatively at him tonight.

The advice she had just given Roselina went for her as well. Be careful, be cautious and do not let your heart be broken.

And yet—she still wanted to reach out and touch Josiah's hair.

Would it be so horrible to forget caution for one night, begin with it again tomorrow? Really, she had already abandoned it so what did it matter?

Gracious, what a feather she had for a brain. She did not even know that Josiah wanted to have his hair touched.

While she was wool-gathering, several people stepped between her and the rest of her group.

She tried to catch up, but the effort was futile. Each second put her further and further behind them. Using the Duchess's hat feather as a beacon, she made slow progress down the stairs.

The room suddenly flared in cold white light. By the time her eyes adjusted, thunder rumbled over the roof. Through the open doors she heard voices exclaiming over the sudden deluge of rain.

'You seem to have been parted from your company, Lady Olivia. Allow me to escort you home.'

Cold air washed in from the open doors and up the stairs, but her chill had not to do with the temperature.

'Nonsense, Lord Waverly. They are at the doors waiting for me,' she said, which did not keep him from reaching for her elbow.

She neatly avoided his grasp.

'I will take you to them, then. There is a back stairway which will get you to the front more quickly than the stairs will.'

'You are a man with a fast reputation, my lord. The very last place I will go with you is into a back stairway.'

'I guarantee we will have a diverting time.'

It would be useless to discuss this with him. Taunting her was all a part of his cat-and-mouse fun.

As luck would have it, Lady Greene, who was an avid conversationalist, was on the step behind. Olivia moved to the side and let her step down between them.

As she had hoped, the Baroness struck up a conversation with Waverly, which gave Olivia a chance to put several people between them.

She needed to get to her party and quickly. The Marquess had been correct about the back stairs. With him delayed by Lady Greene, she would be able to escape down them and be reunited with the Duchess's group as quick as a snap.

She made her way back to the upper landing. With the crowd thinned out it was an easy matter to get to the stairway. Being lit by sconces, the two flights down were not perilous. At the bottom and down a long hallway there would certainly be a door which opened to the lobby.

She was only halfway down the hallway when she heard the stairway door above squeak open. There was nothing for it but to exit one of the doors that lead to the alley before Waverly—and that had to be who was opening the door—spotted her.

She went out the closest one and shut it softly.

Cold rain hit her head, soaked her hair and washed over her face.

Lightning blanched the alley. The thunder seemed very close, but further away than the first strike had been. Oh, but the rain came down in a torrent.

In an instant her gown was a ruin. What a mess she was going to make of the Duchess's carriage.

She started to run, her slippers splashing in puddles that grew deeper by the second.

Looking down, she did not see the large figure coming towards her, but she did hear the running footsteps.

All at once a coat covered her head. Everything went dark until a face popped under and lifted the coat, making a makeshift umbrella of it.

'It's only me.'

Only Josiah Steton, who always seemed to be there in the instant she most needed him.

'What are you doing here?' she asked, beginning to shiver.

'I came to get you.'

'I see that.' Rain hit the coat he held over them, but cold wind blew in sideways. 'But how did you know where I was?'

'I lost you in the crowd. Then there was Waverly pushing his way towards the side door up there. He seemed in an all-fire hurry. I figured there must be an alley door so I came looking.'

'Do you come after every damsel in distress?' She asked this in jest, but only to lighten the deep emotion washing over her. She knew it was not only the weather making her shiver.

As a widow she put on an independent face, even to herself. While she could not deny the man made her shiver, he also made her feel watched over—safe and cherished.

'It is you I came after, Olivia, only you.'

Lightning flashed again, thunder rolled away in the distance but she felt as though it was rolling through her.

'We should go back to the others,' she said because it was oh, so sensible.

Her comment might have been more convincing had she not reached up to touch his rain-slicked hair and sighed out loud.

'Yes, we ought.'

And she might believe his answer if he were not drawing a line down her cheek with his finger, tracing the shape of her lips with his thumb.

'Josiah, I cannot—' But she could and she wanted to.

'Joe, I'm just Joe.' His head dipped an inch closer to her face. She felt the warmth of his breath, which stole hers quite away. 'You can if you wish it, Olivia. And the bald truth is, on my part, I wish it very much.'

'I'm afraid… What if—?'

But what if she did not? Would she shun joy for ever? Would she allow Henry Shaw to reach beyond the grave to rob her joy today, just as he had done with her past?

No! She would not.

'Be gone, wicked shade,' she whispered.

Joe began to back out from under the coat, but she caught his coat, drew him back.

'I was not saying that to you.'

'Ah, good then.'

The warmth of his breath returned, but only for an instant. The gentle pressure of his lips came in its stead, igniting a delightful simmer under her skin.

He dropped the coat. She heard it splash on the stones. He drew her closer, one arm around her back and one hand cupping her head. He tasted like—like—in the moment it escaped her.

The alley faded away, puffed into mist. Indeed, the only real and solid thing she was aware of was being kissed—nearly devoured—by a cowboy. Being dressed in the highest fashion did not make him any less of one.

Joe Steton was rugged to the bone. The most elegant of gentlemanly apparel would not change him.

Tangling her fingers in his hair, she realised how very grateful she was for it.

The crunch of carriage wheels on wet stone sounded at the end of the alley.

Joe let go of her with a softly whispered curse that she took no offence to. Had she not been raised a lady she would have uttered it, too.

'They've come for us, I reckon.' He stooped to pick up the coat.

The carriage door opened and one of the men with their party peeked out. 'Ah, you've found her, then!'

Oh, indeed he had. He had found more of her than anyone knew. He had unearthed a part of her that she had buried long ago.

What no one could know—well, perhaps Joe knew it—was that inside, she was laughing, twirling jubilantly and quite over the moon.

There was not much she feared more than that.

By the next morning the storm had moved on, leaving behind clouds and scattered drizzle.

At least the storm involving lightning and thunder had passed.

There was another one going on inside Joe which

could not be cleared by pacing the parlour. Roselina, sitting at the secretary and writing a letter to Ma, was giving him odd glances, no doubt wondering why he was behaving so strangely.

So he went out, collected his horse from the livery and went for a ride in Hyde Park.

It was the thing to do, he'd heard. To ride out in the morning and socialise—be seen.

Which was not the reason he was in the park. Giving Blue some much-needed exercise wasn't it either.

He needed good clean air and outdoor movement while wearing his familiar Stetson in order to think clearly.

By sugar, he sure didn't seem to be able to think right in the blamed top hat. With any luck the rain had ruined it beyond fixing. Same for the tight black boots that had lost their sheen to a mud puddle.

Glancing about, he noticed he was travelling in the opposite direction of the other riders. That was fine since he did not want to converse with anyone but himself.

He needed to give himself a good, stern talking to. Set what had happened last night right in his mind. He hadn't gone looking for Olivia with the intention of kissing her. He only meant to see to her safety.

If she hadn't looked so appealing with water washing her hair out of its coiffure, with her face slick with raindrops, her lips dotted with them, or if she hadn't been shivering, he might not have.

He shook his head, heard the tap of drizzle on his hat brim. It wasn't true. All those reasons were excuses.

Kissing her had been on his mind for a good long while, since he'd first come across her in the cemetery.

Blue snorted at another animal passing, its rider genteelly attired. Joe tipped his hat by habit, not really paying attention to the gesture. The fellow tipped his in return and rode on.

Whether the gent smiled or not, Joe did not notice, being eaten up with guilt for what he had done.

If Olivia thought he offered more than a kiss, he was a cad. He ought to have fought against the need to be so close to her. Resisted it—a true gentleman would have.

Just went to show he was too rough to be turned into a silk purse. He might manage a show of it for the time it took his sister to find what she was looking for. After that he would go back to acting the fellow he really was.

In the eyes of proper society, he was the son of a baron. What he actually was, was a heathen, following his desire about like a bull with a ring in his nose.

Apologising for his behaviour would be right and proper, except that he was not sorry. It was more that he was repentant, which was a far different emotion as far as Joe was concerned.

He would never be sorry he kissed Olivia. The memory of it would stay with him when he took his last breath. But he was repentant for what damage his indulgence might have caused her.

'Come on, Blue.' He patted the horse's neck, then turned him for the livery. 'I've got some forgiveness to beg.'

After breakfast, Olivia called for the carriage and went shopping. Fencroft House felt as though it was closing in on her, as if the air was stifling and the ceiling pressing down.

With Victor busy at his lessons, there was nothing with which to occupy her mind. Which was far more occupied than it ought to be—with things it ought not to be. The more she indulged in thoughts best forgotten, the more a muddle her mind became.

Last night, holding hands with Josiah had made her oblivious to the fate of the shepherdess and her flock, but his kiss—well, that made her oblivious to anything needing attention this morning.

Purchasing a new gown was something that would take time and require concentration.

Surely giving her full attention to silk and brocade would help her forget the scent of the cowboy.

Mr Creed assisted her down the carriage steps. It was not right that it was Josiah's face she saw smiling instead of the driver's. She blinked hard to clear the image.

As she entered the shop, the first thing she spotted was a dress in shades of green and amber. There was no way she would not see again the way Joe—Josiah—had been looking at her while holding the coat over them and waiting for her to give him a signal to kiss her.

It was wrong. She should not have done it, yet she had never felt such a connection with a man before. Certainly not with Henry The Unfaithful.

Roselina had been correct when she'd said that Joe would be loyal.

She could only pray that she had not given him hope where none existed. For all the joy and elation she had felt in the moment, she did not mean it to indicate a commitment to him.

Vowing a future to a man was not something she was ready to do. Most especially to one who would be leaving London at the end of the Season—perhaps sooner given all the attention Roselina was receiving.

There was but one thing to do, she decided while fingering the fabric which was the shade of Joe's eyes.

That was to confront him this afternoon. Admit it had all been a huge mistake.

And, no, that was not a tear she just whisked from her eye.

Olivia did not watch for Josiah crossing the garden for his afternoon lesson.

Her time would be better spent reviewing today's instruction in how to converse with a lady while not speaking of matters of great importance.

After all, one did not want to offend delicate sensibilities. Which was rubbish, of course. Ladies were as capable of carrying on an intelligent discourse on social issues as gentlemen were.

In many cases, more so.

For all that she tried to keep focused on teaching absurdity, it was not uppermost in her mind.

Figuring out how to be forthcoming with Josiah was. Especially given that she was not being completely truthful with herself.

Telling him she had made a mistake in kissing him was what she needed to do, but she could not, in truth, say that it was.

The memory was one she would cherish. However, she could not indulge in that behaviour again.

'It would be unwise.' She sat down suddenly in the chair at the garden table, drumming her fingers on the notes she would give him of what was, and was not, proper dinner conversation to have with a lady.

'What would be unwise?'

She spun about, surprised that he had come in without her notice even though she had been expecting him. Clearly she had been dwelling on what was unwise—revelling in it, more to the point.

'Good afternoon, Josiah. It has to do with your lesson today.' Did she seem collected, as if last night had not shaken her walls? 'I was thinking it would not be wise to speak to a lady about politics. We have delicate conditions which might be thrown out of balance if we heard that politics was nasty business.'

'Politics might throw anyone off balance.'

And while the subject of off balance was fresh, it was time to discuss why it was.

'Sit down and we will go over these notes.'

What a coward she was. Life's circumstances would not change because she feared speaking of them. She had done what she had done in kissing him. Now she would do what she must in order to make sure it did not happen again.

If she meant to avoid a broken heart, she must avoid becoming too attached to the man who could break it.

She pushed the notes across the table, but he did not even glance at them.

With the way his gaze was so intent upon her, she could only wonder if he meant to kiss her again.

That would not do, not at all.

'It would be much preferable to speak of fashion and—'

'I owe you an apology, Olivia.'

As much as she agreed that they should not pursue what they had begun, she did not wish for him to have been unmoved by it.

In the moment she would have sworn he had been as overcome as she was.

'No need for apology, surely. We were both rather overtaken by a moment. It was simply a temporary lapse of good sense that we will think no more of.'

'I will think of it—always.'

It was as if she had been struck dumb. How was she to reply to his honesty? This was not a time for truth. It was a time to present what needed to be the truth.

'The fact is, Olivia, I can't say if it's a pleasure or a heartache, remembering. But I ask your forgiveness if I led you to believe I could offer more. My place is not here in London.'

'And mine is not away from it. I completely understand.'

Of course she understood. It was only sensible to do so.

But then again—he had just said he would think of their kiss—always. There was no unsaying that.

The notion that he would remember her years down the road from now, possibly even yearn for that kiss, put her off balance. Left her utterly confused.

The very last thing she wanted was to be off balance or confused.

Such a state would make her vulnerable.

'Please,' she said with false flippancy. 'Think no more of it. I am a woman of some experience, after all, and am not misled by a simple kiss.'

'Was it so simple for you? Because it was not for me.'

'As I said, think no more of it. We will carry on with your lessons as if it never happened.'

When, she wondered, had she become so adept at prevarication?

'Does "think no more of it" mean the same thing as you forgive me?'

'It means, there is nothing to forgive.' She waggled the instructions on proper conversation in front of his nose. 'Shall we carry on?'

He took it from her, glanced at it for a moment.

'Seems to me it would be better not to have a conversation with a lady at all if this is what we will be talking about. We will both be bored as snails in a foot race.'

'You might discuss the opera with her.'

His response to that advice was to grin at her.

Evidently he did not regret caressing her fingers any more than he did kissing her.

Maybe he did not have regrets, but she did and they must be dealt with. Wondering what if this, or what if that, did not change the fact that his life led one way and hers another. Trying to do so was a sure path to heartache, which was one road she would not stumble down again.

'I am glad that we have come to an understanding about last night,' she said because even though she had momentarily diverted the conversation away from the subject, she wanted to put a final word on it.

Indeed, she wanted him to understand it was her choice as much as it was his.

An equal and sensible meeting of minds.

If she felt the same tonight in the quiet stillness of her bed, she would be beyond delighted—and surprised.

It seemed that the new Olivia, the one who wanted to dance, sing, and kiss the cowboy, made her presence known in quiet times when the real Olivia let her guard down.

Perhaps she ought to remain awake, recalling the faces of Henry's mistresses. That would keep star-dancing Olivia in her place.

For the next two weeks Joe spent time with Olivia, attending his lessons dutifully, studiously. Somehow he managed not to kiss her, but the temptation was there like an itch under his skin.

During that time of becoming socially educated he

had also learned to greet Roselina's callers with civility. It would not do for him to behave with less friendliness than the dog did. Apparently Sir Bristle thought them all worthy.

Naturally, Sir Bristle was most partial to the one Joe harboured the greatest resentment for.

'Young Lord Mansfield,' he murmured, watching from an upper window while the young man paid his daily visit.

In the absence of Ma, Olivia had volunteered to act as Roselina's chaperon. He could not express how grateful he was for it. Had Joe been chaperon, Roselina would probably have no suitors.

Except that dogged one. How old could he be? Not much older than Roselina, surely. Could he even provide for her?

Watching the two of them laughing and having a fine high time made him irritable.

He would rather look at Olivia, so he did. She sat beside the fountain, reading a book. Pretended to, anyway. Even from up here he noticed her attention focused discreetly on the ridiculously young couple.

And a good thing she did. Of all the boys coming to call, his sister seemed most drawn to peach-faced Mansfield, and he—well, besotted only began to describe the look on his face.

Joe ought to go downstairs, join Olivia in her surveillance.

The trouble was, his attention would be all for her. Keeping up his mask of indifferent camaraderie was no easy thing.

There was an understanding between them. He was obliged to live up to it. But by sugar, he was becoming more attracted to her, not less. He might appear to be the soul of cordiality but there was more to his friendly smile than she knew.

He'd spent more than a few hours wondering what he would do if it was not his destiny to return home.

If, for whatever inconceivable reason, he did not, would she want him?

Didn't appear so. Unlike he did, she probably did not hide anything behind her smile. It was what it appeared to be.

And yet he saw the way she was with her child. A woman who loved so deeply was not likely to limit that love to only one person.

Blame it, he had no business wondering if there was more to her smile. He was going home and grateful to be doing so.

Funny, but the thought of going home used to make him feel rather buoyant. Ever since he had kissed Olivia, thinking of going home almost gave him the sensation of sinking.

Now he was being ridiculous. There was nothing he wanted more than to go home, to ride across the open range and lasso a calf or two.

Down below, young Mansfield bowed over Roselina's hand in taking his leave. He lingered over it, but Olivia did not glance up from her book in censure. Perhaps he ought to rap on the window.

Finally Mansfield did walk away, but not without casting moon-eyed looks back over his shoulder. At last he closed the garden gate behind him.

Ah, just there, he saw Olivia's shoulders shaking in what had to be suppressed humour.

In the instant, Victor dashed across the Fencroft terrace, scrambled over the low stone wall that divided it from the rest of the garden, then ran like mad towards his mother.

She caught him up, twirled him about in a hug, kissing his cheeks without ceasing.

One day some fellow was going to be the lucky recipient of all that love. Resentment over some imagined man ought not turn his stomach sour, and yet it did. The reason why did bear dwelling upon.

Joe Steton was not meant to be her man. He was going home to Wyoming and nothing could deter him from it.

He had nothing against London, except maybe the foul city air, but this was a town for gentlemen—a town for his father. Some day he would be required to take care of the family estates, but that time was far off. When the day came, he would do what his father did— travel between the two—but in the end it would be the ranch that roped his heart.

The hell of it was, Olivia had roped and tied him, as well.

Even if he did change his mind about where home was, there was nothing to say that she wanted him.

It was a wicked situation to be in and it grieved him.

Roselina skipped into the room, looking as happy as he'd ever seen her.

It was not for him to cloud her joy with his own inner turmoil. His job of the moment was to see that the fellow she chose was a good match for her.

After that—or perhaps before—if he could manage, he was off to the north to see to Haversmere Estate.

Once everything was settled there, he hoped the state of his own heart would be more peaceful.

Chapter Nine

'I'd rather be playing poker,' Joe grumbled while sitting across the card table from his sister.

'So would I. However, whist is what most gentlemen play and you will not want to seem inept at it. It's an easy game to play if you pay attention.'

'I'm sorry. My mind was wandering.'

'And I know where to.'

Perhaps she did, but he did not wish to speak of it so he pretended to be studying the cards.

'To Olivia,' she continued, ignoring his attempt to avoid the discussion. 'That is the way of it when one is in love.'

'I'm not in love. And how would you know the way of things?'

'Of course you are. You just have not recognised it yet.'

'But you do?'

'It is rather obvious.'

'I cannot be in love with her. There is no future for us.'

She waved her hand between them, signifying that in her opinion this important detail was irrelevant.

Sir Bristle turned his face towards the door, lifted his nose and sniffed. His tail thumped heavily on the rug.

Voices, speaking softly, rose from the first-level hall.

Joe had no doubt that his expression looked as puzzled as Roselina's did.

Sir Bristle stood up from the rug, then trotted to the doorway.

'Who could be calling that he would be acquainted with? And at this hour?' For clearly whoever it was, was someone he knew.

Light-sounding footsteps tapped quickly up the stairs. A small, black-gowned figure stepped into the room.

'Mama!' Roselina exclaimed.

His sister jumped up from her chair, ran to Ma and held her tight, hugging and weeping joy all over her. 'I cannot believe you are here!'

In her excitement, Roselina failed to really see their mother.

She was dressed head to toe in black. Her eyes were clouded, her mouth turned down in sadness.

Esmeralda Steton was in mourning.

Pa was not with her.

Moonlight streamed through Olivia's chamber window. Sitting up in her bed, she watched the eerie and yet beautiful play of light and shadow in the room.

It was late. She ought to be sleeping, but something was amiss, although she had no idea what it might be. There was just a persistent sense of foreboding, or unrest, which was not due to anything she could identify.

The house was quiet. Victor was asleep. She knew because she had checked in on him three times since she had tucked him into bed.

None of the servants seemed to be up, either, which sometimes indicated that someone was ill.

The house was peaceful. She was not.

Flinging off the quilt, she went to her mother's chair, snuggled into the cushions and gazed out the window at the garden below.

Perhaps with daylight the disquiet would go away.

All of a sudden, she sat up tall and stared hard out the window.

Someone was in the garden.

Josiah sat on the bench beside the fountain, his face buried in his hands. His shoulders shook as if he were weeping.

But why? Something was very wrong.

Roselina! Had something happened to her?

Olivia ran towards the chamber door, snatching her robe from the bed in passing. She stepped into her slippers while dashing down the hallway and nearly tripped over the hem of her robe.

By the time she neared the fountain, she felt sick with dread, her stomach squeezed in a horrible fist.

He must have heard her steps on the stones, the rasp of her laboured breathing, but he did not look up.

'Joe?'

Head down, he reached for her. His hand trembled. She rushed forward, clasped it and sat beside him. Turning sideways, he wrapped her up, buried his face in her neck.

While he was not weeping, his tears dampened her collar. She stroked his hair, held him close and rocked him like she would do Victor when he was hurt.

Although this was not like holding Victor. Hugging her child close, caressing his hurts away, was not the same.

The need to offer Joe comfort was more compelling. She could no more walk back into the house right now than she could send her baby away while he was still clinging to her.

Clearly, Joe was in need of her.

Whatever troubled him went far deeper than a scratch. This hurt was much worse, she feared, and not so easily consoled.

After a long moment, she patted his back and drew slightly away, but only far enough to look into his eyes.

They were red and puffy. Even in the moonlit shadows, the intense grief gripping him was clear to see.

'What is it, Joe? What has happened?'

He shook his head, tried to speak, but could not.

She drew him to her again, whispered close to his ear, 'I'm here. Rest your heart, I'm here.'

Yes, just so—she felt the tension leave his body as he sagged into her.

Hugging him close felt so right, so natural. Letting him weep against her was an act of deep friendship— and perhaps more than that.

Something rustled in a nearby bush. A young kitten ventured into view, but spotting them, scampered for shelter.

She wanted desperately to ask after Roselina, but did not dare. He would speak when he was able. Between now and then she would simply be here, hold him and pray that her presence gave him ease.

It seemed a long time passed before he drew a deep breath, leaned back against the bench and stared up at the moon.

'My father.' His voice was hoarse, as if the very words ripped his throat. 'He's gone—dead.'

Not Roselina, then. Her relief vanished from one heartbeat to the next. Joe loved his father.

'I'm so very sorry.' Common words to console uncommon grief. She only hoped he felt how sincerely she meant them.

He nodded, silent again. He drew her close to his side, curled his arm around her, holding on to control but barely.

The kitten came out again, crawling stealthy towards them. It batted at the tassel on her slipper, then dashed off once more.

She was grateful for it. Sometimes in the midst of overwhelming sorrow something so normal kept the world from flying apart.

'How old do you think it is?' Joe asked. Not because he really cared to know, but because the asking enabled him to take a step back from the edge.

'Only about six weeks, I imagine.'

'I wonder if Victor would want to play with him.'

'He would, of course, but he's asked for a steer.'

He looked at her then, fresh tears shimmering at the corners of his eyes. 'Our mother came from America to tell us. She is with Roselina. I think they have both finally fallen asleep.'

'You should try, Joe.'

'No. For me, sitting out here makes it seem like I'm keeping watch. Don't know what for, but it seems right to do it.'

'Shall I watch with you or would you like to be alone?'

'Stay…please.'

She nodded and it was the last either of them said for several minutes.

'He didn't suffer, Ma said.'

'It's a comfort knowing, I think. It was for me when Oliver passed away. He was happily playing cards and then—he was just gone. I'd swear he was still smiling over the winning cards he was about to play. But Oliver was nearly always smiling.'

She reached up and twined her fingers in his where they lay on her shoulder. In the moment she found she needed comfort as well.

Grief had a way of sneaking up on one, bringing up the hurt all over again.

'We knew Pa was not feeling as strong as usual, but no one knew how sick he was. The doctor said it was probably his heart and such a slow decline it was hard to notice day to day. He went to sleep one night and then he didn't wake up.'

'Your poor mother. She must have been devastated.'

'Ma is small, like Roselina, but as strong as a prize fighter when she needs to be.'

'Also like your sister, I think.'

'They do know their own minds.'

'I'll pay a call tomorrow to offer my condolences. But only if you think it will be a comfort. I would not want to intrude.'

Very gently, he squeezed her fingers. 'I cannot speak for anyone but myself, but, yes, I would find it a great comfort. Please, Olivia...do come.'

'I will then.'

For a long, quiet time they looked at the moon.

'What do you think, Olivia? Are they up there somewhere, can they see us down here, know what we are up to, how we ache for them?'

Of course she did believe that. Had she not heard her brother laughing at her from time to time? And if he was laughing it meant he was happy.

'I'm completely certain of it. No one is more convinced of it than Victor is.'

She shifted her gaze from the moon to Joe's face.

Pure, clean light accented the lines of grief at the corners of his mouth, bringing back too clearly the feel of having her heart cleaved in half in the hours after her brother's death.

Oddly, she had not felt that way when her husband died. Then again, perhaps it was not so odd.

'You will know why he believes it,' she said, continuing with her thought.

'That his uncle sent me? If it is true, I'm flattered. If nothing else, I'm greatly complimented that Victor would feel that way about me.'

'I only hope his attention—oh, honestly—his devotion—is not a burden to you.'

'No, he is a sweet child. His attention could never be that. Don't worry, though, I will not lead him to believe there is anything Heaven-sent about our meeting.'

Olivia blinked, pressed her lips tighter to keep from—well, she did not know what—but there was her brother's laughter. She heard it as clearly as she heard Joe sigh.

'He'll believe it is true no matter what, Joe.'

'Will you keep doing that?'

'Doing what?' What was she doing other than sitting here and being a friend?

'Calling me Joe.'

Oh, she had been doing that! And doing it so naturally that she was not aware of the slip. She could hardly switch back to calling him Josiah now. Not even if she wanted to. Which, to her surprise, she did not. It would be awkward.

'I'll call you Joe.'

'Good, then.' He leaned his head so that his cheek rested on her hair.

For a while all she could hear was his quiet breathing, feel the rush of it stirring her hair.

'Will it always hurt so much, do you think?'

'I think so, but from what I can tell it will not happen as often—and, as odd as it seems, sometimes it will make you smile.'

'I feel like I will never smile again. I know that's wrong, but it hurts so blamed much I don't know how to see my way through it.'

'Live little moments between the sadness, I think. As time goes by the living gets longer and the sadness shorter.'

'If we didn't love so much, it wouldn't hurt this way.'

'And yet we choose to love.' All of a sudden what she said, and said with all sincerity, hit her hard. This was not the way she had been living her life since Henry's betrayal. To the contrary, she had hidden from anyone who might cause her heartache.

'I suppose, when you look at it just so, it is a privilege to grieve so deeply.' Oh, please let this make sense, she thought. 'Some people never love enough to be able to ache this way.'

'A comforting pain?'

'Perhaps, yes—and yet it hurts all the more for it.'

He began to quietly weep. He was so still about it that she would not have known except that her hair was being dampened by his tears.

She sat still, silently holding his hand because sometimes the wave of sorrow needed to be ridden until it left you breathless, gasping on its barren shore—and yet after it somehow able to breathe again.

After a time he let go of her, but only long enough to change position so that he was gazing down at her.

He lowered his mouth and kissed her, very slowly, very gently.

'What are you doing?' she asked, his tears salty on her lips.

'Living—for just a moment—I am living.'

Joe came into the dining room the next morning, not to eat, but because his mother was there.

He did not expect to see Roselina up and dressed, but she was, sitting close to Ma and staring at a slice of toast on her plate.

Ma was slathering jam on it and telling his sister she must eat it.

Seeing him come in, she stood, came to him and kissed his cheek.

'Good morning, Joe.' She tugged his arm, leading him towards the dining table. She pointed for him to sit so he did.

Ma turned towards the sideboard, industriously loading a plate with food. She set it front of him, but he had to look away. Sadly there was no escaping the mingled scents of eggs, ham, jam and clotted cream.

Ma looked well. But, of course, she had had a bit of time to adjust to what had happened—no, not adjust. That might never happen, but to come to terms with it.

Joe wished time would somehow advance to this time next year so he would feel—what?

Better, was all. Just better. And he had last night, in the brief instant he was kissing Olivia. For those few seconds the pain lessened.

'You must eat, my boy—look, Roselina has licked every bit of jam off her toast.'

'Can't stomach it, Ma.' There was something he

needed to ask, had to know. 'It has been more than a month since Pa—' it hurt to even say the word '—since he died. You ought to have sent a telegram. We'd have come home right away.'

'I suppose I ought to have, you deserved to know first thing, but it was—when it came to it, I simply could not put those words into print. This was news you needed to hear from a heart that loves you.' She clasped her hands in front of her, looking at them both as if she needed absolution.

'It is all right, Ma.' Roselina gave Ma her bravest smile. 'I'm glad you told us first hand.'

'It is just as well that I am here, my loves, otherwise you might starve.'

Without looking at his plate, Joe shoved a fork of something in his mouth. Ma looked strong and in control, but it had not been so long ago that she would have been where he and Roselina were this morning—trying to cope with a world dumped on end.

He ate until the food was half-gone because the last thing he wanted to do was cause his mother more heartache than what she had already been through.

Apparently satisfied that he would not starve, she turned her attention on his sister. 'Are you happy here, Roselina? Have you found a young man who suits your fancy?'

The way Ma smiled and talked like life was normal made him think it might be that way again. All they needed was time to come to terms—to say goodbye.

'A few.' Roselina blushed when she said so.

'I cannot wait to hear about them.' Ma kissed Roselina's cheek, reached across the table and squeezed his hand. 'We will go on. It might not seem like it now, change can be difficult. I understand this, but change we must.'

One change would be that they would be going home before Roselina married her nobleman.

Needs were that they must depart for home as soon as possible. The running of the ranch was all up to him now. Perhaps he could hire a reliable man to oversee Haversmere. Yes, was there not already a fellow who did it for Pa?

Or surely Olivia would know someone.

Olivia—he had not thought to part company with her so soon. Knowing he must hit him hard. Like a blow to the gut. There was only so much parting a man could take in a short amount of time.

He would not think of it now.

'I'll arrange passage for home this afternoon,' he said, surprised that he was not more eager to do it. 'I'm sorry, Roselina. I know how you and Ma had your heart set on a fellow from here.'

Roselina nodded, accepting his decision with a great deal of grace. She really was one of the best people he knew. Lord Mansfield was not likely to take the news half so well.

'Joe.' His mother touched his hand, patted his knuckles. 'You are Baron now in your father's place. You are Haversmere.'

That detail had crossed his mind along with a thousand others over the past day. The importance of it dimmed, being jumbled up with everything else pressing upon him.

As Joe grew up, his father's title had seemed something from another world—a duty he attended to each year. Even though Pa had discussed it with him, taught him what was required of a baron, to Joe, his father was a rancher first. His life in England seemed no more than a duty he attended to in order to spend the rest of the year at home with his family.

'I'm Joe Steton from Wyoming.' There was nothing more to say in answer. 'I always have been, Ma.'

'Not always, you were born at Haversmere. The place is your birthright and your sister's. Haversmere was always close to your father's heart. He would not have left at all, you know, except that he feared for you.'

'Why would he?'

'Your grandmother was adamant that it was the wet climate that killed your mother—you know that much.' Yes, Pa used to talk about it. It seemed his grandmother had let everyone know her opinion of Haversmere and of Pa. 'In his grief he half-believed it. Do you have any memory of falling in a river, Joe?'

He shook his head, not sure what that had to do with anything. He had a queer feeling in his gut when she asked, but no memory of such an event.

'It is not surprising. You were very small. But you took sick afterwards, extremely sick. You must imagine how that scared him happening so soon after your mother's death.'

'He never talked about it.'

'Well, I believe it is because he was looking forward and not back. We were building our new lives, son. But you must understand that he still loved Haversmere. It never quit feeling like home to him.'

'I can understand it.'

Ma reached down to pet Sir Bristle, who was asleep halfway under the table near her feet. He had the distinct feeling she was avoiding his gaze.

'I will not let Pa down. I'll care for everything the same as he did.'

'Yes, and you will do it well.'

An odd sensation—a new odd sensation—fisted his gut. Something in his mother's words did not set right.

She looked back up at him, her fingers clenching the dog's fur so tight her knuckles turned white.

'I have sent your father's body to Haversmere for burial.'

Joe's heart began a slow crawl up his throat.

Roselina stood, her hand clutching the lace collar of her gown.

The silence in the room was broken only by Sir Bristle's tail sweeping the rug.

'Why, Mama?' Roselina asked.

'It was your father's wish. He used to tell me it is what he wanted.'

'We will bury him there, then.' The unsettled feeling continued to grip his gut. 'Is there something else, Ma? You don't look yourself.'

She stood up, pressed her hands to her middle. Joe thought she tried to contain their trembling.

Why would she be trembling?

'As much as it was your father's wish to come home, it is my wish to not be separated from you ever again. There will be no ocean between us. Our home will be Haversmere.' She took a very deep breath, let it out in a rush. 'I have sold the ranch.'

He might have remained where he was for hours, stunned and disbelieving, had Mr Bowmeyer not entered the room.

'You have callers, my lord. Lady Olivia and Master Victor.'

* * *

For as brief as Olivia's visit had been, Joe found that her presence grounded him.

In the instant when he thought he could not go on, her smile encouraged him—reminded him he could.

Even Victor's presence felt like a salve. When the little boy tugged at his jacket, wanting attention, he could not very well dive into a pit of sorrow.

The visit was short and he had not had an opportunity to tell Olivia of the ranch being sold. For some reason it seemed important to share the news with her.

'Some reason' being obvious when he gave it a few seconds of thought. Olivia Cavill Shaw was important to him. She was the one he could speak to when everything was chaos. He'd had friends, he'd had lovers, but in Olivia he had both.

Although he did not reckon she saw herself as such. But they had kissed which made them more than mere friends.

This afternoon, so many questions ate at him. His mother had explained, but still, he needed to speak more about it with her.

Why would she do such a thing? Sell his home—his life?

At the moment Ma was in conversation with Mr Bowmeyer, but as soon as she finished Joe went to her.

'Will you walk with me in the park?'

'Thank you, Mr Bowmeyer. I do appreciate your service.' Bowmeyer nodded, then left the parlour. 'A walk will be lovely, but I only have a short time. I'm to meet one of your sister's beaux. Lord Mansfield—do you know him?'

He helped Ma put on her coat before they went outside. Even though it was sunny this afternoon, there was a chill.

'We have met, first at the opera, and now every day since. Are you sure Roselina is ready to receive callers?'

While they crossed the street a nippy breeze bit through his shirt and pebbled his flesh. He ought to have worn a coat, but blame it if he didn't need a distraction from what was going on inside him.

He couldn't say that he welcomed the discomfort, but he did need it to keep from living completely within his head.

His mother slipped her hand into the crook of his arm when they entered Hyde Park.

'Perhaps we should have brought Sir Bristle along. I have truly missed that dog.'

'Everyone would think he was a wolf on the prowl. Better to keep him inside.'

'London is very lovely. Your father always said it was, especially in the spring.'

'Mayfair is, but parts of the city are not so blessed.'

'Yes, I've heard that as well. From all I understand, it is quite nice up north, though. Did you know your father always told me Haversmere was a bit of heaven on earth?'

'I wonder why you never came with him?'

'I could not have an ocean between us. I felt the same then as I do now. We are family and meant to be together.'

'I hear what you are saying—but, Ma, the ranch was your home as much as ours. Why would you sell it?'

She stopped walking, placing her small hand on his vest. There were blue veins showing in skin that looked more fragile than he recalled.

'Listen closely, Son.' Brown eyes the colour of melted

chocolate pleaded with him to. 'I did not make the decision easily. Nor did I make it out of grief—and believe me, I did and do grieve your father. But you must understand that the ranch is not my home. You and your sister are my home. The thought of being separated from either of you—I could not. I think perhaps you did not realise how difficult it was for me over the years. Every time your father went away I feared it might be the last time I would see him.'

'I did not know you worried, Ma.'

'Good, it was my intention that you would not. But crossing an ocean is risky business—it was even more so years ago. I never knew if he would come home safely until I saw him galloping up to the front porch. And even then—Joe—there was always a part of him that remained here.'

'I didn't know that, either.'

'You were a child, such a thing was not for you to know. Then later you assumed he felt the same as you did about the ranch. Why would you not?'

She straightened his vest, then they walked on.

'All you ever knew was the ranch, but think of it, Joe, Haversmere has been home to the Stetons for many generations. Had your mother not died, your father would have carried on that way and never come to America.'

'You are my mother.'

'And you are my son. It is why I sold the ranch.' She crossed her arms over her middle while they walked. 'I could not have you go away every year like your father did, especially with Roselina in London, married and having babies. I could not have.'

A gentleman nodded in passing. Somehow both he and Ma found an answering smile.

'Don't you see?' she continued. 'You would have

found yourself as torn as your father was, once you married. Besides, it is only fitting that your children be raised at Haversmere.'

Marriage—children?

Olivia's face flashed in his mind. The image of her smile felt like refuge. It did not seem a bit odd that he should see in her the home he no longer had.

He would be saying some goodbyes in his heart over the next few days—to the land and the herds—to the hands who had worked side by side with him.

At least he would not be saying goodbye to Olivia. She was the bright spot in all the heartache.

'Who did you sell to?'

'Our neighbour, Tom Holden. We already shared grazing land so, when he offered to buy me out, it was only natural to say yes. Of course, at first I did not. Truly, Joe, I gave the matter a great deal of thought. The land transfer won't be official for another week or so, but I have given my word on it and I will not go back. It is the future we must look to now.'

He nodded and they walked on without speaking. She probably knew thoughts and emotions were whirling around inside him with the chaos of a tornado.

'There is a bit more you should know.'

What could there possibly be? Had she arranged him a marriage, or purchased him a commission in the Royal Navy? Sold Sir Bristle to a travelling circus? What?

'A letter came from the estate manager at Haversmere. Something is not right at the estate and he is asking for your father to come with all haste.'

'What isn't right?'

'"Mischief afoot" is what he wrote.'

'Did he mention what it was?'

She shrugged. 'Very little, but one thing he did say

is that planks from a bridge over the brook had been chopped halfway through. Three lambs fell in the river and had to be fished out.'

'There must be more to it than that for him to ask Pa to come quickly.'

'According to your father, mischief near Grasmere is a rare thing. It was only ever the increasing number of tourists tramping here and there that troubled him. So he did take the estate manager's concern seriously. As weak as your father was when the letter came, he tried to pack a bag—'

She bit her lip, blinked hard and was silent for a moment. 'At any rate, the more quickly we go to Haversmere, the better. It is what your father would want.'

It was not what Joe wanted. He longed for the wide open spaces of home, the rugged land and the tall, sky-kissing mountains, wanted it more than his next breath.

His next breath came, though, and here he was looking somewhat like any other gentleman strolling in Hyde Park.

'What shall we do about Roselina? Her Season has only begun and there are several young dandies vying for her attention,' he pointed out.

Faced with leaving Mayfair, he was suddenly hesitant to do it. It was no great mystery why.

Olivia Cavill Shaw.

'She will come with us, of course. Let's just see which among them will be devoted enough to follow her.'

Would she? There was no reason for her to. Olivia's place—her home—was here. Since Joe did not have a home it hardly mattered where he went, but she had every reason to remain where she was.

But then, Ma had not been speaking of Olivia.

'Mansfield, he might, but most of the young fools are so caught up in high-society posing, they would not be likely to.'

'All the better then. We will see who cares for her.' Ma smiled over at him. 'And what about you? Has there not been a young lady who has captured your attention?'

'Since I thought I was going home I would not have encouraged anyone's attention, let alone sought it out.'

Not that his heart had not become entangled anyway.

'Well, my son, now you may!'

A sliver of something hopeful pierced his gloom. He let the conversation drop while he let it glow for a moment.

'I feel a bit like the Grim Reaper bearing so much bad news, and I'm sorry for it. But I have every reason to believe I will see you happy again. Just give it some time, you will see.'

He thought of the grave in Kensal Green Cemetery. His father had been so distraught he had crossed an ocean in order to outrun his grief, and his fear. Yet Pa had lived a good life, a happy one with Ma.

Surely he could honour his father by doing the same?

'You are far from being the Grim Reaper.' He put his arm about her shoulder, leading her across the street and back to their rooms. 'Facts are what they are. I'm only sorry that you had to face all of that alone.'

'It was—' He figured she was trying to find a way to say that it was all right. It was what mothers did, tried to make things right. But it was not all right. Ma had been to hell and back.

'I've got you now,' he said and felt her lean ever so slightly into him. 'You will not be alone again.'

Chapter Ten

Olivia watched Joe standing at the fountain. He wore the clothing of a man born to society. His hands were shoved in the pockets of the trousers, his shoulders slumped.

He looked sad. But, of course, he was in mourning and it was to be expected. With the day so bright and beautiful, birds singing and blossoms sweetly scenting the air—oh, the contrast must make him feel all the more forlorn.

She ought to do something to cheer him, felt a strong urge to do so, but she could not imagine what.

Not kiss him—again. She knew full well that the only reason he had done it the other night was because he desperately needed an escape from the intensity of his grief.

All she had to offer him now were words—but which ones?

In time life will go on. I'm here if you need me. I understand... All these truisms went through her mind while she watched him. Each of them seemed inadequate.

All of a sudden Victor dashed across the garden,

Miss Hopp in pursuit. He latched on to Joe's trouser leg, hugging tight.

The last thing poor Joe would want was to have to entertain his admirer.

She hurried outside, ready to call Victor to her, but Joe reached down and scooped him up. She stopped where she was because the pair of them were smiling.

Victor squeezed Joe around the neck, then patted his cheek with his plump, half-babyish hand.

'My father is dead, too.'

Needing to know what her child had to say, she listened from a distance far enough away so that her presence would not interfere.

'We have that in common then.' Joe patted Victor's back. 'Let's get each other through it, shall we?'

'I'm not sad, though. I don't cry because I miss him, only because I'm sorry I do not have a papa of my own.'

It felt as though a stone hit her belly. She was not aware that he cried. She had been dreading the day when he would begin to wonder why other children had fathers and he did not. For years she had wondered what she would say. Now in the moment all she wanted to do was weep. Her baby was far too young for this sort of hurt and not a bit of it his fault.

Cursing Henry would do no good since he was dead. But a real man, knowing a child depended upon him, would not have happily slid down the path of dissolution which no doubt resulted in a shortened life.

'I'm sorry for that, too, little cowpoke.'

So far they did not seem to notice her. Neither did they notice Miss Hopp, who stood a distance away with her hand pressed to her mouth.

Did the governess know that Victor cried?

'I don't cry so much any more,' Victor said, looking

very seriously into his hero's eyes. 'That is why Uncle Oliver sent you to me, so I wouldn't. I need a Pa and I reckon you need a boy to cheer you up.'

'I reckon I do, at that. What do you suppose we can play to cheer us up?'

When had Victor begun to use the word 'reckon'? Or to say 'Pa'? But when had he cried and when had he stopped? She thought she knew everything about him and was stunned to learn she did not.

'Big cowboy and little cowpoke go wolf hunting!'

Joe set Victor down, then whistled loudly. A few seconds later the door to the house next door opened and Sir Bristle burst out, tearing across the garden and scattering a flock of pigeons which had been pecking seeds on the pathway.

For all the words of comfort she had tried to summon, it was something as simple as a game that was needed.

Or something as simple as a kiss, she thought, remembering how Joe had sought comfort from her.

A kiss which was not simple at all. On the surface of it, it was a gesture of comfort. But why should it be? What was it that lay under the surface that softened his grief, if only for a moment?

Not casual friendship. Between friends, sympathetic words would suffice.

Watching the cowboys chase the wolf in circles around the fountain, she had to ask herself what it was between them, if not common friendship.

It was important she understood so that she could deal with what was coming.

Joe would be going back to America. The ranch he so loved would need him.

What she ought to do was step in and forbid the bond growing between Victor and Joe.

Yet she stood by, silent and smiling over the laughter and the barking filling the garden.

There would be consequences for it, heartache when they must be parted by an ocean, but she would deal with it tomorrow.

Today she stood in the spring sunshine, smiling inside—happy and grinning with her only worry being whether or not the poor wolf would outrun his pursuers.

Just because the world caved in did not mean Joe would quit his lessons with Olivia.

For the one thing, he wanted to spend time with her and for the other—he was a blamed baron, a peer of the realm. He needed to understand stately behaviour more urgently than he ever had.

Now that his father might be watching from the heavenly realms, he felt a greater need not to let him down. When there had been only an ocean between them, it didn't seem to matter so much. Funny how, with mortal life separated from eternal, he felt a greater need to make his father proud.

Which did not mean he wanted to be Baron Haversmere. He did not. He wanted to remain Cowboy Joe.

What he wanted had little to do with anything any more. The plain fact was, he would honour his father.

And, by sugar, there was Olivia. What his mother had said about him finding someone special—he already had.

Sunshine in the darkness was what she was.

The other night, in that horrid moment when he thought his heart would stop beating and his lungs quit breathing because he did not want to face the next day, hour, or even moment, she had been there to make him want to.

For all that he fought the idea of being baron, there was one bright spot in it. Where there was a baron there was typically a baroness.

He knew he was getting a bit ahead in his thoughts, better to contain them to the here and now.

Just now, it was time for his afternoon lesson.

He crossed the garden. She was not waiting for him as she usually was. She might assume he no longer needed tutoring since as far as she knew he would be going back to America.

He exited the garden by the side gate, then walked around to the front door. The butler let him in with a nod and a word of condolence.

'Lord Haversmere,' he said with a polite bow. 'Please make yourself comfortable while I ask if Lady Olivia is receiving callers.'

Ramsfield's demeanour was more formal than it had been. He didn't care for the change, but supposed it was something he had best get used to.

It took only moments before he heard quick, light footsteps.

Olivia rounded the corner and came into the room, her cheeks flushed pink.

'Good day, my lord.' She presented a small curtsy. 'I'm sorry to have kept you waiting. I did not realise we still had an appointment.'

'Olivia?' He advanced upon her, his strides firm and no nonsense. The butler pivoted on his heel and slipped out of the room. 'I can take this drivel from anyone but you.'

The press of her lips accentuated the delicate brackets at the corner of her smile. 'I did need to hear you say so. After all, I could not presume to—'

'What you can presume is that you are a—' He had to catch his words before he revealed too much. 'A dear friend. You may presume that nothing has changed between us because I bear a title. Isn't yours higher than mine, anyway?'

'My brother's is, but then I married a younger son of—well, it is all complicated muddle. The important thing is that our friendship has not changed. I'm very glad of it.'

Her blush looked pink, pretty and warm. Funny how he felt his own skin flush. Maybe her high colouring was because she was thinking of kissing him. He sure was thinking of it. She had no way of knowing there could be more kisses between them. Many of them if he got his way.

It took him a moment to respond to what she had said because he was so blamed grateful she did not revert to calling him Josiah. By sugar, he nearly hooted out loud.

It would have felt good to hoot. Pa would like to hear him hoot and just knowing so made it seem that he was not so—gone.

'Now that I'm titled, I suppose I'll need even more training.'

At that she looked surprised, which made her lips open slightly.

As yet, she did not know he wasn't returning to America. Nor could she imagine that the ideas he had suppressed as futile no longer were.

When her lips pursed in confusion, he gave himself free rein to imagine them under his, hot and pliant.

'Do you mind if we go to the garden room?' he asked.

'If you like.' Her brows arched. Perplexity wrinkled her brow, but she led the way without asking questions.

'I like it here.' He took off his fancy coat and set it across the back of the chair. He wished he could take off being baron as easily, but here he was.

Not take it all off, though, he thought while walking towards the aviary. Many doors had closed for him with the death of his father, but this one having to do with Olivia had opened.

She followed him to the birdcage, where they watched the feathered creatures flit about.

'How are you today?' she asked, the puzzle lines still creasing her brow.

'Everything is a mess.' He glanced away from the birds and into eyes the colour of the sky. 'Nearly everything.'

'What can I do?'

'Only listen, if you would not mind.'

'Shall we sit? I will ring for tea.'

He followed her to the table, sat down, even though his stomach was still too raw for even tea.

'I'm curious about something,' she said.

So was he—curls, to be exact. They brushed her cheeks, giving her a softer appearance than usual.

'Why do you want to proceed with our lessons when you will be returning to America and much sooner than you expected to?'

'That's just it. I will not be returning.'

Her mouth fell open in clear surprise. He touched her chin.

She caught his hand, pressed it back down to the table. 'Why ever not?'

'My mother sold the ranch to our neighbour.'

Her mouth sagged again, but as soon as he lifted his hand she snapped it shut.

'What a horrible—oh, Joe, I'm so sorry for it. I know how much you counted on going home. You must be heartsick.'

'I could be bitter, if I let myself. But I reckon it's a choice, to live resentful or to look forward to what is next.'

Clearly, Olivia had not made that choice after her husband's infidelity. She lived in fear of handing her heart over to another man—to him.

'A choice? I don't know, Joe. Can one choose to feel one way or another?' She shook her head and the curls brushed her cheeks. He thought of asking why she had—chosen—to wear them, but he refrained.

He longed to know why she was wearing a less-than-severe hair style. It looked pretty and playful. To his way of thinking it might be because her heart was opening.

True, it was a very large step from a changed coiffure to a kinship of the heart, but he hoped she was taking that step towards him.

'The fact of the matter is, I cannot change what has happened. I had no choice in it. But I can, and I do, choose to seek a path of hope and not despair.'

'I believe that one feels what one feels, but truly, I'm glad for your sake that you can do it.'

'Look for the good,' he said. 'It's my new adage.'

'Is it?' Her eyes slanted up with her smile. 'Does that mean you will forsake your Stetson for the top hat?'

'There is no good in it to be found.'

Olivia Shaw had the loveliest smile he had ever seen. It propelled him a step further down his chosen path.

'Apparently you do still require instruction.'

'It's why I'm here.'

It was not at all why, yet he could not tell her he came because he craved her company.

If he did, she might take a step back from their friendship. It was his intention to move forward. To deepen what stirred between them—to make it what their kisses indicated it could be.

It did not take looking past his nose to see they would be right together. In loving touches, of course, but there was more. There was that heart connection neither of them had spoken of and yet knew to be there.

'I'm still as rough as sandpaper. I'd be grateful for everything you can teach me.'

And she would be grateful to be able to help smooth his rough edges. Not that she wanted them erased. Especially not the wink, or the way he wore his Stetson so that his eyes peeked out playfully from under the brim.

The truth was, she enjoyed his company and, for all that she was dreadfully sorry for what had happened to him, she was the tiniest bit relieved he was not going back to America.

Why was that?

If he went home, she need not fear that Victor was forming an attachment which might break his heart.

Because, for mercy's sake, there was no way she would be able to explain to a small boy that he must choose to be happy. That he should simply set aside his tears and be glad that he had known a cowboy at all.

She could not explain it since it made no sense.

Feeling halfway giddy inside because Baron Haversmere would remain in London made no sense either. Better that she did not linger over wondering why it did not.

If she did, what would she discover? Maybe that in spite of all she had learned about the risk of giving herself to a man, she, too, would adopt a new adage?

Hmm, what would it be if she did? *Dance until you trip and fall?* No, rather, *Dance as though you will never trip and fall.*

Yes, if she did adopt an adage she liked the second. It was far more hopeful. Truly, what was the good of having an adage that was not uplifting?

'I have every confidence that you will smooth out brilliantly.'

'So have I, but only with your guidance.'

His forehead drew together in worried-looking lines which made the corners of his eyes crease—but in an extremely handsome way. Really, she did not choose to recognise the fact, it simply was. Her rapid heartbeat and the way she felt so warm inside was also a fact. She did not choose the reaction, it was simply happening.

If there was a choice, she would choose not to be all fluttery inside.

Wouldn't she?

Of course she would! Unless she adopted the adage she had just dreamed up.

'I need to go up north—to Haversmere. Will you and Victor come with me—us, I mean. Ma, Roselina and Mr Bowmeyer are going, too.'

Go with them? She could not possibly. What folly. Why would he suggest such a thing?

'Why must you go?' she asked instead of asking why she should. 'It is the middle of your sister's Season. I think it is not wise to abandon it at this point.'

'Mischief, or so I've been told.'

He gave her the smile that made his eyes crinkle at

the corners. She wished he had not, it tended to distract her.

'But I need you. My lessons are incomplete.'

Why did he have to look at her that way, with his expression so needy, so appealing to her—to her sense of duty? 'The estate manager at Haversmere sent a letter to my father asking him to come quickly.'

'But why?' Why was the estate manager alarmed was what she seemed to be asking, but what she really wanted to know was why he wished for her to go along.

'Damage to a footbridge. A few lambs fell into the water and needed rescuing.'

'Were they rescued?'

'Fortunately, yes. The problem is that the damage to the bridge was done maliciously. The estate manager is worried because such behaviour is uncommon in the area.' His expression grew sober. 'It might as easily have been children falling in. I really must attend to the problem.'

As alarming as that was, it did not mean she could set her life aside and flit merrily away. What would that mean to Victor?

All right, her son would be delirious with joy over the trip.

'I would take it as a great kindness if you would come along—to keep me on my studies.'

He reached across the table, cupped her hand in his, then winked.

'Dance as though you will never trip and fall,' a small voice in her mind suggested. If the voice was in her mind it would know that she had not adopted the adage, only considered it.

'Can we not study when you return?'

He shook his head. 'I'm a slow learner.'

'Only when you do not wish to do something. Otherwise you are quite accomplished.'

Oh! Her hand! It was still lying quite contently in the cowboy's rough fingers.

Something was very wrong. She had certainly not chosen to leave it there. She did, however, choose to yank it back.

'Think of Roselina. She needs for me to present a good face.'

He tipped back in his chair, arms crossed over his chest while regarding her with a teasing quirk tugging the corners of his mouth. She was glad to see it, given how, under his brave face, she knew him to be deeply mourning.

And that right there, the enticing expression, was reason enough she should not go with him. The man was as tempting as a second helping of cake. Worse— as tempting as a kiss in the rain.

If she were not careful, she would actually adopt her new adage. Possibly his adage, too.

Before she knew it she would be looking for the good while in the act of tripping and falling.

'I've no doubt you will behave no matter where I am.'

He plunked the chair legs down on the floor. The humorous cajoling of his expression sobered.

'You must come with me, Olivia. Everything else aside, I will not leave you here to deal with Waverly on your own.'

'I am capable of fending him off, quite capable.'

Although, looking back, she had not been doing a great job of it in the Duchess's garden.

Indeed, every time the man had given up pursuit of her it was because Joe had been present to scare him away. Her sharp tongue was not much of a weapon against one such as the Marquess.

No, from all she could tell, it only increased his desire to have her.

When she thought about it, she would be much safer going to Haversmere. Which in turn meant that Victor would be safer.

So then—her choice seemed to be to instruct a handsome cowboy in the art of courtly behaviour or to fend off a drooling lecher.

She considered her potential adage. Whatever she did she risked falling. All things considered, she would rather fall into Joe's arms than into the Marquess's clutches.

'Will you come?' he asked, leaning across the small table, resting his weight on his elbows.

He wanted to kiss her. She felt it humming in the air between them. She wanted it, too.

She stood up suddenly because if any time was right to learn to resist this man, it was this one.

If she could not, then she had no hope of it, no matter where he went or she did not.

'I'm sorry, Joe. I cannot possibly.'

He caught her hand when she would have walked away.

'Olivia?' His voice was a kiss—to her ears, to her heart.

His gaze held her while she took a step back, freeing her fingers. Oh, but she was not free. How could she be when he continued to kiss her with those exquisitely tender green-brown eyes?

'Come, Olivia, I need you.'

Sitting in her mother's chair, Olivia poked her needle into the embroidered petal of a flower and listened to wind rattle the shutter outside the window. It was a lucky thing she did not stab her finger for all the attention she was paying to the task.

'What were you thinking?' she said, to the chamber apparently, since she was the only one sitting here in the soft glow of lamplight.

Certainly, she was not thinking anything she ought to have been. And they were not thoughts as much as images in her mind. They flashed behind her eyes one after another like a penny slide show.

Oh, there she was taking a lovely stroll with Joe along the banks of Grasmere Lake. And there they were walking hand in hand on a vigorous hike in the fells. No matter what happened, she was not going to kiss him while standing on the peak, gazing at the majestic view below—probably not at least.

From all she had heard, the Lake District was among the most beautiful places in all of England.

Although, it was also very rainy.

Olivia had no intention of finding out for herself, but if she did change her mind, she would need to bring Miss Hopp.

What was to say Miss Hopp would be willing?

Joe had been correct in saying he needed to learn to behave. Although it was not behave as much as repress the wild charm that made her—oh, for goodness sake, he really did need to learn to withhold that wink.

For Roselina's sake.

The sweet girl needed the boon of a dozen beaux to select a husband from. It would not do for her to fall into the false embrace of the first dandy to—ah, but it was not Roselina's folly on her mind, it was her own.

No doubt she ought to go north if only to guide Roselina in her decision. She had her mother, of course, but the lady was as new to society as her daughter was.

For their sakes, she ought to give the offer serious thought.

But then, perhaps Miss Hopp did not enjoy rain.

Indeed, would she not be endlessly drying out Victor's shoes and stockings? And they would be wet since he would find endless pleasure attempting to ride grazing sheep no matter the weather.

'Ouch!' Poking a needle in her finger could be a sign that she should not go—a warning of—

Of finding pleasure in a man's arms—in Joe Steton's arms to be precise?

Everything going on in her mind was second to this.

Joe had spoken of becoming bitter—that he was choosing not to. In spite of all that had happened to him, he was able to smile.

For a very long time after her husband's death and the discovery of his faithlessness, she had not smiled at anyone, with the exception of her baby.

Setting her handiwork aside, she sucked on her pricked finger while looking down at the garden.

Perhaps the warning of the needle had been about closing herself off, allowing her heart to decay.

Bushes lashed about below, making the shadows appear eerie. There was a gate at each end of the garden, but neither one of them was locked.

Joe had been correct to caution her about the Marquess. The fact that she had thwarted his advances did make him all the more eager to press them. While it was true that he had not accosted her recently, he would. It was how he pursued his prey—attack and retreat—time and time again. She had seen him do it to other widows.

Were she to take Victor to Haversmere she would

not need to be constantly looking over her shoulder. Perhaps by the time they returned, the cad's attentions would be settled on some other widow.

She took her finger out of her mouth, the prick only a small red dot on the tip of her finger.

A movement that was not a thrashing shrub caught her attention.

Sir Bristle dashed across the garden, following what appeared to be a ball. Joe walked after the dog. Even from here she could see his slumped shoulders. He must be struggling to walk his hopeful path.

It was late for a game of fetch, but not, she decided, too late to join them in the game.

She caught her coat off the rack and hurried downstairs.

Joe stood at the fountain with his back to her, staring at the blowing spray of water. The moan of wind over the stone path muffled the tread of her steps.

Sir Bristle noticed her and bounded forward with the ball in his mouth, his great tail wagging joyfully.

When Joe turned he was smiling, although she was certain he had not been doing it a second ago.

'It's awfully dark and windy to be outside,' he commented.

'And yet here you are.'

He took the ball from Sir Bristle and threw it. 'Dog needed exercise.'

And Joe needed time to think, to deal with his heartache.

What an admirable man he was, to stand there and smile at her—to follow a path he did not want to travel and yet do it with such courage.

Olivia had not been courageous in her trial. She had folded up on herself, stuffed away life's joy as if she were packing a trunk which she then slammed and locked.

What she was beginning to suspect was that Victor's cowboy had the key to her trunk and was prying at the lock.

All of a sudden she wanted to push the lid open and burst out of her trunk, to laugh out loud, to twirl and sing.

To dance as if she had no fear of falling.

'I've come out into the dark and the wind because I want to ask you a question.'

'Shall we sit?' He indicated a bench with a sweep of his hand.

She shook her head. The temperature was falling quickly and she had only brought her light coat.

'Joe, do you know how to dance?'

'Does a frog know how to fly?'

She laughed out loud and it felt so very good.

'Truly? You do not know any dances?'

He shook his head, his lustrous hair tossed madly in the wind.

'All I do is stomp about. Roselina says ladies hide when they see me coming.'

'This is a problem, a severe one. Did you know it is required of a gentleman, to be proficient at dancing? Why, it is bad mannered to attend a ball not having the skill.'

'I'm afraid then that my sister and my mother will be put to utter shame.' He shrugged, tossing the ball to the dog again. 'Unless someone teaches me before the Duchess's gala I will appear a disgrace.'

He was smiling when he said it so she could not help but return the warmth. And it was warmth—delightful and very wonderful.

'It appears that I must go north with you, then. I would not see your sister's suitors scattered to the wind on your account. When shall I be ready to travel?'

'Will the day after tomorrow be too soon?'

'No. I'll make arrangements.'

Now that she had made her decision she felt good about it. But more than good, really—she felt giddy, all bubbly inside with anticipation.

She could not recall the last time she had felt this way. It had certainly been before her marriage.

'Goodnight, then,' she said to Joe because he just stood there, coat lapels flapping nosily against his shirt while he stared at her.

She turned to go back inside, but he caught her hand. It felt so very solid and warm wrapped around hers.

'Thank you.' Rather than letting go of her, he drew her in, slowly, giving her time to resist the coming kiss if she chose to.

Well, she did not choose to—not this time.

He placed their joined hands behind her back, drew her so close that there was not even a breath between them.

'You will not be sorry, I promise.' His mouth lowered, but she rose up on her toes to meet him.

Wind tugged them, snapped her skirt and his coat. The thud of Sir Bristle's ball hit the stones near her skirt.

Cowboy Joe gave her a fever, a chill—an assurance that no matter what, as long as she stood here in the circle of his arm she would not fall.

His mouth left her, but slowly. 'I look forward to learning everything you have to teach me.'

'About dancing?'

He nodded, released her hand, let his arms fall away from her.

'The most important thing is to not step on your partner's skirt. It would not do to let her trip and fall.'

'Better get back inside, darlin'. You are starting to shiver.'

She was. But it was not caused by the cold wind alone.

Nodding, she turned away and hurried back towards the house.

'Olivia?'

She stopped, glanced back over her shoulder.

'I won't let you fall.'

'I know,' she murmured, then hurried on her way.

Going through the dark garden room, she found that she was excited to tell Victor of their coming adventure.

No doubt, in his joy, he would dash about whooping like a cowboy.

But what she hoped above all things was that she would not whoop about with him—as eager for a spot of fun as he was.

Just because she had unpacked her miserable old emotional trunk did not mean she could leap about laughing.

She was a mother, a woman of great responsibility. And yet, there was that young girl inside her, tentatively swishing her skirts and feeling free for the first time in years.

What harm could it do to let her frolic for a bit? Tomorrow would be soon enough to pick up her mantle of responsibility.

Tonight she was going to visit the girl she used to be.

Chapter Eleven

Haversmere

It had been full dark when Haversmere Manor came into view. From a distance, moonlight reflecting off the aged stones had made it stand out against the dark surrounds. To Joe it had seemed like a soft grey pearl shimmering in night.

Rising, swirling mist gave it an enchanted feel.

Everyone had been asleep except for Joe, Olivia and the driver.

Not wishing to awake the rest of the party, he had not said anything. Olivia nodded at the house and smiled at him. Although, after enduring such a long trip, she might smile at any place offering a bed.

The housekeeper and the butler must have heard the carriage wheels on the driveway because they had hurried down the manor steps and ushered everyone inside.

Naturally, they had been expecting Pa. It was a hard thing to have to give them the news, to listen to their quiet weeping.

It brought back his own tears and Roselina's—even Ma's—although he had not seen her shed many.

Grief was not something one got over all at once. He thought maybe you never did get over it completely, not until you were reunited with your loved one on the other side of life.

It was that thought which gave him the courage to smile and think forward rather than behind.

Coming inside the house last night, he had hoped to feel some sense of home. It had been at one time. No doubt he had been happy here.

All he had felt was relief to get a bite to eat and then to fall on the bed in the master's chamber.

Surprisingly, he'd slept well, then risen before dawn eager to explore Haversmere.

On his way outside he'd heard a bit of noise coming from what must be the kitchen, but other than that the house was silent.

It wasn't light enough yet to see things as more than the dark blurs of trees and the lighter shade of the path that led from the house to—he did not know where to— but he was about to find out.

He heard rushing water. River Rothay, Pa had said. It sounded cold and fast. Not at all like the slow mean- der of the Cheyenne River that cut through the property back—not back home—not any longer.

Pa used to talk about this river, how he loved the fresh sound of it and how many large brown trout he had fished from it.

Joe wondered if it was so different from fishing on the ranch. No doubt it was since everything about Great Britain was different than Wyoming.

Please, let something feel familiar. He was pretty sure that had been a prayer.

If he could recall the smallest thing, it might make it easier to call this place home. In order to best serve the people living and working here, he needed find a bond with the land.

He wanted a sense of belonging to a place. That it was his to care for in a way more than simply what his new title required of him. He'd had that feel for the land in Wyoming, perhaps he could have it here as well.

The closer he got to the river the more clearly he heard the flow of swift water. It was the only sound at this time of morning. Whatever night creatures lived here were already abed for the day and the birds had not yet risen.

He crossed a stone bridge, watching the dark water rush under it, then away towards Grasmere. Some niggling feeling of familiarity poked at his heart, but not so strongly as to call it a memory.

If he could summon a memory or two, it might make it easier to settle in.

Only a flash of something from his very young life might make him feel like he belonged here.

Since he had been only three years old when he left he did not expect to remember much—but anything would help him.

Stepping off the bridge, he spotted a large red structure with sunlight beginning to graze the peak of the roof.

The shearing barn! Somehow he knew what it was. Beside it, only a hundred yards to the east, was the barn that housed the estate horses.

That was a start, he supposed. Perhaps memory would build upon memory and Haversmere would come to feel like home.

Walking past the sheep barn, then across the meadow, he looked forward to visiting the horses on the way back.

Far in the distance he spotted a few campfires. Shepherds keeping warm in the early morning chill, he guessed. While he walked along through fresh-smelling grass, the campfires went out one by one. Sunshine rose over land more green and lush looking than any he had ever seen.

All of a sudden he had a sensation of rolling in the meadow, of grass tickling his nose. It might be a memory, but then it was so vague, it might also be something he longed to do in the here and now.

By sugar, Victor would enjoy rolling down the grassy bank. As soon as the day warmed he would bring him here and they roll in the grass together.

He was going to enjoy teaching the child things. While he was not Victor's father, Joe felt a draw to watch out for him—teach him things a boy ought to know.

Must be because the little cowpoke had claimed him.

It occurred to Joe that perhaps the boy did not know how to swim. He was young for the skill. It would be important for him to know how. The river would be a danger if he didn't.

Joe had fallen in the river, although he did not recall the event. It did not take a vivid memory to know that such an accident would be terrifying. His heart kicked against his ribs at the thought of it happening to Victor.

Looking past acres of pasture land, he saw the mountains—the fells, as folks here called them—coming alive with daylight sliding down from the ridges. They were not nearly as tall as Wyoming's, but he thought they appeared as rugged.

One day he would like to hike up, look down on everything. Maybe Olivia would go with him. He reckoned she would enjoy the view, seeing all the grandeur below as a soaring bird would.

London was vastly different from Haversmere.

After walking about another half-mile, he came upon a lake, its water deep, clear and reflecting the trees growing on its banks. The images were wavy with the breeze that rippled over the surface of the water.

Pa had talked about this lake, called it a mere because it was small.

Since small did not mean shallow, Victor would certainly need to learn to swim.

Joe bent down to waggle his fingers in the water. It was far too cold for swimming. He figured a stern warning about the danger of both the lake and the river would have to do.

It felt a fatherly thing to do, to warn the boy about the danger the water posed. Funny how it gave his heart a warm turn, knowing it fell to him to protect his young friend.

Not that his mother had not done a fine job of it for five years, it's just that a boy needed the guidance of a man's hand.

In the past he hadn't thought a great deal about fatherhood, except that he'd had a father and loved him. Lately something had changed for him in that regard.

Ever since a blue-eyed package of mischief had wrapped his small arms about Joe's neck and claimed him, blamed if he did not feel lassoed and branded.

Not only by the boy, but by his mother. From the first he had been attracted to her, who would not have been? She was a lovely woman and any man would seek her company.

Any man who cared to look past her thorny attitude in regards to men.

Joe Steton cared to look—cared to look even more deeply than he already had.

Now that he had something to offer Olivia, he felt free to pursue the intimacy they were both sparring around.

Winning her over to his way of thinking would not be an easy thing to do. He figured it was not her heart he needed to win. The bond between them was already there and for all its fragility was quite genuine.

Rather what he needed to win was her trust.

The breeze stirred the grass and carried another noise with it, so faint he stopped and listened hard.

Bleating. It sounded soft, forlorn and not far distant.

He hurried forward, a bit towards the right, and discovered a pair of black lambs huddled together in the grass.

They were quite young, their umbilical cords still attached. Poor little critters were shivering.

He took off his coat and wrapped them up in it. What had become of their mother? There must have been a predator of some sort. Nothing else could have made her abandon her lambs.

Odd, though—glancing about he saw no signs of a struggle.

'Don't worry, small beasties, you will be warm and fed in no time.'

He did not know a great deal about sheep, but he assumed any nursing ewe would take them to suckle.

It was a lucky thing that Sir Bristle had not roused from his spot on the floor beside Victor's bed when Joe went out. He had never seen a sheep. Joe wondered who would have been more startled, the lambs or the dog.

Victor would not be startled. He would be overjoyed.

'Will you two help me?' he asked of the lambs. Fortunately they were no longer quaking. 'If you cosy up to Victor, make him happy, his mother will be, too. My hope is that in turn she will cosy up to me.'

One of the lambs stuck its dark nose out of the coat and gave a soft bleat.

'You think I have a chance, then?' He touched the velvet-like nose. The lamb licked his finger. 'You must be hungry. How did you end up out here, anyway?'

Mischief, perhaps, as the estate manager's letter had suggested. But directed at innocent lambs? It didn't make much sense.

More likely a predator. But one so stealthy that it left no evidence of struggle or a kill?

He had not met any of the shepherds yet, but he would have a lot of questions when he did.

By the time he made it back to the barn the lambs had fallen asleep. The sun was fully over the horizon now—which was not to say it was warm.

Someone had lit a fire in the stove at the far end of the barn. Joe walked past the long row of sheering stalls, then set the lambs down in front of it to warm.

Footsteps came into the barn, then stopped abruptly.

'Lord Haversmere!'

Joe glanced up and spotted the silhouette of a man standing in the doorway. It was impossible to make out his features until he stepped further into the barn. 'I offer my heartfelt condolences on the loss of your father. He was a fine man and we are all grieved by his loss.'

It was going to take some time before he became accustomed to being called 'lord'. In his heart he would always be just plain Joe.

'Thank you, sir.' He stood up to shake the man's

hand, but then wondered if it was appropriate since the man nodded his head in deference to the title.

'Welcome to Haversmere. I am Willie Smythe, the estate manager.' He glanced at the lambs with a frown. 'Will you know, sir—did your father receive my letters about the troubles of late?'

'My mother received them. She delivered them to me. Mr Smythe, is trouble so rare here that a broken plank on the bridge is suspect?'

'Quite so, at Haversmere this does not happen. I see to the safety of all our bridges myself. In fact, I inspected the damaged bridge the day before the lambs fell in. It was solid.'

'So you believe someone is sabotaging the estate?'

There was a stack of wood crates close at hand. Joe took two down, sat on one, then offered the other to the overseer.

'I am that certain of it, sir.' Mr Smythe tugged on his ear and shook his head. 'But I'm sure I can't tell you why.'

'I found these two about an hour ago.' He nodded at the lambs. 'They were alone in the pasture near the lake. Can you tell me what predators might have taken their mother?'

'Hereabouts, grown sheep have no predators.' Mr Smythe stood, then went to kneel beside the sleeping lambs. He picked one up, turned it this way and that. 'Not even a day old, I'd say. I've a guess who their mama might be. But as to how she lost them? I fear it is more of the mischief I wrote about.'

He set the lamb beside its twin, then resumed his seat on the crate.

'I only hope you will remain here until the mystery is solved, my lord.'

'My family and I are not returning to America. We will be making our home here.'

'Ach, but the cattle ranch! Your father was devoted to it.'

'Indeed, he was. But as it turns out, my mother was more devoted to my sister and me than a piece of land and so she sold it.'

'Ah, well, might I say, sir, all of us will be glad. We have sore missed having our Baron in residence over the years.'

Mr Smythe was older than Joe was. Could he perhaps remember him from when he was a child here? Did he recall his mother? Perhaps he could unlock some of the memories Joe craved.

'How long have you been employed here, Mr Smythe?'

'Near on twenty years, sir. This is home to me, as I hope it will soon feel to you.'

'Thank you—I only ask because I would like to find someone who knew me when I lived here. I was young and have no memory of any of this. I was hoping there might be someone who might be able to refresh my mind.'

'Old Widow Shoemaker, she would be the one. She was the cook here in those days and even up until five years ago. She lives by your good graces in a small house between here and Grasmere.'

'I will pay her a visit.'

'You won't need to. She comes every day to sell her eggs.'

Joe stood up. No doubt breakfast was being served and people would wonder where he was. He bent over to stroke each of the lambs.

'These will be all right?'

'If Izzy is not their mother, another will take them

in. But I will admit it makes me uneasy thinking someone got close enough to the sheepdogs to be able to take
them without raising an alarm.'

'Perhaps it is someone they know.'

'Aye, my lord, that's the part that makes my gut
crawl.'

'You may rest easy now, Mr Smythe. I am here and
will put the mischief to rest.'

'I'm that grateful.' Smythe tipped the brim of his hat
when Joe took his leave. 'And, sir—for all that Haversmere is different than where you came from, I hope that
you and your family will be happy here.'

'Thank you, Mr Smythe.'

Walking from the barn towards the manor house, Joe
paused a moment on the bridge. He looked at the large
house with its stone walkway, then glanced back at the
pastureland surrounded by the fells.

Smythe was correct in saying the Lake District was
far different than Wyoming. But the plain fact was, it
was no less breathtaking.

Beauty was beauty and came in many forms.

And now Haversmere was his. People depended upon
him to make a success of it.

In the beginning, his only obligation had been to
learn to dress, walk and speak like a gentleman. And
that for only the time it took some fellow to offer for
his sister.

Now he was a baron. The weight of his new role did
sit heavy on him.

Someone came out the front door and stood on the
porch. She waved her hand in greeting.

It was Olivia, dressed in a yellow gown. The way she
smiled made his heart leap. How many times could the
sun rise in one day?

* * *

Perhaps Olivia ought to have asked her maid to come north, but in the moment and with everything happening so quickly, she had not. It was kind enough that Helmswaddle had packed her trunk in haste. The maid deserved to have a prolonged holiday.

As a result Olivia must now dress herself and arrange her own hair. This was not something she was accustomed to doing. All her life she had had help. Which did not mean she was helpless.

Although Miss Hopp would be willing to assist, Olivia would not ask.

One could only imagine what Victor would be doing while the governess tied a ribbon in Olivia's hair.

A ribbon? What had made her think of wearing such a frill? Something had because, staring at her open trunk, she saw three of them draped across her petticoats. They had certainly not purchased themselves.

She had worn the yellow lace at breakfast. Perhaps this afternoon called for blue. Indeed, from her second-storey window she could see a small lake and her blue gown was a near match to the water, although the fabric did not glitter or reflect anything.

She removed the blue gown from the wardrobe, spread it across the bed. It was casual and perfect for her walkabout with Joe.

After putting it on, which was a bit of a challenge without the help of her maid, she looked in the mirror.

Oh, dear. By no means could she style her hair the way Helmswaddle did, even if she had the time.

As it was she was nearly late.

A blue satin ribbon would simply have to do. She tied her hair in the ribbon and let it fall where it would.

She closed the door on her small but pretty room, then walked down the hallway towards the stairs.

The staff at Haversmere took dutiful care of the house. Even though Joe and his party had not been expected, everything was in order as if they had been.

Fresh flowers filled vases on glossy tables along the hallway. The scent of polished wood was as pungent as the flowers were.

In all, the house was comfortable more than formal, made all the cosier because of the smell of bread baking in the kitchen.

She walked past a library with the doors standing open. A small fire in the hearth would make it a welcome spot to read a book.

But then, she was not here to indulge in reading, but to further instruct Joe in the art of gentlemanly posturing. Now that he was Haversmere, a genteel appearance was all the more crucial.

Not that he wasn't already a gentleman, he was to the bone. All he required was a spit of polish. That and to learn to dance.

Clearly the manor house, while grand enough, was not intended to host grand balls. In the process of exploring this morning she noticed a room that would serve for an evening soirée which, unless you were the Duchess, was quite adequate.

No doubt the room had gone unused for a very long time. From what she understood, Joe's father had conducted his business without social fanfare, his wife and hostess living across the ocean.

For not having a mistress, the manor house seemed to be running efficiently. It was apparent that the staff treated the place with care and respect.

If there was a prettier place on earth than Haversmere, she could not imagine where. The home was both grand and inviting—the grounds pastoral.

She had heard the area's praises described by poets and travellers and now knew the words to be well deserved. Joe could not help but find his home here.

Surely in time he would come to love it as much as he had loved the ranch.

Even she, having been here not even a full day, was wishing she never had to leave.

Olivia rounded a corner on the way to the hall and nearly collided with Joe's mother, who balanced a cup of tea on a book she was carrying. The fire set in the library hearth must have been meant for her.

'Good day, my lady,' Olivia said, putting out a hand to steady the tea.

'Why, hello, Olivia. I trust you are finding your way about?'

'I've only become lost once or twice.'

'Only three times for me. But isn't this a lovely house? It is my first time seeing it with my own eyes. My husband described it to me and I half-feel I know everyone, but to see it first hand is a grand thing.' A shadow muddied the rich brown shade of her eyes. 'Looking back, I wish I had come with him on occasion. Of course I could never have put an ocean between me and my children. As you can see, I still cannot. But you are a mother so you will understand.'

'Completely, Lady Haversmere. And am I correct in assuming the need to be near them does not change because our children are grown?'

'It only gets worse, my dear. They go where they will and not where you direct them to.' She sighed. 'I can't tell you how odd it feels to be called Lady Haversmere rather than Mrs Steton.'

'I hope you do not mind.'

'It makes me feel rather high-hat.' She smiled, winked. So that was where Joe learned the gesture. 'And something of an imposter.'

'You should not. I suspect that Haversmere has dearly missed having a mistress to fuss over. From what I can tell, the staff is delighted to have you.'

'As I am delighted to be here, the title notwithstanding. I'd act like a loon in a swamp if that is what it took to be with my babies.' She blew on the tea, took a delicate sip. 'Ah, there is one of them now. Unless I miss my guess he is looking for you. Enjoy your outing.'

With a nod and a smile Lady Haversmere made her way to the library.

Olivia stepped out on to the porch, securing the ribbons of her bonnet under her chin.

Her hair felt oddly wonderful blowing out from under it in the fresh cool air.

Joe met her at the foot of the banister. He had plucked a rose from one of the many bushes growing beside the porch.

'Good afternoon, Joe.'

'It is a good afternoon.' He winked then tucked the rose into the brim of her hat. 'I think it's the same colour as the gown you wore this morning. I'd have picked something the colour of your eyes, but I'd have had to pull down the sky to do it.'

She smiled at the outrageous compliment as if it were the most natural thing in the world to do.

For some women it would be, but for her it was the most unnatural thing.

'Are you always such a flirt?'

'That wasn't flirting, just observing a fact.'

Whatever he chose to call it, she liked it in a way she

had not done in a very long time. The teasing expression warming his gaze gave her the flutters.

One thing was certain, no other man had ever—or would ever—give her the sensation of a feather born along on the breath of—of a kiss.

What a fancy thought. If she was not careful, she would write it down and become a silly poet.

He caught her hand, tucked it into the crook of his elbow. Life seemed more casual at Haversmere. Perhaps she could have come out without gloves. If she had, she would have felt the warmth of his fingers curl around hers. But, no, touching him skin to skin was a bit much to think of right at the moment.

Given that she was already a fluttering feather afloat and within a breath of becoming a sonneteer—well, it was enough to deal with right now.

'Where are we going?' she asked, looking about. It could only be to somewhere green and lush.

'There's a small lake past the shearing barn. Would you like to see it?'

'I did see it from my window. But I want to see everything on your estate. The area really is as lovely as people say.'

Even though they walked slowly, remarking on this flower or that tree, they made it to the lake's edge in under half of an hour.

'This might be the most beautiful spot I've ever been in. Look, Joe, how it reflects the trees as if the water were a mirror.'

A sleek, swift bird flew low over the surface, making it seem that there were two of them. When the bird skimmed the water it nearly seemed that the wings grazed each other. Then the bird lifted up, leaving its match to vanish in the lake.

'I've brought some cheese.' Joe drew a wrapped package from his coat pocket. 'Crackers, too, if they aren't crumbled. Would you like to sit beside the water?'

He led her through ankle-high grass. 'I found a pair of lambs without their mother this morning. Right over there.' He pointed to a place where the grass was bent. 'Poor little critters weren't even a day old.'

Joe took off his jacket, then spread it on the grass for her to sit on. He sat beside her. Taking out the cheese and crackers, he divided them.

'Oh, look, Joe!' she exclaimed while removing her gloves and hat. 'It's a red squirrel. See it digging about in the grass where the lambs were.'

'It's got some small treasure. Shall I see what it is burying?'

'Victor will be overcome with joy if it is a treasure.'

Joe got up went to the spot. The squirrel dashed off. Joe squatted down, poking his fingers about in the grass. He came back with something curled in his fist.

'Not much in the way of treasure. A button only.'

She took it from his open palm and held it up, watched the brass gleam in the sunshine. 'It has an unusual shape, not round, not square.' Nearly pumpkin-shaped better described it. 'I imagine whoever lost it will not find a replacement.'

'It might have come from anywhere.' His brow wrinkled in thought. 'But it might have come from whoever took the lambs from their mother.'

She gave him back the button.

'Poor sweet things.' She and Victor had visited them this morning. 'I don't know who was happier at being reunited, the lambs or their mother.'

'From all I could tell it was Victor.'

'It was a very lucky thing that the estate manager

located the ewe. Had he not, I fear the lambs would have spent the night with him in the nursery,' she said.

'You are a lucky woman to have a boy like Victor. He is good natured and full of adventure.'

'I cannot say I do not worry about his high spirits getting him into trouble.'

'Probably will, it's all a part of being a boy. I wouldn't worry, he will grow to be a fine man.'

With Joe as an example to grow by. The thought came to her before she could stop it. She ought to stuff it back where it came from, but it was such a lovely thing to imagine, she could not manage to snuff it. The best she could do was not say so out loud.

Neither of them spoke for a moment. On her part it was because she was listening to birds sing, feeling sunshine on her loose hair and simply enjoying Joe's company.

'What do you think of the baronetcy? Is that the right word?'

'That refers more to your title. But if you mean the land? Quite honestly, Joe...' she took a nibble of cracker, a nip of cheese and chewed them together '... I think it is the prettiest place I have ever been. I think you are going to be madly happy here once you get used to it being home.'

'Perhaps I could be. If I can only remember something of my past, it might re-establish a connection.'

'Try closing your eyes and your ears if you can—just breathe in. I've heard that smell brings back memories quicker than anything.'

'Has it worked for you?'

She smiled because how could she not? 'I've not admitted this to anyone before, but sometimes I sniff Victor's hair, right behind his ear, because in that spot, he still smells like my baby. I go right back to the time I held him and rocked him.'

Of course there had also been the times she caught the scent of a woman's perfume and it reminded her of the times her husband had returned from 'visiting his ill mother' looking flushed with pleasure.

For once, looking back on it did not rob her of her joy as it usually did. That was odd—and wonderful.

Puzzling, too. Why did the memory not crush her the way it used to?

Perhaps it was because everywhere she looked, beauty was reflected.

But maybe not that. Beauty was pleasant and could be found anywhere if one looked for it.

More, it was looking at Joe that made her happy. The way he smiled at her, his eyes squinting against the sunlight and a wave of hair cutting across his fore-head—well, some beauty went beyond what one beheld and shot straight to the heart.

He closed his eyes, then cracked one back open. He arched a brow in question.

'Yes,' she said. 'Like that, but for longer.'

Closing the eye again, he took a deep sniff, then let his breath out in a slow hiss.

'Well?' She leaned towards him, eager to know if it worked.

'Hmm…' He leaned towards her, sniffed again. 'I smell cheese—on your lips.'

And then he kissed her.

And she let him.

She should not do it. The more she kissed him the more she wanted to.

It was only a kiss—with a wonderful man who was

not going back to America—and so she gave herself over to it. Let him fill her up with—

'I did smell something, Olivia.'

'You did? A memory of your childhood?' She could scarcely believe her advice had helped.

'No, it was not the past I smelled. It was the future.'

Chapter Twelve

The next day found Olivia and Victor, along with the Stetons, riding towards Grasmere in the open carriage to visit a renowned bakery. Even in London, society praised Grasmere Gingerbread. Rumour had it that it was the best in the world.

Olivia was eager to discover if it was true.

The world's finest gingerbread was not the only thing she wished to discover. What had Joe meant when he talked about seeing his future? Ever since he had uttered those words, she'd felt a bit off balance.

It seemed that he had spoken in reference to her, but he had made no further comment on it and she had certainly not.

What else then? Perhaps he had been referring to a new business venture having to do with cheese. It was what he had claimed to smell, after all.

She nearly snorted out loud because she knew very well he was not going to become a cheese maker. He had been alluding to a future with her and no doubt about it.

Trying to imagine it had to do with cheese was a foolish way of denying what was going on between them. Or how poignant his comment had been.

It would be wise to guard her thoughts lest she embarrass herself—truly, cheese?

'Isn't this a lovely quaint town?' she commented, and not simply to distract her attention from the man sitting across from her.

The first time they had travelled through Grasmere it had been dark. Today she noticed how charming the village was. One could easily spend the whole day visiting shops and tea houses. While the village was not exactly bustling the way London was, it was busy with tourists. There were lovely inns and enough restaurants to draw visitors from all over.

The carriage stopped in front of the bakery. The aroma coming from inside was so delicious smelling that Victor began to bounce up and down on the seat in anticipation.

'I'll make our purchase and we'll take it to that grassy spot beside the river we passed on the way into town.'

'Thank you, Son, that will be lovely.' Esmeralda smiled at Victor. 'Will that suit you, my boy?'

'Grandly, my lady.' His words would have been more convincing had Victor not slouched down in the seat and crossed his arms over his chest.

Her son disliked being apart from his cowboy.

'Perhaps I can take him inside with me? He can help carry our purchases.'

Victor sprang up from the seat, grinning as if only a second ago he had not been a perfect image of petulance.

'Very well,' she answered because she could hardly say otherwise. Besides, she did trust Joe with his safety. 'Victor, it will be up to you to make sure Lord Haversmere does not buy up the whole shop.'

'I'll make sure!' He all but leapt into his hero's arms when Joe reached for him.

Watching the pair of them walk across the path and into the shop, her heart swelled. Her throat tightened because her sweet small boy was trying to walk with the same cowboy swagger that Joe did.

What exactly was it that Joe smelled for his future? She knew—in her heart, she did know. The prospect of what it might mean made her insides quake.

She would need to go very slowly in this. With Henry, she had rushed into marriage, beyond eager to give him her heart. This time, it was not only her heart to be considered, it was Victor's, too.

A few moments later, Joe walked out of the bakery, holding Victor's hand and carrying a large box. All of a sudden she did not want to go slowly. She wanted to run towards life, arms open and rejoicing.

Roselina laughed at the sight of Victor gazing up at her tall brother while telling him something that appeared to be important. Whatever Victor had to say was so fascinating that neither male had thought to wipe away the jam and crumbs smeared on his mouth.

It didn't matter, really. What did matter was that Joe laughed and ruffled Victor's hair in a fatherly way. Olivia was not sure she had ever seen anything that stole her so completely away.

'I imagine—' Esmeralda's eyes shone with affection when she spoke '—my son has a very hard time saying no to your son.'

Evidently he did, if the sticky remains of a treat before his treat were anything to go by.

'Joe will make a wonderful father one of these days.' This remark she punctuated with a blatant, brown-eyed wink.

'I know my brother rather well, Olivia.' Roselina waved to Joe and Victor. 'He would be an excellent father to Victor as well as an amazing hus— Who is that woman?'

'I'm sure I don't know.' Esmeralda's eyes narrowed in speculation. 'And why is she scurrying after Joe and Victor?'

Indeed, why was she smiling so brightly—brazenly, in fact?

Olivia did not like the icy hot chill creeping over her skin. She knew it all too well.

Jealousy, or rather fear of it, had been her constant companion for the past six years.

She would not succumb to it again. Why should she?

Joe Steton did not belong to her nor she to him. He was free to pursue the attention of any woman he chose.

Although, she had rather thought—

'Hello!' the lady called.

Joe, being in deep conversation with Victor, did not seem to notice.

The woman was undeniably attractive. Her unbound auburn-hued hair caught the sunshine and glimmered. At least she was not younger than Olivia was—although why it should matter, she could not fathom.

Olivia must bear in mind that in spite of four kisses and how she felt about them, Joe did not belong to her. Oliver had not brought Victor a cowboy and neither had he brought one to her.

'I wonder,' Esmeralda murmured. 'What occurred to prevent her from dressing properly?'

'Lord Haversmere!'

'How does she know who my brother is?' Roselina asked with a frown. 'But I imagine word spreads as quickly here as anywhere. People will know that Pa has passed away.'

Joe took another half-a-dozen steps before he stopped to acknowledge the woman's greeting.

'My lady?' Joe tipped his Stetson.

The woman clapped her hand to her heart, tapped her chest with her fingers while smiling.

Joe did not appear to notice how she was not so innocently drawing attention to her bosom.

Roselina noticed. Olivia heard her utter a word that a lady ought not. Esmeralda must have noticed as well because she did not correct her daughter's language.

Flirts came ten a penny, so why was it that this one rankled? Her hair, perhaps. The colour was an echo of—no, she would not remember it.

'I have been so anxious to make your acquaintance, Lord Haversmere.' She extended her hand for Joe to shake. 'I'm a fellow American!'

The sight of the woman, her bare hand in Joe's, made Olivia's stomach queasy, but since she did not want to appear a shrew, she smiled. Really, more than that she did not want to be a shrew!

She had put all of that behind her. If she trusted Joe, and she did, she had no call to feel anything but gracious towards the woman.

If only seeing the woman leaning in so close to him did not make her feel so green and irritable.

Jealousy was something she had fought to put behind her, but here it was, clinging to her like a disgusting shadow.

It mattered not that Joe had given her no reason to feel this way. It could only be that her heart was flawed, damaged.

Josiah Steton was a handsome, charming man. Now that he was Haversmere he would be even more sought after by women.

This well-endowed beauty was only the first of many who would try to win him for themselves.

It would be wise to hold on to her heart. Keep it safe within her chest until—oh, well she did not know until when.

'My name is Prudence Lapperton. I am the propri-etress of a lovely inn here in town,' the smooth voice nattered on. Olivia tried not to eavesdrop, but stand-ing as close to the carriage as she was it could not be avoided. 'We are kindred spirits, are we not, both of us being American?'

Had the harlot purred when she said it? Perhaps she had not, but because of Olivia's rather green emotional state it seemed so. What Olivia needed to do was bite her uncharitable tongue—or thoughts, as it were.

Joe handed the box he carried to his mother, then lifted Victor back into the carriage, glancing briefly over his shoulder while he climbed in. 'Good day, Miss Lapperton.'

'Oh, it's Mrs, my lord.' She walked beside the car-riage when it slowly moved away. 'I'm a widow. Please, if you are in town and wish a place to stay rather than make the long trip home, my doors are open to you.'

'As I recall it,' Roselina said, 'the drive was little more than half an hour.'

'Perhaps if you only wish to get away from estate business? I'd be pleased to introduce you to—'

Her voice faded as the carriage picked up speed and left her behind.

'That woman has set her cap for you, Brother,' Rose-lina said with a glance over her shoulder.

Following Roselina's gaze, Olivia saw the widow waving her arm and grinning, her bosom a-jiggle.

It was uncharitable to notice. Olivia was doing her best to be a more tolerant person, but—

'But she has lost her cap,' Victor chirruped. 'See, her head is bare.'

'Indeed she has, sweet boy.' Esmeralda hugged him and kissed the top of his sunshine-blond hair.

'Victor Shaw, not another bite of gingerbread for you.'

'But, Mother, it is the best in the world. The baker said so.'

'Just because it is the best does not mean it will not make you sick.'

Joe sat on the blanket spread beside the river, listening to the conversation. Not to the words as much as the sound of Olivia's voice and Victor's answering one.

Mother and son had grown to be special to him. In the short time he'd known them they had walked smack into his heart. Indeed, and that was exactly where he wanted to keep them.

'Lay your head down. Take a small nap.' She stroked his hair when she said it.

'But, Mother, I—'

Olivia pointed to her lap and the billowing folds of her skirt. In spite of his objection to napping, the child was asleep within moments.

Joe wondered if the time would come when she would invite him to lay his head where Victor's was. If she did, he was pretty sure he would not drift off to sleep.

No, rather he would simply lie there and look at her face, hold her hand. He'd snuggle his cheek against her soft belly and sigh in contentment—for a little while.

Given his head would be where it was, and that he

was a man full grown, by sugar, it would not be contentment uppermost on his mind.

Better not to even think of what else, not with his mother and his sister chatting so close by. It would be indecent.

Courting Olivia was his intention, but he would need to go slowly with it.

Blamed Lapperton woman. He had noticed Olivia's reaction to her—had felt it when she had withdrawn from him. Until that woman forced her blatant, suggestive attention on him, Olivia had been, if slowly, coming to trust him. Over cheese and crackers at the lake she had let him close to the heart of her.

He'd felt it when the fear of being betrayed caught her heart in its fist and squeezed. The damage her fickle husband had caused would not be healed without time and patience.

Joe had time. He had patience. He also had what Olivia needed most.

Loyalty.

He would give her that no matter how many Prudence Lappertons threw themselves in the path of his title.

There would only ever be one woman for him. If he could help it, Olivia Shaw would not end her days a bitter widow.

'So many people have approached us this morning to offer condolences. I believe we ought to host a celebration in honour of your father's life.' Ma glanced back and forth between him and Roselina.

'I believe Pa was very well loved.' Roselina's eyes grew moist when she said so.

'I know he was.' He would have been. While to his

family he was a Wyoming rancher, to the folks here he was one of their own, their Baron.

As Joe now was. He had an obligation to the people living at Haversmere. If only he could remember something—anything—that would give him the devotion he needed in order to serve them the way he should.

He could serve them without it. But they deserved to have someone who felt a part of their world. Had their best interests at heart because he cared about Haversmere—about them.

'I agree. It would honour Pa and help us, too. We need to become accepted here.'

'Nothing grand.' Ma tapped one finger on her chin in thought. 'But intimate—to remember your father and to become acquainted with our neighbours.'

'I'll need your help, Olivia,' he said. This gathering could work to his advantage in more than just getting acquainted with the local folks. Perhaps by spending a lot of time with his teacher, he could win back the trust the widow had shaken.

'If you ask me, my brother still has much to learn.' Roselina shook her head as if he had learned nothing over the course of his instruction.

The plain fact was, he had learned far more than he ever expected to. How to dress and how to speak were only a part of it.

He had learned that Olivia Steton was a dedicated mother—a loving one. Also that her son was endearing in every way a boy could be. He had learned that she was a determined instructor.

He had seen her angry, seen her patient. Seen her wary and seen her surrender her heart—to him. He had seen her away turn from hurt and betrayal to trust—in him.

Most of all, he had learned that he was in love with her. Not that he could admit it. It was too soon for such a revelation.

As things now stood, Olivia was not ready to discover she was going to become his wife—that Victor was going to be his son. It might seem this decision was sudden, but looking back he knew it had been in the making for a while now.

It had taken seed in Kensal Cemetery. But the night in Fencroft garden when she had held him while he cried—he had loved her then.

Sitting here now, he knew he always would. From this moment on he would not be the same.

Turning his gaze towards the river, he watched the water rush past. What he was really doing was hiding his expression. He was choked up with emotion and did not want anyone to suspect it.

'Your brother is actually doing very well, I think.'

She thought that? He felt like preening at her defence of his social skills.

'There is one thing he is stubborn about, though.'

'What? I'm not stubborn. I'm pliable.'

'Not when it comes to your top hat. You refuse to wear it.'

'And since I will continue to do so, your work with me remains unfinished.'

'And have you learned to dance yet, Joe?' Roselina asked.

'My dear Olivia, I fear your work with my son might take a lifetime to accomplish.'

Thank you, Ma.

A rainy day and a young boy trapped inside amounted to nothing but trouble, no matter that this was a spacious manor house. Olivia feared for each porcelain vase of flowers. It was inevitable that at least one of them would crash on the floor when Victor galloped down the hallway on his imaginary horse.

Given that he might also yank down a curtain in pursuit of an outlaw, she was only able to give half of her attention to the conversation she was having with Roselina.

It was unfortunate because Joe's sister seemed rather morose today and it was unlike her to be so. Olivia would like to discover what was behind it but there was a sudden thump in the hallway.

'Yee haw! Got you, you lowdown bag of fleas!'

'I'm sorry, Roselina.' She stood up, then hurried to the doorway. 'I had better find out what he really captured.'

Not a bag of fleas, for sure. She was certain he had not learned the expression from any of his books. Either he had made it up himself or heard it from Joe.

A bag of fleas, indeed. She could not help but smile. Her son really did have a fine imagination.

Warm breath skimmed the top of her hair. A quiet laugh tickled her ear. 'It's a lucky thing that pillow is going to jail, otherwise we'd have bugs all over,' he said.

'Your home is so well kept I pity the flea who tries to set up house here.' Olivia laughed, too.

'I'm taking Sir Bristle on a walk to the barn. Would you and Victor care to come with us?'

'I can't think of what I would like more. It will be a relief to get him outside.'

Which was not all the truth. She would like to toss her arms around his neck, express her thanks for the invitation. She would like that more.

Of course, her heart would go soft at the feel of him

so firm and strong under her hands. The scent of him so close would fill her nose and her knees would knock.

She feared that taking things slow with this man might prove to be futile.

'Thank you, we accept,' she murmured, clasping her hands in front of her. She would not hug him because, futile or not, she must at least try to remain level-headed.

Had she forgotten how to keep a man at a distance? She had not forgotten the need to do so.

If only Mrs Lapperton had not stirred up those old memories of being betrayed. She struggled to remember it was Henry who had done the damage, not Joe.

Walking towards the shearing barn listening to the pinging of raindrops on the umbrellas, she tried to rebuild the emotional wall she used to have.

It was the safe thing to do. The sensible thing.

Ah, but the rain was against her. The steady drum brought her back to the moment Joe had kissed her in the alley behind the opera house.

In that moment nothing in her past had mattered.

Fortunately Joe opened the barn door before she let herself believe it again.

The past did matter. One learned from one's past.

Of course, her past had not been with Joe. Had it been, the lesson would have been different.

She gave herself a good mental shake. They were together in the barn for one purpose only, to let Victor romp about without having to worry about damage to the house.

A spot of fun was all she was going to think about.

For a large space, the shearing barn was cosy. The scent of fresh straw in the stalls and wood burning in several stoves filled the air. With the weather churning outside, everything in here seemed all the more snug.

Sir Bristle's ears swivelled to attention when he heard the bleat of a lamb. He wagged his tail, stirring a puff of straw dust.

'I reckon he likes lambs.' Victor whooped, then galloped towards the stall where they lay with their mother.

The dog trotted after him, seeming so good natured she nearly forgot he had knocked Lord Waverly flat, then stood over him as if he wanted nothing more than to devour him.

The ewe, apparently used to being herded by dogs, did not seem alarmed by Sir Bristle sniffing her babies. Victor stepped into the stall, sat down, then picked up the one he had named Annie Oakley. He settled her on his lap and sang softly to her.

'Come and sit with me.' Joe caught her hand and led her to a bench near one of the stoves. 'I have something to say to you.'

While he held her hand? She really did need to snatch it back.

'It's about the woman in Grasmere.'

If there was one thing she did not want to discuss, it was that brazen person. She was having the devil of a time forgetting her as it was.

Prudence Lapperton had smacked Olivia back to a time when she'd felt threatened. The woman scratched at the wound she had striven so hard to heal from—and she had done it with pointed fingernails.

Old Olivia shivered fearfully, warning the new Olivia to be cautious.

But of Joe?

She wriggled her fingers out of his hand. 'What about her?'

'I want to know why she made you uneasy.' His voice was low, nearly a whisper.

'Unless I'm wrong, she made us all uneasy. Roselina and your mother were annoyed at the way she was acting overly familiar with you.'

'I imagine not. They are not used to such women. Pa was always loyal to my mother. He never gave her a reason to doubt his faithfulness.'

What a blessing it would be to feel confident of a husband's loyalty. She thought she had had that confidence once, had blindly and wholly given her trust only to have it crushed.

'Ma and Roselina were annoyed. But it was more than that for you—you felt threatened, darlin'.'

It made her uncomfortable to know he could peer into her heart so easily. Truthfully, she desired an intimate connection with Joe, but not, perhaps, as much as she feared it.

'What reason would I have to feel threatened?'

'You know what reason.'

She did know, yet she shook her head to make him think she did not. Why was she hiding from him, especially when she did not truly want to?

'There is something rare between us, Olivia. It's tender and it's growing.' Normally, Joe had a light in his eyes that reflected his cheerful nature. It was not there now. 'But for all that it is remarkable it is also wounded. If that woman had not waylaid us as she had, it would not be. When you saw that she was interested in me— or more likely my title—it frightened you.'

He was wrong in thinking Mrs Lapperton's interest had to do with his title. She was only the first of many women who would be seeking Joe's attention because he was an exceptional man.

This was not something she could accept.

'All right, it did frighten me, Joe. I honestly thought I was finished with—with the ugliness my late husband left me with, but it seems I was wrong. The widow, she bore a resemblance to the woman who held my husband while he died in her bed. I would be lying if I did not say I was shaken by her.'

'Do not fear me.' He cupped her chin, gazed at her as if he saw her trepidation and looked right past it. 'Trust me, Olivia. I will never betray you.'

Footsteps shuffled through scattered straw on the barn floor. The steps stopped a short distance away and someone cleared his throat.

Joe withdrew his hand, turning on the bench to see Willie Smythe wringing his hat in his hands.

'What is it, Mr Smythe?'

Joe reached for an overturned barrel, pulled it closer, then indicated that the estate manager should sit down.

'I'm that sorry to interrupt, sir.' In spite of it he sat down. 'There's a problem among the shepherds and I fear it will come to a bad end.'

'What is the nature of this problem, Mr Smythe?' Joe leaned forward, a frown cutting his brow.

Olivia had to catch her breath. Joe might not feel like a baron, but watching him while he listened to the estate manager, oh, he did look it. He was so very confident, so self-assured, his noble bloodline was evident.

'Ach, it will sound silly to you. It did to me at first, but the lads fear there is a ghost behind the recent mischief.'

'A ghost?' Joe's brows shot up.

'Your father's ghost, God rest his generous soul.'

'Perhaps we should discuss this out of hearing of the

boy.' Joe rose, walked several paces away, then stood with his arms crossed over his middle.

Olivia followed, too, because who would not?

Closer to the barn door the rain sounded louder and she could hear the wind moaning under the eaves.

Well, the timing of that was odd.

'Tell me what you know, Mr Smythe. I would like to understand what has happened to make them think such a thing.'

'At first it was the broken bridge, then a branch fallen from a healthy tree and that with the weather as still as can be. Then the lambs vanished from their mother's udders and were whisked away to be left by the lake.'

There had also been a button left by the lake. She kept quiet about it, though, confident that Joe remembered and would deal with this as he would.

'What is there about these events to make them think it is the work of the supernatural and not plain mischief?'

'It's just that the happenings were odd and when the boys counted back, they figured the strange things began to happen at the time the old Baron died.'

'And do you believe this is happening because of a shade?'

Mr Smythe did not answer at first, but drew the tip of his boot in a half-circle in the dust on the floor.

'I think I do not—especially in the broad light of day. But I would not quit even if I did believe it. I can't explain what's going on, though.'

'But the others? They are speaking of leaving Haversmere?'

Willie Smythe nodded. 'Sitting out by the fires at night, they tell stories, some far-fetched, but others— well, the lads tend to be superstitious.'

'I'll have a meeting with them. See if I can explain how there are natural causes for it all.'

'I'm glad for it, my lord. They are reliable shepherds. Some of them have grown up here. We would be hard pressed to do without them.'

Mr Smythe nodded to her, then to Joe. He rolled open the barn door, then paused to looked back at Joe. Heavy rain had turned the area beyond the door into a vast mud puddle which Victor was going to take great delight in.

'Oh, and you will need to explain why that hay-stack—' he wagged his finger at a hay pile which stood no less than eight feet high '—moved from the right side of the barn to the left overnight without anyone hear-ing or seeing a thing.'

Joe sat down on the divan in the library, stretched his legs towards the fire and wondered what problem he should consider first.

After dinner the ladies had gone to the parlour to stitch dainty-looking flowers on pillow cases and to talk about whatever things women did, leaving him on his own.

With Victor being put to bed by Miss Hopp and the servants going quietly about their business of the eve-ning, the house was quiet, pleasantly tranquil.

Tranquil to his mind, at least. He suspected the ser-vants were wondering what might go bump in the night. Gossip about Haversmere being haunted was spread-ing fast.

He'd noticed more than one maid glancing over her shoulder while hurrying down a long hallway.

Joe took off his boots, waggling his stockings at the fire while deciding which of his pressing issues to deal with first.

The one most compelling had to do with Olivia and her fear of trusting him. There had to be something he could do to make her trust him—although it was not him she distrusted. He knew that. There was more than one ghost to be dealt with.

One was a fabrication, but the other? Henry Shaw, curse the man, was quite real as a spectre from the past.

How was he to battle a dead man? He knew of only one weapon against the hurt the fool had left behind.

Love. His banner over Olivia would be love. And he would win.

He would also show his employees he was a responsible leader once he got to the bottom of the business involving a fabricated ghost.

The phantom was missing a brass button shaped somewhat like a pumpkin and that was all he knew about him. He wasn't the spookiest of spirits. Sabotaging a bridge, kidnapping lambs, and sawing a limb off a tree were acts of mischief and nothing more.

So far the 'spook's' reason seemed to be to frighten rather than harm.

Blamed if he knew why, though. Didn't make any sense why someone would want to put everyone on edge.

One thing was certain, it was not Pa come back to cause mischief.

He crossed his arms over his belly, which was still humming happily over dinner. He closed his eyes and was about to drift contentedly away when he heard the rustle of a skirt.

'I am sorry. I did not mean to intrude.' The last voice he would consider intrusive was Olivia's.

Sitting up straight, he turned to her with a smile. She

always made him feel like grinning. He waved for her to come and sit beside him.

'Looking for a book?'

'The nights can get rather long without one.'

'I can recommend some excellent poetry.'

'No doubt.' She frowned, but her lips pressed together so he knew she suppressed a smile.

The thought popping into his mind was that the night did not need to be long. The reason why not was better left unsaid for now—but not for ever.

One night they were going to sit right here and read poetry together. His thoughts went soft, drifting away while he watched her bite her bottom lip in thought.

She hesitated in accepting his invitation to sit down, but in the end she did. Not quite beside him, but close enough for easy, friendly conversation. Close enough that a sideways scoot would bring them shoulder to shoulder, hip to hip.

'You ladies finished your stitching quicker than I expected.'

'I put mine away early. I felt your mother and sister needed time to talk alone.'

'What's wrong with Roselina, do you think? She hasn't seemed herself today.'

'I know what is wrong, just not what is to be done about it.'

'Is she ill?' That was an alarming thought. Roselina was never ill.

He relaxed when Olivia's mouth quirked in a dimpled smile. 'Not in the way you think.'

'Oh, good then. But what is it?'

'You remember young Lord Mansfield?'

He did. Just the name made him want to growl. With

exceptional effort he answered pleasantly, 'I remember him.'

'The boy has done nothing to deserve that scowl, Joe.'

Scowl! Was he not displaying a perfectly agreeable grin?

'Then why is my sister distraught?'

'She misses him, of course.' Olivia shrugged, as if anyone would know this. 'And she expected him to follow her to Haversmere, but, as you can see, he has not.'

By sugar, that news left him confused. On the one hand he was put out with the fellow for making Roselina sad by not showing up, but if he did show up Joe would be no less put out.

'What do you think? Tell me true, Olivia, is he good enough for her?'

'I know he is suitable. He will be Earl one day, of course. To his credit, he does not have a fast reputation as some of the young men do. And he is not ancient, but of a good age for her.' Then she sighed as if this were bad news. 'I think he does care for her, but I am not the best judge of a young man's heart.'

If ever there was an invitation to discuss her past, this clearly was one.

He shifted his position on the couch so that he looked straight at her. He lay his arm across the back of the cushions, a call for her to move closer if she chose to.

She did not, but sat with her hands folded on her lap.

'On the contrary, Olivia, it seems to me that, given your past, living through what you have, it gives you a better sense of what is in a man's heart.'

'Perhaps it might be so.' She shot him a quick, sidelong glance. 'Had I not spent the past several years trying my best not to see a man's heart.'

Just like earlier, she wore her hair down. He wanted to touch it because it looked like a fair, silken waterfall gliding over her shoulder.

What kind of insanity would make a man stray from her bed?

'I could not begin to know how to advise Roselina. I'm sure your mother will know what to tell her,' she said while gazing at the fire in the hearth.

'I can't help but wonder what my mother would tell you.'

'What do you mean?' She snapped her attention away from the flames. Her wide, blue-eyed gaze settled fully on him.

'What would she advise you—about me?'

'Not would, Joe. Both your mother and your sister have made sure to tell me how very loyal you are.'

'Loyal as a bee to a spring blossom.'

'I rather thought my husband was like a bee, flitting from spring blossom to summer blossom and then on and on. To him London was one vast meadow waiting to be pollinated.'

'That was a bad illustration. I simply meant—' He got up and began to pace in front of the couch. He needed the right words to show her who he really was, but blamed if he knew which ones would work magic—which it was beginning to seem like he would need in order to—

'It was wrong of me to compare the two of you,' she said with a resigned sigh. 'I beg your forgiveness.'

As apologies went, it was acceptable, yet not terribly heartfelt. She had stated a simple fact. As far as he could tell she had not had a revelation as to who he was.

He spun about, gripped the mantel tight and hung his head. The bond they had begun to forge was slipping away. No matter what he said he could not seem to prevent it.

He heard the shift of her skirt when she stood. His fingers pressed hard on the wood, turning white to the bone.

If she walked out of the library, this would be the end of it—of them. He feared the tenderness between them would fade to indifference.

Then she touched his shoulder, the pressure of her hand light, hesitant. He straightened, turned, looked down and saw moisture standing in her eyes.

'I do not want to feel like this, Joe.' She blinked, then swiped her wrist across one eye. 'If it was a matter of choosing, I would not let that woman, what she makes me remember, come between us. But—'

He cupped her cheeks, felt the moisture dampen his palms. She tried to turn her face away.

'Olivia, no. Look at me, darlin'.' Her nod was so hesitant he barely felt it. 'Look into me—see me. I will never betray you. I will fight for you. The demons that woman stirred up, I'm at war against them. They will not have you—I will.'

Her lips parted as if she meant to reply, but then did not. Whatever she meant to say, he would never know. But he knew what she did not say: 'No.' She hadn't said that one word which would reject his declaration. Far from it—she slipped her arms about his ribs, leaning her head against his chest.

'Never doubt it, darlin'.'

She sniffed. Her hair slid against his shirt with her nod, a nod which meant she was at least hearing him.

He tipped her head up to kiss her and lasso her heart back to him.

Lightning flashed beyond the parlour windows. Thunder pounded—at the front door?

A woman screamed.

Of all the blamed luck!

Joe did kiss her, but quickly. Letting go of her, he dashed out of the library to see what had befallen Haversmere.

The tap of Olivia's footsteps hurried behind him.

One of the maids, Betty, clasped her hand to her heart. She stared at the front door, her face as pale as the ghost she must think was on the other side. An overturned bucket of water flooded the stones near her feet.

The pounding resumed, so forcefully it shook the door in its frame.

'Don't open it, my lord!' she cried. ''Tis a spirit come to call, for certain. I heard him moaning and wailing.'

Roselina and Ma rushed into the hall.

Joe walked towards the door. 'In case it is only some poor soul standing in the rain, I will open up.'

Betty looked pale, ready to faint. She buried her face in her apron.

The sooner he got to the bottom of the supernatural nonsense, the better. Taking a firm hold of the door, he drew it open wide.

Joe would rather have seen the ghost of his father walking in than the pitiful dripping form of Lord Mansfield—an opinion his sister did not share.

Roselina dashed forward and would have hugged him, but before she could he went down on one knee. He reached into his pocket and drew out a ring.

'Roselina Steton, I love you to distraction. Will you marry me?'

For a moment the only sound was the drip, patter, drip of water hitting the floor as it came off Lord Mansfield's finely tailored suit. He removed his sodden top hat and placed it over his heart. Evidently in haste to make his declaration he had momentarily forgotten the ugly black thing.

'I would,' Roselina said coyly, as if she had not been pining away for the fellow, as if her eyes were not alight with joy. 'But I simply cannot, not without Lord Haversmere's blessing and I imagine you have yet to seek it.'

Mansfield pivoted on his knee. 'Please, sir, I beg you—have mercy on me and say yes. I promise I will treat your sister well. Truly, she has my heart and I will perish if I cannot also give her every day of the rest of my life.'

'I accept your proposal.' Roselina opened her arms.

Lord Mansfield leapt up, nearly slipped, but righted himself. He caught his brand newly intended in a joyful hug that had both of them hopping up and down in jubilation.

Their giddy laughter showed how very young they were. He envied them.

But had anyone noticed he had not given a yea or nay to the union? Of course, he hadn't expected his opinion to have a lick of influence in what his sister decided.

Which went to show that Mansfield was the right fellow for Roselina to marry. Given the poor fool's appearance he had apparently gone through some trouble getting here.

It came as a surprise to find that Joe did, in fact, admire the young man.

'Betty,' Ma said. 'Kindly bring Lord Mansfield some towels.'

Joe felt a tug on his sleeve. It was Olivia and she was smiling.

'Did I make the right choice?' he asked.

She laughed and he thought he had never heard a nicer sound. 'Your silence covered it either way.'

Roselina, both feet now on the floor, kissed her betrothed right in front of them, then turned to Ma to show off her ring.

'You asked me what I thought about him a little while ago?'

'You didn't answer. Your past kept you from being a good judge.'

'Seeing them now—yes, Joe, I think they will suit.'

How long would it be before Olivia thought Joe would suit her? He had to believe she would, eventually.

At least it was what he hoped—no, prayed—to be true because, like Lord Mansfield, he thought he might perish if he did not give her every day of the rest of his life.

'Are you ready to learn to dance, Joe? I am fairly certain this wedding will be sooner rather than later.' In his imagination the bride was Olivia. 'This cannot be put off any longer.'

'Tomorrow.' He would have said tonight, but it was getting late and it would be unseemly for anyone to know his attention was not for anyone but his sister.

Betty hurried back into the hall carrying a stack of towels, her face red and embarrassed.

Tomorrow he would need to do something to put this nonsense about ghostly doings to rest.

Chapter Thirteen

Morning sunshine streaked through the window curtain of Olivia's chamber, casting the shapes of roses on the bed.

'Mother, hurry!' On his knees, Victor bounced on the mattress.

'Almost ready.' She tugged on her skirt while giving her appearance a glance-over in the mirror. Once again she would need to wear her hair unbound.

If Helmswaddle were here Olivia would have asked for a dozen curls. Ever since last night she felt curly—bouncy and light-hearted.

Something had shifted within her and it felt—

Well, honestly, she felt like she used to a very long time ago. Looking forward to the day, she expected good things to peek out from around every corner.

The knockdown Mrs Lapperton had unknowingly deflated her with no longer stung. She would delve deeply into the reason why, but Victor was hopping about like a grasshopper, impatient to be on their way.

In the end the precise reason for her change of heart did not matter, as long as it had changed. Besides, it had not likely been only one event to open her eyes to the true-hearted character of Joe Steton.

But that was not right. Early on, her eyes had been open. Anyone could see he was trustworthy. It was her heart which had stubbornly chosen not to see him.

'Joe is going to ride his horse without us,' her son whined.

She ruffled Victor's hair. 'Do you not recall that he promised to wait for us?'

He nodded, his expression so very trusting. 'A cowboy never breaks his promise.'

Or a heart. At least this cowboy did not.

'There's your bonnet, Mother, put it on quickly. We'll need to run to the stable as it is.'

She looked at the pretty headpiece hanging on a hook and decided that while fashion demanded she wear it, the sunny, warm morning did not.

'I'll race you to the hall, my son.'

Victor's eyes grew round, his face flushed with excitement. 'You know how to run?'

He dashed off and was halfway down the hallway before she could call out behind him that she used to be quicker than all her friends.

By the time she got to the hall she was out of breath, but from laughing as much as running.

'I won!' Victor danced in a circle, pumping his fist in the air. 'Can't wait to tell Joe!'

Olivia stopped laughing when she spotted Betty and another maid standing in front of the big clock in the hall and wringing their hands in their aprons.

'Is there a problem?' Olivia asked, her breath still short.

'Oh, yes, my lady! The clock has stopped.'

'Is there not a key to rewind it?'

Betty opened her hand to reveal an ornate brass key. 'I daren't use it. You see, it is stopped on the exact minute the Baron's mother died, Lord rest her sweet soul.'

The only thing odd about it was that someone recalled the exact moment. It had been a great many years since the lady's tragic passing.

'Has it been some time since the clock has been wound?'

'It has, but,' the younger of the two maids said, her fingers trembling, 'this can only be the work of the— well, I can hardly say it out loud.'

Olivia plucked the fancy key from Betty's hand. She set the clock hands to the correct time and then wound it up. 'I am certain there is no ghost.'

'You ought not have done that, Lady Olivia.'

'No harm will come to me, or to anyone else, because I wound the clock.'

For all that she had assured the women there was no ghost, it was not because she did not believe in ghosts.

Indeed, for Olivia, there had been a ghost.

The shade of Henry Shaw reached beyond the grave, had prevented her from trusting anyone—even her own brother, Heath.

But no more. Just as she had dared to step forward to wind the clock, she would dare to step into the love that Joe offered.

If Henry even lifted a finger from the grave, she would stamp on it—no, better, she would dance on it. She was finished with allowing him to stand between her and love.

And it was love. Joe had not said the word, but her heart recognised it. It also recognised that she had never shared the emotion with Henry.

She had blindly adored him for a time, but words

were all he had ever given her. False words which wounded her as nothing ever had.

Now, here was Joe, who, even without 'the words', had freely given himself.

She opened the front door and took a long cleansing breath of Haversmere air.

As surely as the hallway clock was ticking, the ghost of Henry Shaw was put back in the grave where he belonged.

'Let's race to the stable!' Victor dashed away from her and down the front stone steps. 'I'll go slow so you can win!'

But she had won already.

Her victory over the past made her feel as though she could outrun anyone, dance like a fool on the white puffy clouds dotting the sky and never stop smiling.

But she was not a fool. Not this time.

Since they were to spend the morning riding and fishing, Joe decided to wear his buckskin jacket. It had been hanging in the wardrobe for too long.

He could nearly smell Wyoming on it.

Victor tugged on the sleeve, urging him to hurry with what he was doing, but he didn't.

Helping Olivia on to the saddle of a dark, sturdy-looking horse, he lingered over the job. When his hands rested too long on her waist, he let go, petting the horse's black mane.

This was a fell pony, Mr Smythe had explained. A good-tempered mount that would suit Olivia well.

Blue stood paces away, clearly as impatient as Victor was to be on the way.

Because Blue snorted, and Victor was madly eager

to be put on the saddle in front of Joe, he stepped away from the pony's saddle.

Olivia bent down, indicated that he ought to come closer, that she had something to whisper in his ear. She smelled like the lush pastures of Haversmere.

'I see you, Joe,' she murmured, then sat up tall in the saddle.

Four words and his life seemed to fall into place. At least it would once he knew for sure she trusted what she saw.

Joe picked up Victor, set him on the horse, then mounted him.

'Giddy up, Blue!' Victor shouted, then they were off trotting across lush meadows.

The child's excitement raced through Joe, took him back to a time when—

When he sat on a horse in front of his father, shouting and whooping like Victor was now. He remembered—saw so clearly the land falling away, heard the pounding of hooves tearing across the meadow, clods of moist dirt flying every which way. He seemed so far off the ground, as if he were flying. He felt his father's laughter on the back of his neck and his strong arm curled around his ribs.

Victor let go of the saddle horn, spread his arms wide and flapped them.

'I'm a bird!' he shouted and it was Joe's turn to laugh.

He had to do it through a leak of tears, though. To remember something of his past here at Haversmere squeezed the emotion right out of his eyes. Hopefully this was only the beginning of recalling his past here.

They rode for the river to do a bit of fishing and to let the horses rest.

Olivia spread a quilt on the grass, then set out lunch

while he and Victor sat beside the rushing water and dipped their fishing lines in the water.

These moments had to be a reminder of what Heaven held in store. By sugar, it could be nothing less.

Victor's line tugged down, jerking in a battle with an unseen fish.

For a second it was not Olivia's son on the bank, leaping and shouting, it was Violet Steton's son.

It was not the grown-up Joe cheering for Victor's success, it was his own mother. He saw her so clearly it nearly brought him to his knees. She wrapped him up, lifted him off the ground and said how proud his father was going to be when he saw the catch.

'Joe?' Olivia called out, then began to rise from her spot on the quilt? 'Are you well?'

He nodded, not quite able to express how very well he was.

Victor bent over the fish flopping about on the bank. 'Can I eat it, Joe?'

Then, just like that, Joe remembered how elated he had been eating the fish he had caught that long-ago day.

'Let's see if you can catch enough for all of us.'

An hour later, seven trout lay on the bank. Victor knelt beside them, no doubt picturing a feast.

After Victor's excitement calmed, the three of them sat on the quilt to eat the lunch Cook had sent along. With a great yawn and a pat to his belly, Victor fell asleep, his head on Joe's lap.

His blond hair rustled in the soft spring breeze. Joe touched the strands, felt the lingering warmth of sunshine in the curls. The desire to protect this child felt nearly physical. If a natural-born father felt any different he'd eat his hat—the top hat—not the Stetson.

'I'm beginning to remember things,' he said quietly. 'Just now, watching your boy sleep, I recall what it felt like to lay my head on my mother's lap and just drift away. Nothing has ever felt so peaceful as that, I think.'

'Victor will remember this and you in the same way.'

The question was, would Joe be remembered as a cowboy he once knew or the father who held his small hand, watched him grow and helped him to become an honourable man?

'What did you mean when you said that you saw me?'

She scooted across the quilt so that they sat shoulder to shoulder, both of them gazing down at Victor.

'I see you, Joe, who you are.' She looked at him then, her eyes catching the blue of the sky—or maybe it was the other way around. She touched his cheek, gently drew one finger along his jawline. 'What it means is—I love you.'

'You won't be sorry, darlin'.'

Never, not one day or minute would she have cause to regret what she had just told him.

'I know that. I would hardly hand you my son's heart if I did not.' She covered his hand with hers where his fingers still nestled in Victor's curls.

'I love you, Olivia.' Simple words and yet powerful—life-changing. He bent low, whispered against Victor's plump pink cheek, 'I love you, too, Son.'

Olivia started to cry, but she was smiling so the tears pooled in the corners of her mouth.

A breeze came up so Joe snatched up his jacket, settled it over his and Olivia's shoulders, drawing them close. The jacket's shadow cast a patch of shade over Victor.

Funny, but the leather no longer smelled like Wyoming.

Later that afternoon Joe rode Blue into Grasmere. It wasn't his first choice of where he wanted to be. No matter that the village was as charming as the poets claimed it to be, he would rather be at Haversmere, wooing Olivia.

First thing, he would to pay a visit to the jeweller. He had a marriage proposal to make. For it, he needed a ring, along with something for his boy.

His boy! If the grin on Joe's face got any wider, it might pop his ears off.

The idea of having a wife and a son filled him with such high spirits folks were bound to wonder why his feet didn't touch the stones when he walked.

A proposal while they sat beside the river earlier today would have been nice, appropriate for the moment, but he had hesitated.

Appropriate was fine, but something well thought out, planned to make the moment even more special for her would be better.

To ask 'the question' during a romantic waltz, the steps slowed down for the intimate occasion, would be a thing to cherish for ever.

She hadn't taught him to dance yet, but he would shuffle about as best he could. Olivia deserved nothing but to feel cherished.

Joe tied Blue to a post in front of the bakery. The scent of gingerbread drifted out of the open door. He would bring plenty of that delectable bread home.

The image of a small crumb-dotted mouth warmed his heart.

'Lord Haversmere!' He recognised the warbling voice, blame it. 'I have been beside myself hoping to see you again.'

'Good afternoon, Mrs Lapperton.' He ought to say how nice it was to see her. It would be the thing a gentleman would say. 'I hope you have been well.'

That sounded polite enough. He did not wish the woman ill after all. He just did not wish to be in her company.

'As well as I might be, I suppose.'

Of all the bad luck! She fell into step beside him while he walked towards the jeweller's shop.

'A widow on her own can only be well enough, do you not think?'

'It depends upon the widow, I imagine.' Olivia was doing a fine job of running Fencroft in her family's absence. He would point that out, but did not wish to engage her in conversation. 'Is there something in particular you want to discuss?'

That was a rather broad hint that he did not wish to linger in her company.

'How did you know?' She took a deep breath, no doubt a strategy intended to lift her bosom to its best advantage. It was not the first time he had seen a forward lady use the tactic. 'Perhaps it is because we are both Americans and share an affinity.'

That was unlikely, but he did not express the thought out loud. All he wanted was to be on his way home—to Haversmere.

It was interesting how being away from the estate made him long for it in the same way he had longed for the ranch.

Returning memories were binding him to Haversmere much more quickly than he expected. He had to have been happy here as a child.

It might not only be the past deepening his connection to the estate. Thoughts of spending the future here with Olivia and Victor might be causing it as well.

'Have you come to spend a day or two at my inn?' The shameless turn of her mouth made it clear why she wanted him to.

'I prefer the comfort of my own home, Mrs Lapperton.'

'Of course, but may I say how sorry I am for the trouble at Haversmere?'

'What trouble do you mean?'

'Why, the haunting, of course. Naturally, I do not believe it. But some folks here? Anything that is not easily explained they deem to be of the spectral realm. Don't you know, I heard someone only this morning claim they saw Mr Wordsworth and his sister, Dorothy, strolling arm in arm into the bakery.'

'You need not be concerned for Haversmere. It is not haunted.'

'No doubt that is true. I only hope you have better luck convincing your staff of it than poor Mr Miller did. When his inn appeared to be haunted, they all quit. Tourists were afraid to lodge there and he went bankrupt—penniless.'

'Is there some reason you think the same will happen to Haversmere?'

'Naturally not, not with someone like you in control.' She cast her gaze over him in a slow, lingering perusal that made him feel all but violated, right here in broad daylight. He was only grateful that Olivia was not here to witness it.

She'd said she trusted him and he believed it. None the less, after all she had been through over the years, trust would be a fragile thing for her.

'Good day, Mrs Lapperton.' He supposed he ought to tip his hat. It would be the gentlemanly thing to do, and Olivia had gone to great lengths to transform him into a refined fellow.

For the sake of all her hard work, he did it—but he could not bring himself to smile before turning towards the jeweller's shop.

'Just one thing, Lord Haversmere,' she called after him. 'You might be relieved to know that Mr Miller did not end up as destitute as he might have. My late husband left me with a great deal of money and I was able to purchase the inn. It is more successful than ever.'

'That is fortunate. Again, good day.' He continued on, but she caught up, snagging the fringe on his coat sleeve.

'I'm telling you this because I am interested in opening another inn and Haversmere is a perfect spot for it. I will pay handsome money for the property.'

'Haversmere is not merely property. It is home to my family and to many others.'

'Those are the very words your father told me.' The woman was still smiling, but something, a shadow or a dark thought, crossed her eyes.

'You asked my father to sell?'

'Indeed I did, this time last year.'

She sighed again, but her attempt to draw attention to her prominent feature was wasted.

Joe tipped his hat to a woman passing by pushing a baby in a pram, which was far more pleasant than being toyed with by the widow.

'I'm certain he would have, had he not—oh, but he did pass away and so—'

This time he did not wish her good day or tip his hat. He spun away without a polite parting word.

What Joe was certain of was that his father would not have considered selling Haversmere any more than Joe would.

There had been a time when he might have entertained the idea. The funds would have allowed him to purchase another ranch in Wyoming.

No longer, though. Not now that he was beginning to see a life here—to recall the one he'd had.

All of a sudden he recalled something. It crashed upon him, cut him to the heart.

Joe had sobbed on the day his father carried him away from Haversmere, his tender heart had shattered.

Pa had cried that day, too.

He felt the widow's stare niggling at his back even after he closed the jeweller's door behind him.

Olivia watched Roselina smiling across the trout platter during dinner. And no wonder she was— 'Freddie', as she had begun to refer to her intended, had not ceased grinning at her.

Which in turn made Olivia smile, which also in turn made her happy to be free of the woman she had been only weeks ago.

The bitter, suspicious Olivia would have warned Roselina to be careful about giving her heart away so freely. Indeed, she would and had done exactly that.

Where was that woman? Not here tonight, and Olivia desperately hoped she would never return.

This evening she wanted to do nothing more than rejoice for Roselina and her young man. While it was true that difficult times would come, there was nothing to say their love would not grow even stronger for having faced them.

'I caught one trout for each of us and one more for whoever is really hungry.' Victor counted them out loud, looking as pleased with his fish as Roselina did with her Freddie.

'You should have seen him land those trout,' Joe said. It touched Olivia, hearing genuine pride reflected in the comment.

Seeing the way he looked at her child—loving him, devoted to him—it was only one of the reasons she loved this man.

Even now she could scarcely believe she had revealed how she felt. She had promised herself she would never make herself that vulnerable again.

But she had and did not regret it. Even though she had placed both her heart and Victor's squarely into Joe's care, she did not think she had made a mistake.

Victor's cowboy was a man to be trusted.

'I met Mrs Lapperton in town this afternoon.' Joe addressed the comment to his mother.

A pin aimed its shiny point at her happiness. She neatly deflected it. Even if Joe had enjoyed speaking with the widow, what could she say about it?

Yes, they had declared their love, but they were not bound to each other by an engagement.

An engagement was a very serious matter. If Joe did propose, she would take a long time before giving him an answer.

'I am sorry to hear that, Son. What a disagreeable woman.'

'More disagreeable than the first time we met.'

It was a relief to see him frown in regards to his encounter with the widow. She could hardly deny that it was not.

'She told me she made Pa an offer to buy Haversmere. Did he ever mention it?'

'No. If she did, your father did not take the offer seriously enough to tell me.'

'Let's not think of her,' Roselina declared. 'We have a party to plan.'

'Yes, let's do! We have a great deal to celebrate,' Esmeralda Steton declared. 'Seven fine trout to eat and an engagement to celebrate. As I see it, the gathering ought to be of an open-house style. All our neighbours should be invited, everyone from our own people to those in Grasmere.'

While they ate, Roselina and Joe's mother got down to the details of the gathering: colours, flowers, food, and music.

'It sounds grand!' Freddie said with a grin at Roselina.

'How long do I have to learn to dance?' Joe wiped his mouth on a napkin, glancing about with his brows lifted.

'Not nearly long enough.' Esmeralda shook her head, looking discouraged. 'Two weeks is all.'

Joe stood, reached for Olivia's hand. 'Shall we begin my lessons?'

Now? Oh—well, why not? There was nothing she would rather do than be with her handsome student, teaching him new skills.

'I'll take Victor to Miss Hopp and we will begin.'

'Teach me to dance, too!' Victor dabbed his mouth with the napkin the same as Joe had done, then stood up, matching Joe's posture.

'How would it be if your mother and I put you to

bed and then tomorrow I will teach you what I have learned?'

Esmeralda's gaze shifted between Joe and Victor. Olivia suspected she understood the deep bond growing between them.

Her smile shifted, settled on Olivia. She lifted her wine glass, then winked.

Lady Haversmere was a woman who could look at a person and see the heart of them. But then she was a mother, so perhaps it was not so unusual when it was her children she was looking at.

Olivia had no trouble at all seeing Victor's heart, knowing how badly he wanted his cowboy to become his father.

Chapter Fourteen

Victor did not want to sleep. He begged for story after story, which had been fun up until a point. But Joe had a wedding proposal to make and wouldn't feel settled until it was made and accepted.

Although the ring he'd picked out was delicate and nearly as brilliant as a star, he did not know for sure that Olivia would accept it.

Admitting you loved someone was not the same thing as agreeing to a lifetime with them. Could be she would not want to leave London and live here. It could be that, for all that she felt for him, when it came down to it perhaps it was a born-and-bred gentleman she wanted to spend her life with.

While he chewed over the worry, Olivia sang her boy a lullaby.

He closed his eyes to listen and must have started to doze off because all of a sudden he felt lips near his ear.

Olivia's warm breath skimmed past his temple. Odd how warmth could make a body shiver.

'Shall we discover if you really do have two left feet?' she murmured, then, straightening, walked towards the nursery door, where she cast a glance and a smile back over her shoulder at him.

'It's true.' He rose, then followed her into the hallway. 'We better find a place where no one can watch me behave like a fool.'

'You would only be a fool if you did not try. But really, Joe, you do have a natural grace in the way you move. Dancing should come easily to you.'

'I reckon I'm a puzzle.' He leaned down, kissed her. 'Go get your coat and meet me on the terrace. Let's see if you can fit the pieces together.'

Joe watched her walk away, admiring her straight carriage and the way her efficient steps carried her down the hallway.

Love and marriage went together, didn't they? The same as he and Olivia went together.

Surely she would accept his proposal.

It took but a moment to go to his own chambers, snatch up the ring and the small music box he had purchased in town. On the way out he grabbed his coat, spotting the package of gingerbread. He took it, too, since he did not know where the night would lead and it never hurt to have a snack at hand.

Outside, the night was brisk, but not frigid. The air was still and the sky resembled a ballroom made of stars reaching from horizon to horizon.

He was glad he had decided to wait until tonight to ask her to become his bride.

Hearing steps on the stones, he turned. Olivia carried a cloak in the crook of her arm.

'Are you ready?' she asked.

He reckoned he had been ready all of his adult life. He had never felt this depth of wanting a woman before.

No doubt it was because there had never been a woman who stirred him up the way Olivia did.

'The question is, are you?' He winked, touching his shirt pocket under his coat to be certain the ring was still safely hidden away.

'We have no music so it will be a bit of a challenge.' She set her cloak on one of the chairs that he had shoved to one end of the terrace in order to give them room. 'We will simply have to count the steps.'

'Close your eyes and put out your hands.'

'Why?' She narrowed those wide lovely blues as though she feared he would place a bug in her palm.

'Don't worry, darlin'. It's not a beetle.'

'I adore it when you call me that.' She closed her eyes, but her lips parted ever so slightly, glistening in starlight.

What could he do but kiss them while he placed the music box in her hands.

'It's beautiful!' She touched the ruby on top with her fingertip. 'What does it play?'

'"Sleeping Beauty Waltz". The jeweller says it's new. Have you heard it yet?'

She opened the box. The pretty melody tinkled over the terrace. He was dang sure he was not going to look pretty trying to keep time with it.

'No, I haven't. Oh, but it is exquisite—and joyful sounding.' She closed her eyes for a moment, swaying slightly to the tune. 'I'm certain if you study hard you can learn to waltz.'

He held out his arms because, while he did want to learn, what he wanted even more was to hold her. To tell her he loved her again, to ask her to dance with him for ever.

'Are you that brave, Olivia?'

She opened her mouth, but before she could answer, men's voices intruded, sounding alarmed.

A dozen or more boots thumped across the bridge, coming hard and fast. They dashed towards the front of the manor, but spotting him, they changed course, running for him with their coat-tails flapping as though they'd caught on fire.

'My lord,' the eldest panted while the others glanced behind, left, then right.

The shepherds looked spooked, as if they thought something was going to pop out of the grass and devour them. Perhaps sheep were not as protected from predators as people assumed. One and all, they trembled, the youngest looked as if he had soiled his breeches.

'What is it, Mr Firth?' Little by little Joe was becoming familiar with everyone's name.

'We saw it!'

'A wolf? A cougar?' Had there ever been cougars in these parts? Pa had not mentioned them.

'We'd not run from a beast, sir,' one of them stated, looking offended.

'Ach, no! We would not leave the lambs alone for that,' Mr Firth explained. ''Twas it—the ghost. All of us saw it. It was fearfully white and glowing. It slid from tree to tree, not even touching the ground.'

'It had not proper feet, Lord Haversmere,' said the youngest, shifting his weight from foot to foot, obviously uncomfortable with the condition of his trousers. 'It stared right at us. Shook its fist, it did.'

'It had a fist?' Olivia asked. 'I'd not have thought so.'

'Well, it was a blur, but it did shake something.'

'Am I to assume you are finished with your shift for the night? That the lambs will be left alone?'

Mr Firth glanced at the others who nodded their

heads in what, oddly, looked to be in time with the tinkling notes of the waltz.

'Not all alone. There's the dogs—they stayed. That big one of yours didn't seem inclined to run so the rest didn't either.'

'You can count on Sir Bristle.' Olivia gave the shepherds a look that Joe was glad not to have focused on him. She strode to the chair, snatched up her cloak. 'And on me.'

With a snap, she twirled the cape over her shoulders.

By sugar, he could think of worse ways to spend the night than under the stars, keeping watch with Olivia.

Watching her walk towards the gate which would lead to the bridge and then the meadow, her back straight and her steps determined, he knew she would make an excellent baroness.

He closed the music box, then slipped it into his coat pocket. In spite of this turn of events he still did need to learn to dance.

Seeing her glance back over her shoulder, send a smile meant only for him—he was in even more of a hurry to propose marriage.

'I will expect you to return your flock at dawn. Hopefully, by the light of day, you all will regain some common sense.'

Or they might not, given they had all seen the same thing and could not attribute the vision to fearful imaginations or colourful stories told around the campfire.

'We are that grateful you have come home, my lord. It would not do to face this without our Baron.'

'Gentlemen, you need not worry. I will come to the bottom of the problem and you will see it is nothing unnatural.'

From here he could see the glow of the campfire they

had abandoned. While the shepherds had fled from the spot in fear, it held a great deal of anticipation for Joe.

Repressing a grin, he nodded to them, went out the gate and followed his future across the bridge.

Olivia sat beside the campfire, watching Joe from across a meadow dotted with sheep, some lying down and some peacefully grazing. He was inspecting the tree line in search of anything the spectral prowler might have left behind.

The grove was heavily wooded. It would be no great feat for someone to lurk about giving the appearance of materialising, then disappearing. Anyone already fearful of witnessing such a thing would be terrified.

Seeing him squat down, skim his fingers over the grass, then rise again to do the same thing several yards down, truly, the last thing Olivia felt was fear.

'Isn't he the most handsome man?'

Naturally, the dog had nothing to say, but he did look up, head cocked and tail thumping.

'I really do love him, you know.'

Ordinarily the dog kept watch with the shepherds until about nine o'clock, then trotted back to the house to sleep at the foot of Victor's bed.

She was glad he stayed a bit later tonight. For all that she had never given undue thought to the pleasure of a dog's company, she found she did enjoy it.

Along with a few other things she had not expected to. Late last night she had crept to the library and opened a book of poetry. To her great surprise, it was not as sappy as she expected it to be.

Sir Bristle laid his large head on her lap, rolled his eyes up at her, then shifted them to gaze across the pasture at Joe.

'You really are a good, loyal fellow, aren't you?' She stroked the tuft of soft hair between his ears. 'Rather like your master, I think.'

Some people might not appreciate being compared to a large hairy canine, but it was a compliment.

People ran away from responsibility, as the shepherds were evidence of, as Henry Shaw was to an even greater degree.

'But here you are and so is Joe.'

Walking back across the pasture, Joe's steps were long and bold, a sight to make a lady's heart simmer. Then he stopped, bent to pet a small lamb. She could spend hours watching the shift of his shoulders and the stretch of his bare forearms where he had turned up the cuffs of his sleeves.

'He really is very virile, you know. Or maybe you do not, but I assure you, a man like that? He turns a woman like me quite wobbly inside, which is not the easiest thing to do. And I promise you it is not due to the influence of the full moon.'

Not that moonlight was not exquisite, the way it illuminated the pasture and the woods with a romantic sprinkling of fairy light.

It had been a long time since she had thought of fairies, an even longer time than she had thought of romance.

And yet in the moment all she wanted was to lay back in the grass, count stars and kisses.

But no more than kisses! Not for now, at least. Deeper intimacy would lead to a commitment she had yet to make. One she was going to take her time over this go around.

'Did you find anything?' she asked when he sat down beside her.

'Nothing as solid as a brass button. The grass was crushed in a path near the trees. I'd wager my Stetson against the top hat that it was made by human feet.'

'Speaking of feet, you still need to learn the waltz.' She stood up, brushed a dusting of dog fur from the front of her skirt. She was done with ghosts for the evening so she extended her hand. 'Come, Joe, we can count out the steps.'

His big hand caught hers, the gentle pressure soothing—yet at the same time, exciting. Although not as exciting as his grin—that had her rather heated. He brought her hand to his mouth, turned it and kissed her open palm.

Heat tingled past her wrist, frizzled along her inner arm and somehow swelled through her breast to lodge in her heart.

'Do you love me still?' he asked while coming to his feet, tugging on her hand to draw her closer.

'You are rather brave, stalking through the woods in search of a nebulous creature that lesser men flee screaming from.'

Long fingers tugging her waist, he drew her in.

'Also, it does go without saying that you are exceedingly handsome.'

'I won't mind if you do say it.'

Closer, closer, lips nearly touching—breath mingling warm between them.

'And, of course, you are a very good kisser.'

A point which he then proved. She looped her arms around his neck to make certain he kept on convincing her.

'Do you love me, still?' he asked again.

'I might. First I will need to judge your dedication to dancing. I am not completely won over.'

'I'm a lost man.'

He let go of her, then withdrew the music box from his pocket. He set it on top of a large stone, then opened the lid.

And just like that, the night became enchanted. Sleeping Beauty and starlight—fire glow and sheep calling softly to each other—she half-expected to see a fairy flit over the grass scattering sparkling promises with her wand.

Breathing deeply the scents of fresh grass and sheep's wool, she sighed and gave herself to the moment.

Sir Bristle did not seem to take note of the mood. He stood up, shook, then trotted off for home, probably to sleep at the foot of Victor's bed.

'What do I do first?' he asked.

'You raise your arm, just so.' She illustrated by taking the position he needed to.

With a wink, he copied her stance. 'Now, do you still love me?'

'Nearly.' She placed her fingers in his, then her other hand on his shoulder. 'Place your hand lightly on my waist. Surely you have seen this done.'

With fingers splayed, he touched the small of her back. He ignored her instruction about touching her lightly, but rather caressed her while drawing her close. So very close—his heartbeat tapped her chest.

He must feel hers beating, too. No man had ever felt her heart that way before. She had a feeling—and a very good one—that intimacy with Joe would be a far more wonderful experience than it had been with Henry.

She also had a feeling she would be unhappy— devastated more than that—if he ever danced the waltz with anyone but her. Perhaps she ought not teach him.

'If we dance this way, we will trip,' she pointed out.

'Tumble to the grass, do you mean? Wrapped up in each other's arms?'

'It could happen.'

'We shall go slowly then.'

He swayed, rocking her gently back and forth, the steps deliberately slow. This was no waltz. Nor was it any respectable dance she had ever heard of. It was more of a hug set to the strains of the music box.

And yet it felt akin to dancing, but of the most intimate sort.

'Whoever said you do not dance well was mistaken.' It was only fair to point out the obvious.

'You only say so because I have not stepped on your foot—or tripped you.'

'Down to the grass, do you mean? Where our limbs would become entangled?'

'It would not be my fault if my boot caught on your cloak.'

'It's true. But with arms going who knows where and hands grasping for purchase on—on anything—someone could get hurt.'

'Ah, but if I do this…' he scooped her up, then slowly knelt, bringing them gently to the grass '…the danger will be avoided. Since you nearly love me I will not risk doing you harm.'

'And our hands needn't grasp.'

'Nor our legs become entangled.' His expression indicated he imagined his hands on her hair, curled about her ribs and legs, under her—her bustle.

Even if he were not imagining those things she was doing a smashing job of it on her own.

What she ought to do was get off his lap, but—

'I have never enjoyed a dance more, Joe. And, yes, I do still love you.'

While he kissed her, while his fingers flexed and crept up her ribs, traced lightly over her throat, then tangled in her hair at the base of her neck, the music box wound down.

'Don't go anywhere,' he said, grinning while he eased out from under her.

'As if I could.' What a bold thing it was to admit aloud that she was weak-kneed. But it did seem that she could say anything to him because he was her friend. More than a sweetheart, more than a potential lover or husband even. Joe Steton was her soul's companion.

He walked towards the stone, dodged a ewe going after a straying lamb, and then rewound the music box.

If her heart ever stopped melting over the way he walked—so brawny, so very, very male—it would be because she had fallen into a deep coma.

She hoped he would put her back on his lap, continue the kisses where they had ended, but he did not.

Instead, he knelt in front of her, one knee covered in the ruffle of her skirt. He reached inside his shirt pocket, withdrew a small box. It was white. Moonlight made the velvet shimmer with the soft glow of a pearl.

'Olivia Cavill Shaw, you are the light of my heart. Will you marry me?'

He opened the box. An exquisitely delicate ring winked at her.

Not now! Not yet!

She wanted this—truly, desperately did. But she had vowed to be cautious this time. Last time, with Henry, she had blindly leapt. This time she wanted to proceed slowly, logically—be as certain in her mind as she was in her heart.

The hurt she saw in Joe's expression cut her to the quick.

If only the ghost were real and would fly out of the woods and whisk her away.

Olivia stared at him, silent—eyes wide and unblinking.

He had rushed what was between them and now she was going to turn him down, take her son and go back to London.

Why had he not waited and been sure?

But, no! He had been sure!

Even now he expected her to blink, to smile and say yes with a dozen kisses.

'I want to say yes, Joe, you know I do.'

If he wasn't the worst of cads, he did not know who was. He'd made her cry. It was the last thing he intended, or hoped for, but there she sat with tears streaking down her cheeks.

'I'm sorry, Olivia. I rushed things.'

'Anyone else—' she sniffed '—would not think so—it's me. I'm damaged and—and, are you going to stop calling me darlin'?'

'Never. Now come here to me and you can tell me what troubles you so, what you are feeling.'

She scooted close. He wrapped her up, stroked her back and arms. She wiped her tears on her sleeve.

'I am feeling like a fool.'

'But you have no reason to.'

'Do I not? What kind of woman loves a man so desperately as I love you and turns down his proposal?'

'Are you turning it down?' he spoke the words even though they ripped his throat worse than the edge of a dull razor. Even though he prayed through each endless, silent second that she was not.

She shook her head, wrung her hands in her lap. He caught them both up in one fist, brought them to his lips and kissed her fingers.

'I love you, darlin'. You can say anything to me and that will never change.'

'What I want is to say yes—let's run for Gretna Green tonight and return in the morning married.' This time she wiped her tears with his sleeve. 'But my heart and my mind don't agree on it.'

'That is understandable.'

It was. He didn't like it, but looking at the way her husband had treated her, it was not so hard to figure out. He had been a fool not to recognise she would be cautious.

'It is?'

'Of course. You need to be confident that I will not treat you the same way your husband did.'

'I already know you will not. But, Joe, as soon as Henry proposed, I said yes—the very instant. And then—' She grabbed the fabric of her skirt, fisted it tight and looked away from him. 'Then he made sure I could not change my mind. Young fool that I was, I thought it was greatly romantic and that he simply adored me too deeply to wait for official vows. Looking back, knowing who he was, I realise now what was at the heart of it.'

'Just so you understand, darlin', I had no intention of seducing you even if you had said yes.'

'And just so you know, I have not turned you down—just—I need time.'

He patted his shirt where the weight of the ring box pulled on the pocket. 'In that case, I'll carry this with me so when you do say yes, I can put it on your finger right away.'

'I hope I have not hurt you. Truly, Joe—I do love you.'

'You said you loved me. That does not hurt.' But the rejection did sting—more than a bit. 'Nor does it hurt that we are out here on this glorious, starry night. We can talk until dawn if you like, unless you would rather go back to the house. I can watch the sheep on my own.'

'No, I want to be with you.'

'Good, then, I'm glad.' He hugged her once, then let go and lay back on the grass, watching the stars. If only wishes really could be made upon them. But prayers were far more effective so he sent a fervent one past the spectacular vista.

Olivia lay down beside him. 'Would you kiss me?'

He went up on his elbow, gazed at her face for a time before he kissed her cheek.

'Just so you know, I want more than that. But I'll keep what I want to myself. You deserve respect, darlin'. You didn't get it last time, but you sure as blazes will now.'

'You are the best man I know.'

'You would think so even more if you knew I brought gingerbread.'

'Did you? You truly are my hero.'

The music box wound down, but he did not get up to rewind it. Somehow the breeze whispering over the grass, the whoosh of an owl's feathers swooping low and the bleating of ewes to their lambs was all the music they needed.

For now.

Chapter Fifteen

Olivia sat on a barrel in the horse barn watching Joe instruct Victor in the art of lassoing a post.

It had been more than a week since the night in the pasture and still she had not committed to Joe.

What a fool she was to hold on to past scars. Watching her son having fun with his cowboy made that very clear.

'Look, Ma!' Victor spun about on his heel, shooting her a triumphant grin. 'I caught me a post!'

She nearly corrected his grammar, but found she did not really want to.

Perhaps later—or perhaps not at all.

For the moment she was grateful for a pause in party preparations.

For the event, there were tasks to be performed which she had never been required to undertake. Back in Mayfair there were servants to see to the cleaning, cooking, serving and all the other work that went into casual entertaining.

Of course the difference between here and Fencroft was that Fencroft was not 'haunted'.

Servants did not leave because of an owl hooting in the attic.

It seemed one could not go five minutes without hearing fearful whispers or seeing people glance over their shoulders at the most innocent sounds.

Joe intended to meet with everyone tonight. Over pastries and tea, he hoped to convince them that it was only anxiety making things seem what they were not. He had an oddly shaped button to try to convince them.

She dearly hoped he had more than that, though. The atmosphere at Haversmere was unhealthy.

'I can lasso that spooky shade for sure now,' Victor proudly announced.

'We should talk about that, Son.' Joe sat down on an overturned barrel near Olivia and waved for Victor to take a place on his lap.

Her heart went soft as she watched the pair of them head to head in conversation.

'Folks like to talk. It's kind of exciting to think about something so unusual going on. But listen, none of it is real. There is nothing for you to be afraid of.'

'Willie, the boy who works in the stable, says the ghost is a woman with dark holes where her eyes should be. I reckon I'm scared of that.'

'Listen to your cowboy, Victor,' she said.

Had it been such a short time ago that she had insisted Joe was not his cowboy? It had been, indeed—a very short time ago.

Which only pointed out that she was wise to withhold her answer to Joe. Marriage was meant to last a lifetime and deserved to be given careful, deliberate thought, not jumped into with one's heart wide open.

Her past was proof of that. She wanted to do everything different now than she had then.

'If you hear or see anything that frightens you…' Joe ruffled Victor's blond curls '…you come tell me or your mother. We can hunt down the scary thing and show you that it is as normal as peas.'

'I will. But may I sleep with the rope nearby?'

Joe glanced at her for an answer.

'Yes, you may. But only as long as you do not play with it all night long.'

'Yee haw!' Victor scrambled off Joe's lap. 'I'll practise so that I can capture that black-eyed, snake-haired lady and then folks won't be so scared of everything.'

Snake-haired was something she had not heard before. It must be Victor's contribution to the gossip.

She looked at Joe, shrugging. He arched his brows, gave her a smile that crinkled the lines at the corners of his eyes.

His message needed no words. Victor was going to believe there was a ghost. Nothing either of them could say would make a difference.

Her son could be a stubborn little boy.

Had he not insisted all along that Joe was his cowboy? And had she not just called him that?

In this case, though, no matter how firmly he believed he would lasso a wraith, it would not happen.

The wind whipped around the corner of the house and whistled under the eaves while Olivia tucked Victor into bed that night.

Admittedly, it did sound rather haunting.

Victor left the rope looped around the bedpost. Whether it was in dread or anticipation, she could not tell.

'You need not send in Miss Hopp to sit with me. I'm getting too grown for it.'

'Are you?' she asked and kissed his forehead. For some reason what he said made her want to weep. Her baby was growing too quickly.

She could have another baby.

The sneaky thought nearly made her gasp out loud. Another child was not something she had ever allowed herself to hope for.

'You are not afraid to be alone with all the silly talk going on?'

She was turning down his lamp while she spoke, but even then his eyes looked crystal blue. He was so much like Oliver. Her heart swelled in joy, also in sorrow. Odd how both could happen at the same time.

It seemed her emotions were all over the place these days. How could she expect to make a decision as important as marriage?

She turned down the lamp, went to the door, but paused beside it. Even while she watched his eyes dipped closed.

'Sweet dreams,' she called softly.

'Goodnight, Mama.'

He must be very tired, indeed. When was the last time he had called her Mama?

On her way to the parlour where the family was gathered for the evening, she tucked the sweet sound of his voice away in her heart so that she would never forget.

But the sad truth was, she would forget. Already she could not recall exactly what his first word had been— or the day he had sat up without her support.

If only there were a way to capture those moments, put them in a jar, take them out to view later.

She found quite suddenly that she did long to hold another child to her breast. She imagined it cooing contentedly and gazing up at her with eyes a match to Joe's.

In her mind the baby was a daughter.

Olivia must have been smiling when she walked into the parlour because Joe, Roselina and Freddie all returned it.

'You have the look of a woman thinking about her child,' Esmeralda commented.

Olivia was not certain she had ever met a woman who could see so deeply into an expression.

'Victor just called me Mama,' she admitted. 'It has been a long time since I've heard it.'

'It is the sweetest name in the world. Joe, of course, was too grown to call me that when I became his mother, but Roselina still does every once in a great while.'

Olivia sat in the only empty chair, which was next to Joe's. She placed her hands on the armrests and leaned back into the cushions.

Conveniently, the position of the chairs was such that the armrests of her chair and Joe's aligned. Her little finger brushed his in the smallest of touches, but it was enough to warm her on this cold, blustery night.

Joe cast her an odd, but compelling look. It was as if he read her thoughts even more astutely than his mother did and knew it was not only Victor she had been thinking of.

Then again, she could be reading what she wanted to in the look.

Until she accepted Joe's proposal, she needed to put all thoughts of a new baby away.

'The gathering is going to be grand,' Lord Mansfield declared. 'I look forward to announcing the betrothal.'

This time she knew what Joe's gaze upon her meant.

'Should you not inform your father and mother first?' Roselina asked. 'I would not want them to think

I snatched you away. I imagine they had a British lady in mind for you. One of a rank higher than mine.'

'We live in progressive times.'

'Perhaps so,' Esmeralda said. 'But it does not mean that society always reflects it.'

'I meant this as a surprise,' Freddie said with a great grin. 'But I shall surprise you all now. Before I came here, I told my parents what I was up to. They gave me their blessing, in part because they knew it was useless to do otherwise, but also because they saw Roselina petting a wolf that night in the Duchess's garden. You left quite an impression on them, Rosie. But I sent them a telegram, let them know you had accepted me. They will be here for the announcement.'

'Oh—my word.' Esmeralda looked alarmed. 'I had not taken this into consideration when I planned our humble event. I fear it will not suit an earl and his countess. We have invited all manner of people, lowborn and higher, but not so highborn as your parents.'

'Progressive times, Ma,' Joe pointed out.

'It will be good for them,' Freddie said, laughing.

They had been discussing the party for an hour before Miss Hopp screamed.

Joe leapt from his chair, ran for the hallway before the screech ended.

The terror in the governess's voice was not due to seeing a phantom. He knew in his bones it was something far worse.

Olivia rushed past him, meeting Miss Hopp at the foot of the stairs.

Breathless, the governess gasped out something about checking on Victor and finding he was not in bed. She had spotted him from the window near the river and dragging his lasso.

Miss Hopp had to hurry behind them to finish the story, but running flat out he missed the last of it. He had heard all he needed to. Victor was in danger.

Rain pelted the surface of the river, distorting it. Standing on the bridge, it was impossible to see any disturbance to show a child might have fallen in.

While he stared, Olivia gasped, pointed to something caught in a bush.

Victor's rope. The noose was caught on the shrub, but the long end lashed about in the water.

Joe did not feel his feet while he ran, or his heart, only the rasp of ragged, fear-strangled, breath.

Where was Victor? The water kept its secret.

Joe was dimly aware of Olivia shouting her child's name. Out of the corner of his vision he saw her racing along the bank.

He yanked at the rope, but thorns tangled it further.

Suddenly Lord Mansfield was at his side, cutting the twigs away with a pocket knife.

Joe yanked again and this time the rope slipped loose.

Freddie clapped a hand on Joe's shoulder, pointing downstream.

Something of a lighter shade than the water was being tossed about in the flow. Victor's hair, one instant visible—then a longer instant—vanished.

On the run, he twirled the lasso, but could not judge when to let it fly. The added weight of the rope being wet made a skill that was second nature feel awkward.

His target bobbed, dipped, cried out, then became silent.

Victor would be cold, breathless—terrified. But he

could very likely hear voices when his head was out of the water.

Joe knew it to be true because he suddenly remembered being the child in the river. He'd felt he was going to die, but then his father had shouted at him to raise his arm out of the water. Pa had gone out on a limb bending over the river and snatched his arm, pulling him up and to safety.

From a distance, Joe heard barking—Sir Bristle sensing the danger and tearing across the pasture to help.

The dog would be a lifesaver, able to drag Victor from the river when no one else could. He could, if it were not such a long run from the field. Even with four powerful legs and a warrior's heart, he would not get here in time.

The water was faster than Joe was. The current carried the boy further away. If he did not manage to rope him—

'Victor!' he shouted. 'Lift your arm!'

The small hand shot up, giving him a brief, bobbing target, but it was enough. He let the rope fly, watching as it caught around Victor's arm.

Victor had the strength to hold on. Better, he had the wisdom to wriggle his shoulders through the noose.

Digging his boots into the mud, Joe pulled the rope, arms straining against the current while the wet line chafed his hands raw.

Five feet from the shore Olivia waded in and caught her son up.

The river grabbed her skirt, weighted it. She started to stumble. Then Freddie was behind him, helping him pull on the rope, giving Olivia the aid she needed.

As soon as her knees hit the bank, Joe dropped the

rope, ran forward, then snatched the cold, small form out of his mother's arms.

He was aware that Freddie helped Olivia up, supporting her on a run towards the house, but only dimly.

One thing was on his mind. He remembered how frigid the river was. How it could quickly suck the life out of one so small.

He recalled how, afterwards, the cold was as wicked as the water. How he'd been so numb he hadn't felt the chill. He hadn't felt his pa's arms around him either, but he knew they were there.

Rushing into the parlour, he saw his mother already waiting with warmed blankets.

Joe set the boy down on the hearth so the fire would help keep the blanket warm.

Olivia snuggled Victor on one side and Joe hugged him on the other.

After a moment his teeth began to clack. This was a good sign. His body was trying to warm itself.

'I...nearly...ha-had her,' he said. Blame it if he was not grinning as if he had not nearly drowned.

'Had who, Son?' he asked.

'The frightful...sh-shade.'

'You must have seen it in a dream.' Olivia hugged him tighter, which seemed to help with the shiver. His skin was quickly gaining colour.

He shook his head, which must have been difficult being pressed as tightly to his mother's heart as it was.

'I was already awake. Just sitting by the window and watching. Then there she was, floating right out of a bush. She does have black holes for eyes, like the shepherds say.'

'Your mother is right, Son. It was a nightmare. You

thought it was real and went to the window to look. Your mind was still dreamy. Isn't that right?'

'Nope—she was real. I tried to catch her after I fell in the water. I had her, too, for a little while.'

'What do you mean?' Olivia set him away from her, staring at him, her distress reflected in the narrowed slant of her eyes.

'When I fell in the water she grabbed my hand. I tried to keep hold of her, but she's a slippery ghost. She was reaching for me again, but someone screamed and she floated back into the bush.'

'She ran away? Left you in the water?' Olivia's face flushed the purest shade of angry he had ever seen.

'Umm, umm, she floated. Saw it with my own eyes.'

'Your eyes were watery, Son.' Joe pointed out. 'It would look that way—but what did her hand feel like?'

'Like any other hand, but quite cold.' His eyes went wide and he grinned. 'Like cold bones, all clackety and sharp.'

'Victor Shaw! You must tell us the truth.'

No doubt he thought he was. But he was of an age where such a thing might seem as real as not.

Joe recalled thinking he saw an angel when he was being carried away in the river. She had rushed along the bank, calling his name. He remembered thinking it was his mother's voice, even though at that time he no longer remembered what her voice sounded like.

'Did it wear a ring? Did you see one or feel it?'

He frowned in thought, nodded. 'I didn't see it, but I remember something hard hurting.'

Joe picked up Victor's hand, cradled it for a moment, grateful to feel the warmth returning.

'Let me see?' He curled the plump little fingers back,

saw a red welt at the base of his fingers. When he bent for a closer look he spotted a tiny scrape.

A ring with a stone. As clues went it wasn't much. Many people wore rings with stones—men and women both.

Olivia drew his hand closer to her, peered at the cut. Her face was splotched in patches of red.

Joe had to tamp down on his rage the same as he knew Olivia was doing.

Someone had attempted to pull Victor from the water, but had turned tail and run like a coward when they feared being caught.

All of a sudden this ghost business was no longer simply a nuisance with folks being afraid and quitting their jobs. This had nearly proved fatal for a sweet and innocent child—*his* sweet and innocent child.

Olivia might not have decided it was official yet, but Joe had. Someone had left his son to drown. They would pay for that.

'Looks like you did see a spook after all, Son,' he stated, drawing on calmness from some impossible place. 'And you nearly caught it! You were as brave a boy as I've ever met. But the problem with it is, your mother was frightened—look at her, Victor—she is still trembling. We need to make sure our women never feel scared. I need your promise—your word as a cowboy—that you will not try to catch the ghost again. If you see it, come to me and we will see what is to be done together.'

Victor sat up tall. The blanket fell away from his shoulders. 'I promise, Joe.' Damp blond curls shimmered when he nodded his head.

'I'm proud of you, Son.'

'This has all been grandly exciting,' Olivia said,

her voice deceptively light. Clearly she did not want to frighten him more than he had already been.

For all of Victor's bravado, Joe knew it was a great deal of bluster.

Not only did he know, he remembered it first-hand.

As rumours went, this one spread more quickly than most. The facts became distorted before the sun ever came up.

Eight servants were ready to quit because of what they had heard. What a surprise it was to find that a ghostly spectre had slithered into Victor's room during the night, snatched him out of his bed and put a spell on him which then compelled him to leave the house and leap into the river.

It was past time Joe summoned this meeting. If things went on as they were, he would have only a handful of servants working for him this time next week.

The employees gathered at the foot of the steps, huddled into their coats against the wind.

His intention had been to invite everyone inside, but a third of them refused because of the stopped clock and the ghostly visit to the nursery. No one seemed to notice that the clock had been ticking happily away ever since Olivia wound it.

The cook, a wonderful woman who thought the rest of the staff had lost their minds, poured tea and passed it about. Joe listened to her as she went about the task, telling one fearful fellow he was addled and another pasty-faced woman she was hysterical.

Behind the crowd Joe could see far into the distance, past emerald-coloured fields dotted with grazing sheep, beyond the blue lake, all the way to the rugged fells.

Not so long ago he believed there was no place he could love as much as he did Wyoming.

He was wrong. Seeing it all now—the land and the people—his heart further shifted. It was as if roots that had been ripped out were growing again. The soil of Haversmere was every bit as dear to him as the soil at the ranch had been.

With his family standing on the porch behind him— and he counted Olivia and Victor among them—he understood this was where he belonged.

He was Baron Haversmere. The folks looking up at him belonged to the estate and the estate belonged to him. The realisation was humbling. Having a title might be a thing to make a man feel puffed up about himself. It only made Joe unsure because under it all he was just a cowboy.

Here in the moment it was going to take some fancy talk to convince some of these people not to flee their home. Without knowing exactly what he would say, he began with something to the effect of home sweet home and deep roots, courage and dedication. He told them he was convinced the ghostly appearances to be trickery on someone's part and he promised to get the bottom of the mystery.

At the end of it, those who said they were leaving agreed to wait. Others felt somewhat reassured that the haunting was not real and, if it was real, Baron Haversmere would protect them.

When they walked away it was just him and Ma left standing on the steps. She slipped her arm through his, gazing out at the pastureland.

'You make a wonderful baron, Son. Your father would be so proud.'

'I never expected to feel my place here. I was wrong.'

He covered his mother's hand with his and gently squeezed. 'In case you have regrets about selling the ranch, I think you did the right thing, Ma. I'm glad you did.'

'You will be even happier about it once you convince your young lady to marry you.'

'I've been trying.'

'I'm glad to hear it. And you will succeed. Any fool can see how much she loves you. But, given what she went through?' She went up on her toes, kissed his cheek. 'I got over my past when I met you and your father and she will as well. In the meantime you need to shave. Gentlemen do not grow whiskers.'

Olivia must not have got around to mentioning that grooming flaw.

She would, in time.

In time she would get around to many things. All he need do was wait, be patient and trust in answered prayer.

Chapter Sixteen

Olivia was relieved that the afternoon of the party arrived without further mischief from the ghost. Perhaps the vile creature felt a dash of remorse for abandoning a child in peril.

Remorseful or not, she would gladly throttle whoever had left her son in the river.

Thankfully fearful employees had stopped fleeing their jobs.

The only dampener on the party was the weather. It was damp. The damp weather was a dampener. The humour of it nearly made Olivia chuckle in spite of the wind-driven rain tapping at the windows.

London was a rainy place—the Lake District was more so. Parts of it, she had been told, were even wetter than Haversmere.

Luckily, she found rain rather pleasant, but that was only a small part of what she found pleasant. Lately, she found life exceptionally agreeable in spite of the haunting nonsense.

Victor was, well, happy to be his cowboy's sidekick—yes, sidekick was the word her son was now fond of using.

But cowboy's son would be better.

Cowboy's wife—Baroness Haversmere—would be...well, she could scarcely imagine how wonderful it would be.

And suddenly, standing here among a throng of people, chatting, eating and drinking, she knew, beyond any doubt, she wanted to marry Joe.

What a fool she had been to allow hurt and fear be her guiding star. Just because she had rushed into marriage with Henry did not mean she needed to drag her feet with Joe. What idiocy had made her think so? Joe would be no less wonderful for her waiting to accept his proposal. He was who he had always been and who he would continue to be.

She loved Joe. She adored him for the man he was, not because he could fulfil her fairy-tale dreams of happily ever after. All right, he actually could do that, but she no longer had an innocent, untried heart. She knew what love was and what it was not. What a fickle-minded, stubborn-hearted woman she had been!

But no more. She had squandered too much precious time as it was. She glanced about. Where was her Baron?

Oh, just there, all the way on the other side of the room, speaking to the estate manager. It was hard to miss the troubled look shadowing his face.

Mr Smythe was scowling, shaking his head while he passed by vase after vase of spring flowers on his way out of the room.

The next person to approach Joe was smiling, gesturing with her hand at the decorations she, Esmeralda and Roselina had taken such care in planning.

It was a relief to see Joe returning her smile. Perhaps the matter with Mr Smythe had not been so urgent after all.

In a moment she would know for certain. She walked across the room towards Joe, but in her mind she was waltzing the distance to the tune of 'Sleeping Beauty'. Not a true waltz, but the more intimate one Joe had taught her.

Thought of in the right way, she had been Princess Aurora—asleep to joy until a cowboy baron's kiss woke her to life.

One thing she knew for certain, she was no longer cursed by the memory of a dead man. Now that she had woken, no one would be able to put her back in the miserable trunk she had created.

She was only steps away when Lord Grantly and his Countess waylaid her.

'How lovely to see you again, Lady Olivia,' the Countess greeted her with a bright smile. 'It seems ages since we encountered each other at the opera—but it has not been, not really. Time just goes by so frightfully quickly, does it not?'

'Frightfully.' Unless one was waylaid in conversation. In that case it ticked by slowly. 'And what a pleasure to see you, as well.'

If they had not been previously acquainted it would have been easier to keep the conversation short, thrifty. But, no, they had mutual friends who must be mentioned, them and their lovely children—their prosperous estates. And of course there was the happy betrothed couple to be rejoiced over.

By the time she was able to gracefully end the conversation, Joe was no longer in the room.

Olivia ducked into the hall before anyone else could engage her attention.

Since Joe had been discussing something with the estate manager, she suspected he might have gone to one of the barns.

It would be wise to go upstairs and get her coat. At that moment she did not feel like being wise, only following her heart—claiming her man.

Halfway to the sheep barn, she thought that might have been a mistake. She was drenched. Not shivering, though, she was too merry of spirit to feel the cold.

Once inside, she stood for a moment, sluicing water off her face and sleeves. No one was about, but the lamps were burning low. Mr Smythe must be close by, perhaps in his quarters at the far end of the barn.

Hurrying that way, she spotted something odd. Far back in one of the stalls it glinted under a short pile of straw. By the looks of it the thing had been hidden and in a hurry.

She bent down, brushed the straw away. My word—it was a woman's gown, brown and plain, but with the most unusually shaped buttons.

One of them was missing.

The phantom was here! The wicked person who had left Victor in the river was close by and no doubt planning to cause a scene at the party.

She nearly shouted for Joe, but thought better of it. She wanted the person to be caught, not alerted.

Olivia picked up the gown, tucking it under her arm. She dashed the length of the barn, carefully checking each stall.

Convinced the wretch was not in this barn, she went out the back door, ran the short distance to the horse barn.

Before she drew the door open she heard voices, indistinct, but clearly male and female.

Luckily, the door made no noise when she stepped inside, then closed it behind her. Even luckier, she did not scream, probably because she suddenly felt cast in stone, watching Mrs Lapperton walk towards an open stall. She heard Joe's voice, but whatever he said was spoken so softly she could not hear distinct words.

The hussy wore nothing but a shift. Hands on her round hips, she swayed into the stall.

Olivia could see nothing of what went on. Oh, but her mind supplied dozens of images of Henry tangled with various lovers—in sweaty sheets, on carriage seats and rugs in front of blazing hearths.

If she could move, she would vomit on the floor— weep and fall to her knees. Rip her gown and lament her situation. How could she have fallen for Henry's trickery again? She would shake her head to clear her brain, but her neck was stiff. She could not move.

'Not Henry,' whispered a still small voice in her heart, struggling to make it to the surface of reason.

Joe. She knew him, believed in him. This was her Joe.

The woman chuckled deep in her throat. Straw shuffled, indicating that she was taking short, slow steps, no doubt to make her hips sway seductively.

'You and I,' the voice crooned, sickly sweet. 'Imagine it—picture it, my handsome lord, the pair of us together—right here in the straw—'

This was enough! There had been a time when Olivia gathered her misery about her, huddled in a corner hiding from truth like—she did not know what like for sure, but something weak and unworthy of womanhood. She began to feel herself again—arms, legs and heart began to rally.

Spirit rising, she curled her fists, muttered under her

breath, 'Thank you, Henry'. His betrayal had given her backbone, strength forged in heartache. How had she not recognised the bitter gift for what it was? Now that she did, she would use it.

Joe would never succumb to that woman's treachery. She knew who he was—principled, reliable. He was hers! And he was waiting for an answer to his proposal. Oh, but he was about to get it.

As good fortune would have it, a bucket of water was within reach—it was a wonder she had not stumbled on it when she came in. She swirled the water with her fingertips. Good, it was nice and cold.

Mrs Lapperton was purring when Olivia stepped up behind her.

When the water hit her back, the wicked creature screeched. As far as Olivia was concerned, the outrage sounded akin to music.

It was as if the bucket of water had been dumped on every woman who had ever wronged her by dallying with Henry. Vindication made her feel like laughing out loud. So did seeing Joe backed up against the wall, brandishing a shovel in front of him.

Mrs Lapperton spun about, breathing through her teeth. She appeared good and stunned.

Fine, then. Olivia tossed the dress at her. 'You are missing a button.'

Joe dropped the shovel, cursing under his breath. 'You—!' He cursed again, using a worse word, but of course it was not foul enough.

Olivia planted herself between him and the widow. 'I will marry you, Joe.'

'You will do what?' He had to have misheard. His ears failed to recognise the *not* part of the phrase.

'I will become your wife—tonight.'

He leapt, wrapping her up tight to make certain this was real and not a figment of his desire. Real! As soon as he kissed her, felt her give his love back, he knew it. She clung to him as tightly as he held on to her.

'This is not how it looks,' he said when he found his breath. 'I promise it is not.'

'It looks rather like you were about to clobber the strumpet with the shovel.'

'She did have me cornered. Lucky thing you rescued me before I had to fight my way out of the stall.'

'In the future, you can count on me to douse anyone trying to corner you.'

They laughed, kissed again.

Prudence Lapperton gasped, a reminder that, regrettably, they were not alone in the barn.

'I hardly find having water dumped on me a matter of humour. I'll catch my death of a chill.'

Olivia went suddenly rigid. She did not step away from him, but pivoted in the circle of his arms.

Lapperton yanked her dress over her hips, scowling as if she had just cause. The woman was about to discover the error of her thinking.

'Did you give my son a thought after you left him in the river? How chilled he would be if he even survived drowning?'

'I'm certain I do not know what you mean. And it is rather unbecoming of you to call me names.'

'You fear names are the only weapon I can use against you that will not end up with you lying unconscious on the floor? But since I am to be married tonight, I would rather it be you in jail tonight and not me.'

Lapperton's fingers trembled over buttoning her

dress, snagged on the empty buttonhole. He couldn't say it was not a gratifying sight.

It was a fortunate thing he had decided to keep the brass button with him. He had not known the moment proof would be required, only that it would be.

'We found this near the lake where you left the lambs.'

'Once again, I have no idea what you are talking about.'

The door at the end of the barn crashed open.

'I found it, my lord—just like you—' Mr Smythe stood in the doorway gripping a white sheet with holes cut out for eyes. 'It is her—ach, good deduction, Lord Haversmere.'

'The lot of you have lost your minds!'

'Darlin'?' Joe said and could not resist giving Olivia a quick kiss with the asking. 'Is Constable Rollins still in attendance?'

'I believe so. When I left he was bringing your mother a glass of punch.'

'Shall we see what the lawman has to say about it, Mrs Lapperton?'

'Say about what? You can hardly keep your people from fleeing a ghost by blaming it on me.'

'You are, by and far, the most despicable woman I have had the misfortune to meet.' Olivia stepped nearly nose to nose with her, clenching her skirt in her fists. Clearly she was within an inch of punching the woman. He would not try to stop her if she did it. 'And you can be assured, I have met some of the worst. If you think this is about simple trickery, you truly are the fool you appear to be. The crime which we will present to the constable is attempted murder. Everyone here tonight will learn how you walked away from a little boy, left him to nearly drown in the Rothay.'

'Mr Smythe, please escort this person back to the house. We will join you there in a moment.'

As soon as the door closed behind them, Joe cupped Olivia's cheeks, turning her face so that he could better see what was in her eyes.

'Say it again.'

'She is the most despicable woman I have ever met— or exposing her wicked treatment of Victor—and how did you put it all together?'

'Neither one of those.' He kissed her. 'The other.'

'I will marry you, Joe.'

'Tonight—you said that, too.'

'Have the carriage readied. It is not so far to Gretna Green. We can be married before breakfast.'

He hugged her tight, then held her at arm's length to better judge the answer to the question he had to ask.

'Have you taken the time you need to decide this, darlin'? It was not coming upon the widow and me like you did that forced your choice?'

'Firstly, I have wasted enough good time as it is.' She tipped her head, smiling at him in the way that made her eyes slant. 'Secondly, I was on my way to find you, to tell you how desperately I do want to marry you. So, no, my decision had nothing to do with that.'

'I'm relieved—but blame it—you must have felt betrayed all over again.'

'Oh, I did—but not betrayed by you. It was the oddest thing, it felt as though Henry sprung out of his grave to wound me again. But, Joe, he no longer can. And that is because of you. Even when I saw her trying to seduce you, I knew you would not succumb.'

'Never—there is no one else but you, darlin'. There never will be.'

'I know—and I feel the same—but why was she trying to seduce you?'

'I'll tell you about it on the way back to the house.'

He lifted his coat over their heads. While they hurried from the horse barn, rain beat on it. It reminded him of the time he had kissed her in the alley beside the opera house.

Stopping, he kissed her again. 'Do you remember?'

She nodded, grinned. 'I was falling in love with you, even then.'

There was no better place than this to go down on his knee, so he did. When he opened the velvet box, withdrew the ring and proposed again, she held out her hand, waggling her finger at him.

He stood up, eager to call for the coach. 'Tonight—Gretna Green.' It was what she had said and he would hold her to it.

'Tonight.' She hugged him tight. 'Let's get to the house, Joe. On the way you can tell me what Mrs Lapperton hoped to get out of all this.'

They dashed through the sheep barn to avoid some of the rain.

'What she wanted was Haversmere. I think she planned to turn it into an inn. I'm pretty sure she did this haunting business once before to a fellow who owned an inn in Grasmere. She did try to purchase Haversmere from Pa, but he refused, she told me that much.'

Coming out of the sheep barn, they were hit by rain again—not that he minded, not as long as he could hug his betrothed close beside him.

'So when your father would not,' Olivia said, holding tight to him, 'she began haunting Haversmere the same as she had the inn?'

'It appears so. I can only wonder how she did not get caught.'

'Slippery ghoul. But you and Mr Smythe did catch her.'

'It was because of him that we did. He came to me because he spotted Lapperton in an area she had no business being in. Since she had expressed that interest in buying Haversmere, to me and to Pa both, and been turned down, I wondered if she might try to entrap me—force a marriage to get it.'

'She did act forwardly around you. She must have thought it a surer way to get her hands on the estate than haunting it.'

'I said as much to Smythe and he agreed. That is why I made a show of going out alone, just to see if she would spot me and follow. It gave Smythe time to look about for anything that might be amiss, any small odd thing that might give her away.'

'What luck that he found her costume! You will increase his salary?'

'By however much you instruct me to, Lady Haversmere.'

Crossing the bridge, Olivia stopped to stare at the Rothay rushing swiftly away towards Grasmere.

'I think she is all the more wicked for wanting to help Victor and then choosing not to. More, perhaps, than if she had outright meant him harm.'

'Come, let's go inside and see her come to justice. Further justice, by sugar.' Taking her hand, he squeezed it. 'I cannot recall ever seeing anything so gratifying as when you doused her with water. You, my avenging angel, were impressive.'

They came into the house, their clothes dripping on the floor. They were barely noticed, though. Conversation buzzed since Prudence Lapperton's entrance a few moments ago would have given everyone a great deal to gossip about.

'Rest assured, Joe, the next time a woman tries to compromise you, or hurt our children...' she used the plural casually, but to Joe the word was a miracle. He could think of nothing more wonderful than giving his son sisters and brothers '... I will be impressive again. Society will quake at my wrath.'

Baroness Haversmere snuggled into the plush coach cushions, feeling utterly content to simply sit and listen to the wind whistle about the conveyance.

A shaft of moonlight washed the interior in a soft glow. Outside trees lashed, branches cracked, but here inside? She could not recall ever feeling so peaceful—so blessed.

Joe had tried to give the driver extra pay for sitting on top in the elements, but he had refused it, adamant that he was that grateful to the Baron for ferreting out the ghost—even more grateful that he had given up America for Haversmere.

Everyone was pleased Joe had chosen to make the estate his home, grateful to call him Baron.

Olivia yawned, but did not bother to cover her mouth, the only people in the cab to see her were her husband and her son and they were sound asleep, snuggled together and exhausted.

It had been twenty-four hours since they had left Haversmere for Gretna Green and she did not expect to make it home until dawn. She did not mind, of course. Not as long as she could watch her cowboys, see how

Joe wrapped his new son up in his arms, how his breath stirred Victor's hair while they slept.

She tried to preserve the sight to memory because she was certain nothing had ever touched her in quite the same way.

Having Joe as her husband was beyond joy—a dream she hadn't hoped for—but perhaps not as much of a joy as seeing her baby with a father. As incredible as it seemed, they were a family.

Victor had wasted no time after the vows had been uttered to remind her to thank Uncle Oliver for all of it.

Even now she did not believe her brother had any more to do with it than that it had been his grave they were visiting when Joe rescued Victor.

Clearly it did no good to say so to her son. He believed it more now than he had then.

It was understandable, she did have to admit it was, given he did have the cowboy he expected to have.

Whereas she married the gentleman she never expected to. Indeed, she had not believed such a man existed. Lord Haversmere was not the façade of a gentleman—no, he was honourable to his core and she completely adored him.

She closed her eyes to look back on the past day. So many visions came to her mind.

The first was hearing Constable Rollins declare that although he could not arrest Prudence Lapperton for portraying a ghost and scaring everyone, nor was there enough evidence to prove she had neglected to rescue Victor when she could have, he stated quite clearly that what she had done was reprehensible.

He also gave his opinion that it would be well for her to seek another town to live in because no one would welcome her in Grasmere. Further, it was the opinion of nearly everyone that she ought to give the hotel back to Mr Miller since she had all but stolen it from him.

Of course, it remained to be seen what did become of the woman. Public opinion might not be a thing that influenced Lapperton overmuch.

At the end of it, Olivia was done with the widow, whether she remained in Grasmere or went somewhere else. Because Joe loved her, and she trusted in that love, Prudence Lapperton had no power to haunt her.

Oh—my word! She sat up straighter on the cushion, grinning because she realised Henry's awful women no longer haunted her either. She could think of them without a twinge of pain, or anger even.

Love had freed her.

She would have reached across and touched her husband, but decided it was just too wonderful to look at him, enjoy the sweep of his lashes, the crinkle lines at the corners of his eyes.

After a few moments her eyes grew heavy and slowly closed.

She saw him still in her half-dreamy state—how handsome her groom had been, gazing at her during the vows. There had been a lifetime of promise in his kiss. It had lingered a bit long given that his mother, sister, Freddie, and even Victor were present. None of them seemed to mind if their grins and Freddie's slap on the back were any judge of it.

She drifted towards sleep, watching it all again while the carriage rocked through the wee hours of night.

'Lady Haversmere.' She felt heat skim her ear, then a tender nip on her lobe. No dream but this, but a promise.

Settling beside her, Joe drew her tightly to his wonderfully firm chest. He touched her throat, gently stroking a path from her collarbone to her hip before he kissed her.

'I'll be glad when we reach home and you no longer have to treat me with respect.' How many more hours would it be?

Too many. Perhaps she ought to have accepted Esmeralda's offer to have Victor ride home in their carriage. But at that moment, the three of them had just become a family. It only felt right to be together.

However, in this moment with her groom's hands and mouth giving a preview of what was to come—well, she might have made another choice.

'Ah, Olivia, my beautiful, sweet wife. I do intend to respect you. I am going to respect every…' he lightly skimmed the bodice of her gown, tapped each button from neck to waist '…lovely line and curve of your exquisite body for the rest of my life.'

Mayfair—first evening of summer, 1890

'Are you certain you feel up to going to the Duchess of Guthrie's ball?' Joe asked while they waited in the Fencroft hall for the rest of the family to come down.

No doubt it was her husband not feeling up to it. He was making his first public appearance as Baron Haversmere. The results of her training were to be put on view for everyone to witness.

Given his last reception at the Duchess's home, it was no wonder he felt ill at ease.

'I feel wonderful.' She went up on her toes to kiss him. In truth, she did not feel wonderful, but not as wicked as she had early today. 'If you would like to draw back my hair each morning while our child makes its presence known, you may.'

Light footsteps tapped down the stairs. 'Is Freddie here yet?'

One could only call Roselina joy incarnate—from her smile to the rose-coloured gown which seemed to float about her, she sparkled. And why would she not? For the first time, she and Lord Mansfield were to appear in public as an engaged couple.

The front door flew open wide and the young man rushed in.

'Lord Mansfield,' the butler announced, rolling his eyes and closing the door on the warm summer evening.

Roselina hurried forward, laughing and hugging him tight.

'Thank you, Mr Ramsfield,' she said. 'You may tell him we are at home.'

'Ah, just in time.' Esmeralda hurried into the hall.

Olivia thought her mother-in-law looked grandly elegant. She, too, was to be introduced to society as Dowager Baroness Haversmere.

This was going to be an outstanding night. With any luck, baby Steton would not send Olivia rushing for the nearest convenience.

'The coach has arrived, my lord,' the butler announced, opening the door.

Mr Ramsfield reached for the coat rack, handed each lady her cape along with a smile. When it came to Joe, he handed over his formal coat along with the top hat. The butler arched a brow, then handed him the Stetson also.

'I am so proud of you, Joe,' Esmeralda said, beaming at her son while he went down the front steps. 'Given that you spent your youth running free on the open range, not knowing an earl from a viscount, you have cleaned up rather well.'

Olivia did have to admit it was true—and yet—in the privacy of the bedroom her cowboy was not a bit refined, but wild and quite wonderful.

'But I am even more proud of you, Olivia. I would not have thought my son could be so transformed.'

'Until he wears the top hat the job is not complete,' she pointed out.

Joe tucked one hat under each arm and still managed to hand her into the carriage.

He helped his mother in, then came in and sat between them. Freddie helped Roselina up the steps. The pair of them rather resembled sunshine they were so aglow with their young love.

It was a heart-warming thing to see, but all things considered, Olivia would not change the fact that she had met Joe later. It did not mean she did not feel as aglow as the youngsters did, she was completely aglow. But she also felt grounded in the very best way.

'Should we not bring Sir Bristle in case Lord Waverly is attending the ball?' Roselina asked.

'Have you not heard?' Esmeralda smiled, clearly happy to impart some news about the low-down Marquess. Although she had never had the misfortune to cross his path, she had heard him spoken of.

'What news?' Olivia asked, hoping whatever it was would prevent him from being there tonight.

Now that she was married she was safe from his lecherous attentions, but the evening would be better if she did not have to look at him.

'It seems that his wife has had quite enough of him. She sent him away and did it while in the company of others. They say she collected his secret portraits, displaying them for all to see. What could he do but flee in shame? He is quite cut—is that what it is called when one is banished?'

'Cut or banished—either will suit nicely just as long as he is gone,' she said.

'Perhaps he will go to America,' Freddie said. 'Is not that where it is rumoured that Prudence Lapperton went? They might well meet, she being a widow. I can't imagine a change of location will cause him to change his ways.'

'America is vast and it is unlikely,' Roselina pointed out. 'But one never knows. It is rather lovely to think of justice being served in that way. The pair of them would make each other miserable.'

'I don't know,' Joe said. 'I think if it did happen our sympathy ought to go to the town they settle in.'

The ride to the Duchess's was a short one. The driver opened the door before the subject was exhausted.

It was just as well. Olivia had no wish to think of the man ever again. She tossed his memory on the rubbish heap along with Henry's and his mistresses'.

Esmeralda, Roselina and Freddie went in ahead of them. The butler's voice announcing them carried down the front steps of the mansion.

'Are you ready, Lord Haversmere?' Truly, she was so proud of him. There was not a more polished gentleman in all of Mayfair.

He glanced at the door where the butler waited.

Then he smiled, kissed her quickly and shoved the top hat on his head and held the Stetson behind his back.

He took her arm to lead her up the stairs.

'Wait!'

She snatched the top hat off his head, tossed it back

at the street, where a breeze caught it and sent it into the path of a passing cart.

'It never did look right on you.' She took the Stetson, placing it on his head.

'I love you, darlin',' he said while they went up the steps, arm in arm.

'Baron Haversmere and Baroness Haversmere,' the butler announced in his full deep voice.

All of a sudden Joe stopped, glancing at her in surprise.

'Did you just hear a laugh? From behind us? Directly behind us?'

'Don't worry, Joe. It is only Oliver.'

* * * * *

If you enjoyed this book, why not check out these other great reads by Carol Arens